The Kingdom of Heaven_/

by

Evelyn M. Lewis

Acknowledgements

I would like to extend my sincere gratitude to the following people:

Bette Hertzberg, as without her support this publication would not be possible. My mother, Erin Lembke, for helping edit the manuscript. Lindsey Saur, for being there to bounce ideas off of and resolve plot holes.

And of course Grandpa, for his general editorial comments and advisement on the workings of a helicopter. Any helicopter-related inaccuracies that remain are solely my fault.

Special thanks to everyone else who supported the project in its crowdfunding form, including Rayce Thoms, the Keller family, Katie Glover, Maria Fedina, Sam Freese, my novel-writing teacher Katherine Grace Bond, and many others too numerous to be named who contributed to the book's formation in some way.

Apollyon: Whence come you and whither are you bound?

Christian: I am come from the City of Destruction, which is the place of all evil, and am going to the city of Zion.

Apollyon: By this I perceive thou art one of my subjects, for all that country is mine; and I am the prince and god of it. How is it, then, that thou hast run away from thy king?

- Pilgrim's Progress, John Bunyan (abridged quote)

Table Of Contents

The Settlement

			↑		
1st North-west	2nd North-west	1st North	2nd North	1st North-east	2nd North-east
3rd North-west	4th North-west	3rd North	4th North	3rd North-east	4th North-east
1st West ← The gate	2nd West	1st Central DYNTEC headquarters ↓	2nd Central Central Tower ←	1st East	2nd East
3rd West	4th West	3rd Central	4th Central ← My apartment	3rd East	4th East
1st South-west	2nd South-west	1st South	2nd South	1st South-east	2nd South-east
3rd South-west	4th South-west	3rd South	4th South	3rd South-east	4th South-east

Chapter One

The Tree

I saw a tree, once.

I was ten years old. We lived on the first floor of a tenement building—my mother, my father, and I. I could see it from my bedroom, which had a window into an alleyway. A little helicoptering seed had blown over the walls and into a dirt-filled crack between two concrete blocks.

It was scarcely big enough to be called a tree yet, but I knew what it was, because I had seen pictures of saplings, and the tough brown stem wasn't like the blades of grass that poked up occasionally around the Settlement.

Over three weeks I watched it sprout up. First the thin stem, then, slowly, a single leaf that uncurled hesitantly like a little tongue tasting the air.

By the end of the third week, it was gone. I watched them remove it. They came with rubber gloves and spades.

The next day I told my Educator about the tree. "What are they going to do with it?" I asked. I felt a bit sorry for the little plant, brave enough to try to grow out of doors.

"They'll take it to a conservatory," she said.

"What's a conservatory?" I asked.

"It's a special place where plants are kept," said the Educator.

That piqued my interest. I hadn't known that any plants were kept in the Settlement; I'd been told they were all dead for a long ways round, if any were even still alive on earth.

I wanted to see a real tree, a live tree in full growth, like in books. I wanted to go to the conservatory. I decided I wanted to be a part of the plant removal crew when I grew up.

I never did join the plant removal crew. Ultimately, it was a different path that led me back to the tree.

Chapter Two

Jumping Off the Job Ladder

"Alex."

The Administrator met my eyes, and I flinched. She was a gray woman, not just of hair, but of countenance. Her entire appearance, from the starched legs of her pantsuit to her straight shoulders to her bloodless lips, was like marble; but her eyes were only nearly gray. They were the icy, bleached blue of a January sky, threatening to snow, and her pupils were chips of flint, tiny flecks that suggested she could see past my flesh into my soul, and loathed what she found there.

It was more than enough to intimidate a civilian like myself. To complete the statuesque illusion, her angular body stood a full six feet and one inch.

I looked away, but she continued to stare down on me. "Your résumé is impressive," she said. "Perhaps too impressive."

I shrank. I knew I'd been sent here because of my failures. Only an absolutely desperate case would be sent to the top. There were only two possible ways for this meeting to end. Reassignment, or termination. I crossed my fingers for reassignment.

She took a seat at the polished black table. It stood on metal legs with black rollers at the bottom. I sat down across from her, though unprompted. The room itself was of polished black substance— glass and metal— with narrow seams along the wall panels. Any of them might be one-way glass, but I couldn't be sure.

Her Biometric activated a screen on the tabletop, and she scrolled through my job history. She was in the highest echelon; there was nothing she couldn't see.

"You've been… an Educator. Content Writer. Food Service Worker. Maintenance Technician. Food Lab Tech. It was the Head of the Food Labs that referred you to me." And her gaze was back.

I gave a barely perceptible nod. I could feel the sweat beading up on my forehead. Her eyes were too piercing. If only she would look away.

"That's a lot of jobs. You know, people here are taught to specialize early precisely to *avoid* these types of scenarios." She pronounced "scenario" in a posh way, long on the *a*.

"I'm not lazy," I stressed. "I did my best in every job. I tried. Really, I tried. I wasn't detractive. I was just…"

Reassigned.

"They just weren't a good fit," I finished lamely.

"Five jobs and no good fit."

She was going to kill me.

I probably deserved it. A failed educator, failed content writer, failed food server, failed maintenance technician, failed lab tech. At this rate I'd never be any use to the Settlement at all.

"Please," I begged. "Just give me another chance. I want to work for the Settlement. I'm loyal. I care about the future of humanity; I do."

The Administrator looked away from me for a moment (blessedly), seeming to give it some thought. Finally, she said, "Indeed. I've seen your type before. You're a good person. Everything on your profile is clean—well." Her pale lips turned upwards slightly, though nothing changed in her eyes. "Nobody's perfect. But you're as clean as humanly possible. You're right. You just need to find the right fit."

I was stunned, but relief washed over me. I was right. Thank Earth.

"You're bored. That's all." Her voice took on a patronizing, friendly tone, though still nothing in her face changed. "You have to move on. You want a new assignment. You can't do just *one* thing, can you?"

In the food labs, I'd spent 10 hours per day painting food-growth cultures on to hosting plates. These cultures would later become all manner of colorful facsimiles—hot dogs, cupcakes, salads. It was brainless, but it was last-ditch work for a person who'd been reassigned from four other jobs. Still, I'd thought maybe I could be happy with the chance to work with organic materials. I'd wanted to see the cultures grow; maybe I'd even get to see the cells divide—maybe even into plant and leaf-like materials.

Instead, it was that—just that. Standing at an assembly line, using a paintbrush of clear solution on the plates as they glided by. Nothing ever, ever changed. Day-to-day, hour-to-hour, minute-to-minute, bending, brushing, bending, brushing. It was awful, and when it started to break my mind and my back, I had complained.

"Complained" was a kind word for what I'd done, as in fact I'd cried like a baby. Wept in front of the plant manager during inspection; begged him to let me go. Because of that moment, I now knew that I was a weak person at heart. At the time, I hadn't cared if there were no jobs left for me. I'd hated it so much there that I'd felt I'd rather die than stay another day.

And so, I found out what happens when you jump off the bottom of the job ladder: you get sent to see an Administrator.

Everyone else seemed to manage a normal job somehow. She was right, there was something wrong with me.

My first job had been an Educator, my dream career. As a child, I'd always envied the Educators, since they seemed so self-possessed. They had all the knowledge and all the answers, and the freedom to move about from place to place in just the way that children didn't.

I'd loved the job, but after I confessed scandalous thoughts to a guidance counselor, I'd been reassigned. The full details, of course, are too embarrassing to discuss, but the long and short of it was that working with children had made me feel… *estrogenic.* Motherly. There was no shame in it, of course, since it was confessed and dealt with promptly, but anyone with an estrogenic temperament is forbidden from working with children, and so I was promptly reassigned.

"I have an idea," said the Administrator. "Why don't I assign you to work for DYNTEC?"

I was stunned again. "Dintec," I echoed. Really? DYNTEC was a different dream, the dream of every more adventurous kid in the Settlement.

"You'll have new assignments there all the time," she said. "I challenge you to get bored in DYNTEC. It'll keep you on your toes." Without warning, her lips moved upwards, almost imperceptibly. "Dismissed."

And the meeting ended far more quickly than it had begun. I stood up, my head spinning. I started to back awkwardly out of the room.

"Ah, wait," said the Administrator. "I haven't told you where to go, have I? Their locations aren't listed in the Index like other facilities. Go to Room 200 of this building on Level 12. Cam will meet you there. You won't have to tell him that I sent you."

�֍

Chapter Three

The Theory of Relativity

"Alex."

I snapped to attention at my desk. I hadn't been paying attention— had drifted off again into a daydream about trees, and a conservatory filled with lush greenery.

The Educator raised an eyebrow.

"I'm sorry," I said. "I've missed the question."

"What is two plus two?" asked the Educator again.

Two plus two? I blinked. This was Social Studies, not Math class.

"Four," I said, blankly, hoping.

"Incorrect."

I flinched.

"As I have just been explaining to the rest of the class, Alex, one of the most essential parts of life in the Settlement is choosing language deliberately. It is in this way that we can be sure that we say exactly what we mean, and that we do not place undue strain on our listeners, and that we do not leave ourselves open to any accusation of Detractiveness. Alex, what is two plus two? And this time, please choose your language deliberately."

Now I knew where this was going.

"I think two plus two is four," I said.

"That is correct," said the Educator. "The principle which you have demonstrated," he continued (but I knew this), "is called General Relativity. Of course, in day-to-day life it will not be necessary to apply General Relativity so strictly, but here in the classroom we must train with it for the sake of form, as you put units on equations in Math class, in my Social Studies classroom, any deviation from General Relativity will be graded down appropriately."

He was addressing the class now, no longer focused on me in particular. I looked around, and everybody was safely ignoring me again, so I relaxed. I squirmed in my seat—if only I had just a bit of synth-paper. Not even to draw on, as this would betray the fact that my thoughts were elsewhere. Just to fold, maybe, or tear. I chewed my fingernails.

"In the Settlement, it is permitted to state definitively that 'two plus two equals four.' That is because the vast majority of human beings happen to share your opinion. In principle, however, Relativity keeps us from stating our opinions as fact. We use it in the classroom because it trains our thinking to always remember, with technical precision, that absolutes do not exist."

We all nodded.

And then mercifully the lecture was over, and we broke out the synth-paper.

Educator Jordan passed out markers from a box; we were making cards for the local DYNTEC workers of the 4th Central division.

I took the card and started drawing. I was still thinking about the tree. I put down a curling line; under my fingers it almost became a tree. I forced myself to stop; what was I thinking? This card was going *directly* to DYNTEC, and while I knew that they protected important things like trees and so forth; I'd been picking up sensitive vibes around the subject, like it would be Detractive to talk about. I had a good sense of when to avoid certain subjects. I drew a DYNTEC patch and their little chevrons.

"Do write something on the cards," said Jordan. "We are sending these cards to thank the DYNTEC agents, who put their lives on the line to keep our community safe."

"Are they coming here?" asked one of the boys eagerly. His name was Taylor.

"No," said Educator Jordan.

"Oh," he said disappointedly. "I thought maybe. We had the lab workers come to class last Career day."

"DYNTEC agents can't do that," said Jordan. "They're very busy, and also, their work is very secret and dangerous, so they can't show themselves in public."

I knew that; it would ruin their ability to catch criminals by surprise.

"How is it dangerous?" asked Taylor. He wouldn't have asked if he had no idea; it was clear he idolized the agents a little bit and wanted to hear more. Every child had some kind of obsession; mine was with plants, but if his was with the cool agents, I couldn't fault him.

"They have to fight and arrest dangerous people," said Educator Jordan in a tone no more exciting than if he were listing the times tables. "Detractors, and other types of criminals."

He went on passing out cards.

"Jordan?" said Taylor again a little bit more excitedly, raising his hand a little bit.

"Yes, Taylor."

"What's a Detractor? I mean…" he shrank a bit. "Exactly. I know what it is, but like."

"Good Gaia." Jordan didn't raise his voice or anything, but he frowned a little bit. "You are in the fourth grade. Has no one *ever* given you a proper definition of a Detractor?"

To his surprise, most of the class shook their heads.

I was less surprised. No one had ever *told* me, but it wasn't hard for me to put it together from context by the way people said it. You just know. You just figure it out.

"Kids these days," said Jordan, shaking his head. He leaned back with his two hands on the desk. "Detractive behavior is something that you *do*, but a Detractor is something that you *are*."

The way he said "you" put me on edge.

"Anybody can do something Detractive, or potentially Detractive. This is behavior that does exactly what it sounds like: detracts from the goals of the Settlement. Takes away from the good of society. A Detractor is someone who tells and believes lies; who insists on absolutes, which alienate others; who wants to gather up more than their fair share; who wants to live in secrecy and keep things all to themselves. In their secrecy, Detractors hide the fact that they are violent, malignant, hateful to the entire Settlement, and at their heart they want to destroy us all.

"My goal as an Educator is not only to keep you from doing Detractive things, but to keep you from *being* Detractors." He shrugged a little. "When you grow up, I mean. A child can do Detractive things, but they can't be a Detractor, at least not until they're an adult."

"At the same time, though, we can know a Detractor by what they do. A Detractor is the opposite of a model citizen, and a person doesn't become a model citizen by accident. If you don't work to be a model citizen, you'll always be sliding towards Detractiveness. There's no default! There's no neutrality. You must constantly train your mind to move away from Detractive thoughts and impulses. Even the best person is a mere careless slide away from becoming a Detractor. Anybody could become a Detractor, even someone who was once a model citizen. That's why you always have to pay attention to the people around you."

We all looked around us, at each other, as though we could see Detractors. I shifted uncomfortably in my seat.

"Remember, kids." He smiled. He was one of the only teachers I had who sometimes smiled, though I always felt it was more a private joke with himself than it was for us. "If you see something, say something!"

Chapter Four

No More Worlds to Conquer

Every part of the Central building was largely the same in color and nature. Smooth, gray hallways led to smooth, black rooms. There were plenty of stairwells, but I chose the elevator. It was a seamless ride from the meeting rooms on Level 30, down to Level 12.

At least Level 12 had windows. At the end of the hallway was a narrow view out on the city. It wasn't particularly scenic from this angle, but I thought it was impressive in its own way. I looked down into a deep crevasse between two buildings, an alleyway filled with a jumble of fire escapes.

No building in the Settlement had windows above the twenty-fifth floor. There was a good reason for that too. When our ancestors had built the city, they hadn't wanted to look over the Wall. I guess it was just too depressing for them to have to see the scorched earth, the wasteland that they'd ruined. A total climate disaster had left no green anywhere. No trees. No forests. No fertile land able to produce crops. It was why we'd resorted to growing food in labs. Every job in the Settlement was necessary for the survival of the human race. We had to be completely self-sufficient— a closed system, as it were—while we waited for the Earth to heal herself.

I came to door 200. I had never thought seriously about working for DYNTEC before and was already growing nervous again after my initial relief. The organization was all about saving the world, and stopping crime, and all that. Those were high stakes. High stakes, big guns, cool tech. The name stood for "Dynamic National Technologies, Incorporated," though for most people it had long ceased to be an acronym.

And I was… well… lame. Not exactly badass. Maybe even a bit of a wimp. Hopefully they'd just assign me to a desk or something. Nice and comfortable in a back corner. But no, that would defeat the purpose of keeping me moving, wouldn't it? There was no chance of that. My hand started to shake as I prepared to scan my Biometric.

The door opened.

A man was waiting on the other side to greet me.

"Hi there," he said. "You must be Alex. I'm Cam."

Cam was tall; a good head taller than me and had a scraggly blonde beard. I could tell that he probably worked out. He was wearing something similar to a black track suit and had a smile that was a notch more sincere than the Administrator's, though laced with something that might have been irony.

"Nice to meet you," I said.

"Come on in," he invited me. I followed him. The ceilings were higher here, and running fluorescent lights hung in irregular configurations that were probably somebody's idea of art.

I wondered what part of DYNTEC we were in. Headquarters? Unlikely.

"Welcome to the Level-One gym and training center for DYNTEC," said Cam, answering my unspoken question. "If you're wondering where the gym equipment is, that's on the eleventh floor. You'll probably have to spend a few weeks here before you're ready to go on to any assignments." He looked me over with a critical eye. "You don't seem too excited to be here."

"Just nervous," I said. It was true.

"Don't be," said Cam. "You got promoted to DYNTEC. You're already more powerful than 99% of the population." This seemed to amuse him. He took a seat in a rounded, plush chair by the wall. There were two others nearby. "Think of me as your friend."

He must have seen my skeptical look because he said, "I love welcoming new recruits, doing orientation, and all that. It's my favorite job because I get to be lazy and sit in the cushy chairs." He leaned his neck back on the pillow and put his feet up on the coffee table. "Why don't you sit?"

I sat delicately on the edge of the seat.

"So why did they send you to DYNTEC?" Cam asked me.

I felt my tongue clamming up. "I… I asked for re-assignment from the food labs."

"Oh, yeah. That's one way to get in, I suppose."

My curiosity welled up a little, but I was too timid to ask.

"The other way," said Cam, who evidently loved to talk about himself, "is the way I got in."

"How did you get in?" I indulged him. Perhaps I could loosen up just a little bit around this guy.

"Oh, you know. Usual story. Flunked out of school as a teenager— didn't have much of a head for numbers or memorization. The Administrators caught me exploring around the off-limits parts of the sublevels. I was trouble, but without any real Detractive purposes. Just enough trouble to be useful. They offered me the choice between juvie and working for DYNTEC. I chose to work for DYNTEC."

"Nice," I said, not sure what else to say.

"All right, Alex," said Cam, getting up. "Come on with me, and I guess I'll show you around the downstairs." He got up, and I followed him to the far end of the long room. "That's an interesting name. You were named after a man; did you know that?

I shook my head. "So what?" Most names in the Settlement were gender neutral.

"So what?" Cam laughed. "I like you already. The man you were named after conquered the world. That's your new job."

Now he was saying confusing things. "My job?"

"Well, our job. DYNTEC's job. The world was a lot smaller in Alexander's day, of course. But years ago, we ran into the same problem he did."

"What's that?" I clasped my hands behind my back politely.

"No more worlds to conquer."

"I thought DYNTEC was supposed to save the world," I said.

"Sometimes you have to conquer things to save them," said Cam. "If you don't think so, you're naïve."

Well, I wasn't naïve. I knew you needed control over something to manage it properly. I'd just never heard it put that way before.

We came to a wide set of stairs and started to descend. I still hadn't seen any DYNTEC employees besides Cam.

"We can say more or less what we want here," said Cam, as if reading my thoughts. "The only people who can monitor our profiles and the logs for DYNTEC rooms are the Administrators. And they hardly give a damn about social graces as far as we're concerned. By the way. Has anyone ever told you you're very pretty?"

I reddened, mildly offended. Comments on physical appearance, especially positive ones, were simply not made in the Settlement, except as a form of sexual advance.

"Screw off," I said.

He just laughed.

"I'll report you."

"Try. I just told you they don't care here. Anyway, don't worry. I don't mean it."

That made me even more irritated, for some reason.

"You should try it. Saying something edgy. It's fun."

I wanted to simply clam up, but he was giving me such an odd choice. "No." I crossed my arms.

"Good!" He grinned. "That's good. I like no. No is edgy. You'll have to learn how to say no around here." The grin fell to a smirk. "More on that later."

We had reached the bottom of the stairs.

There was a hallway there, with doorways and various stairs branching off it, and I realized that most of

Levels 10 through 14 must be accessible to DYNTEC employees only. Their largest headquarters was only a block away in the West Central district, but they still had a decent office space in the Central tower. The windows here showed mostly the sides of other buildings, since we were well below the standard height limit. Still, off in the distance, I could see the brown edge of the Wall just above eye level. The sky was a pale gray.

Cam led me aside into a room that was open to the hall with a large tile doorway. The room was octagonally shaped and had a mix of black and white paneling. There was a single swiveling chair in the center, fixed to the ground. Around it was a semicircular arrangement of desks and monitors.

"The first part of your initiation," said Cam, "is that I need to reprogram your Biometric to give you the proper security clearance. Normally we'd do background checks first, but the Administrators have already done extensive background checks on you, and they said you're clean."

"So I've been told." I chewed my lips, feeling as though I was hiding something. What was it the Administrator had said? *Clean as humanly possible— but nobody's perfect.* In retrospect, it was more worrisome. She must have found some kind of dirt on my Profile she had simply chosen to ignore.

"Sit," said Cam.

I sat in the curved plastic chair.

He grabbed my hand. I tensed. He was *touching* me. I couldn't remember the last time I'd been touched by anyone. Surely it had happened by accident, in a narrow hallway or something. But this was different.

He took hold of my wrist and flipped it palm-side up, where the Biometric was implanted. "Activate it," he said.

I tapped my middle finger to my palm. The tiny part of the Biometric that ran close to my skin lit up with a pinprick of bright blue light. The nearby monitor registered it and booted up, displaying my Profile.

Cam picked up a small device from the desk that looked a bit like a barcode scanner and held it close to my wrist. "Don't move," he said. "You have to stay within range while it calibrates."

Then he activated his own Biometric, linked it to a second touchscreen, and started swiping and tapping through screens for an onboarding process.

It only took a few minutes. Once he put the scanner back where it came from, I withdrew my hand.

"There. Now you can come into this building on your own. You can also enter any civilian dwelling, backdoor any civilian's Profile, and check out Level One–approved weaponry."

I could…? Now? Already? I couldn't have been more bemused if he'd casually told me I had been granted super strength and the ability to turn invisible. I raised an eyebrow.

"Oh yeah, baby." He grinned. "We're gonna get you some firearms training."

❋

Chapter Five

Jerked Down the Path of Least Resistance

I was an only child.

My parents' Profiles and genomes were clean enough to have a second, but like most people, they were dependent on the sizeable financial stipend issued for not doing so.

They both worked, of course. They spent their lives devoted to the Settlement and wished the same for me. Therefore, despite the fact that they remained together, and I was fortunate enough to live with them, I was raised more or less by the Settlement from the age of two, when I received the Biometric.

Children in the Settlement were not permitted to go outdoors.

There were many reasons for that, and all of them perfectly valid. Unsupervised minors were always in danger, prone to the formation of subcultures. Subcultures could promote crime, mischief, contraband, or even Detractiveness. Children below a certain age couldn't be held criminally responsible as Detractors, of course, but sometimes they could say Detractive things and spread false rumors without realizing it, due to not yet being fully educated. Hence, it was better to prevent ideas from spreading laterally between minors. The very cohesion of the Settlement could be undermined; and as we all knew, the Settle-ment was humanity's last hope.

None of that meant children couldn't get from place to place, it simply meant they had to use the sublevels.

The sublevels connected all of the buildings in the Settlement. They were also the only place that really counted as "public space", seeing as so many of them were now abandoned and disused.

The sublevels in use were clean and orderly.

The abandoned sublevels were a labyrinthine place. With so many entrances and exits throughout all thirty-six districts, fully blocking off every one of them would have been impossible for even the Admin-istrators.

It was said that some of these sublevels still connected to the outer parts of the Settlement, the districts that had been walled off from the main city and abandoned. I wasn't sure, as I'd never been there—that was an errand for rebellious teens.

In order to curb exploration, a rumor was permitted to grow. There was something down there, our parents told us, something scary. Something waiting on the very lowest sublevel—Sublevel 35—to devour children. The form of the bogeyman changed depending on who was telling the story. Sometimes it was a great green gremlin that ripped children limb from limb and ate them. Sometimes we'd be told a far more reasonable sounding story about contamination with radioactive materials. These still sounded far-fetched to me—the idea of a rock that could kill with energy—before I took Science class and learned about the atom. At any rate, I never went down there, so it didn't matter.

Although the system was supposed to deter rebellion, commerce won a rather large victory for us. There was an underground shopping corridor five miles in length that ran under the city from the 2nd Southwest District to the 2nd Central District. It had several offshoots, one of which bypassed us in the 4th Central where I lived.

The shopping corridor had glass ceilings to let in the light. Glass ceilings! Although most places simply used solar power, no panels can beat the efficiency of direct sunlight.

Kids and teenagers who could escape for a moment would walk up and down the corridor window shopping. None of them could buy anything, since there was no way for them to have any money—their digital cash accounts weren't even issued until they turned sixteen. And they could only loiter for a few minutes before the security would show up to report them to their parents and clear them out. Simply put, the tracker in the Biometric caught anyone who wasn't where they were supposed to be before too much time could pass.

Still, I envied them. I never got away like that since my parents were too upstanding to let me engage in such behavior. I enjoyed walking through the corridor whenever my mother took me to an appointment or extracurricular. It was nice to get a glimpse of the sun.

The schools didn't have windows, but they did have ultraviolet lights to boost mood. And most people used tanning beds. They used to say that you could measure a kid's will to live by the amount of time they spent in front of the UVs. Whether that was cause or effect was a matter of speculation.

Since I was compliant in nature with a strong sense of self-preservation, intelligent enough to get good grades, and had no major ambitions in life, I was more or less jerked down the path of least resistance.

❖

Chapter Six

The Deep End

In a larger room on Level 11, Cam double-tapped a wide pane of glass.

This was the gym; one of the walls was mirrored and this time there were a few other DYNTEC employees around. Most of them were preoccupied with their own workout routine; doing push-ups, pull-ups, or lifting weights with various levers and pulleys.

The black pane that Cam had tapped faded into transparency. Within its surface, an interface of lights and lines appeared. Behind the interface was an astonishing number of guns.

The main display consisted of dozens of short pistols and long-barreled black rifles sitting on a shelf and hanging below on a rack, but there were other types of guns and weapons that I didn't recognize and a few knives with jagged edges that looked quite terrifying.

I'd never seen anything like it before, at least not in real life. I hadn't even seen a real gun, let alone a whole case of them.

"Is this… *all* of DYNTEC's guns?" I asked.

Cam laughed loudly. "No. This is a small fraction of what we own. DYNTEC has enough weapons to subdue the entire city if we needed to. This is the training supply case for Level-Ones. Just scan your Biometric, then pick the one you want from the glass. They're numbered. You have to—and this is very important—you *have to* return it at the end of the day after training."

I nodded.

"Otherwise, there are consequences up to and including termination. Level Two's—like me," his lips quirked, "can check them out for longer periods. So don't worry about me, just worry about yourself."

I nodded again.

"So… check one out."

I looked at him questioningly.

"Go on then, pick one. How about the little black Rivera down there? Number forty-two."

I held my Biometric up to the screen where Cam had put his. The display powered down and booted up again, and I selected "42," where the lines on the case overlapped the Rivera.

There was a small whirring and hissing noise, then a small trap-door opened under the firearm and dispensed it onto a tray, like a high-end vending machine. Cam reached into the tray, grabbed the gun, and placed it in my hand.

I held it awkwardly on top of my palm. It was heavier than I'd expected.

"Cam?" I asked, hesitantly. "What am I going to be *doing* for DYNTEC?"

He laughed again. "Basically nothing. Don't worry about it. You're only a Level One."

***

Cam was right. It did take eight weeks of training for me to buff up even a little bit. Even then, I didn't look that different, I could just run a mile, lift over half my own weight, and do ten pull-ups on a good day. I'd also been working on the basics of martial arts; the punching bag had a few good dents in it, and I was trying to learn how to fight with a knife.

When I wasn't training, I was introduced to the other trainees and agents. Nearly all of them stopped by the gym occasionally, Cam told me. Keeping in shape was a part of the contract. If you let yourself go too much, you'd be let go.

There were other men and women, some older than me, some younger. Most intimidated me at first, but I figured I'd get used to it, so I tried to fit in. After all, I was one of them now.

The culture seemed fairly competitive. There was no reassignment after being in DYNTEC. I realized, not without apprehension, that I'd never met a *former* DYNTEC employee. I asked Cam about retirement, and he said it was possible, but most retired DYNTEC employees didn't advertise their former profession. They could even lie about it if necessary; have their history changed on the Profile.

"Why?" I asked.

"Helps you get along better with the civvies, if you really want to mix back in with them." He shrugged. "We're not exactly well-liked."

"What do you mean?" I was perplexed, I'd never heard anyone say anything bad about DYNTEC.

"You're so innocent," said Cam, and I glared at him. "How about I show you how to do a Profile check," he said. "You spend some more time doing Profile checks, you'll learn what people are *really* like."

So I began to flex my powers as well. Every morning after physical training, Cam would provide me with a list of suspicious persons—so I got that bland desk after all!—and I'd read through their Profiles. I had a backdoor too, so I could see everything the general public couldn't see, and I could read all of their private messages. At first it was a weird feeling.

I never interacted with the targets; that would have been worse. Conversations through the Profiles are like being on the wrong side of one-way glass. Most of the time people don't notice the glass is there. It's only uncanny when something starts moving on the other side.

"The system generates these lists automatically," said Cam. "Just mark the ones you think might be Detractors. Thumbs up or thumbs down. You used to be an Educator. You know what the criteria are."

And Cam was right too. Under the clean and polite public cover, people who'd been flagged by the system tended to be very lacking in the "social graces" Cam had described. And there was a lot worse than that; sometimes just straight-up crime. It was a lot like grading papers, except with the awkwardness of reading people's personal communications.

Some of them were obvious, such clear obsceneities regarding the Administrators and DYNTEC. I was shocked that people could talk this way about them—and well, about *me.* Wasn't I a DYNTEC employee? Wasn't I working to keep them safe from criminals? The first few times, the system showed me these conversations almost devoid of context, and I flagged them without hesitation.

Some of them were obviously Detractors. Any time somebody talked about wanting to leave the Settlement, I knew they were spreading ideas that could lead to the extinction of mankind. We had to wait. We couldn't go out there and leech even more resources off the Earth. Detractors were unbelievably selfish people. Just for a look outside the Wall, they'd doom humanity.

Some were less obvious.

Hi dear, Jamie isn't feeling well today, she has a stomachache again. I don't know what it is.

Maybe it's those cupcakes she had at school for the last two days in a row, do you think they made a bad batch?

If they did they wouldn't tell us, we all know what the damned food labs are like.

This one, I had to think about. They only *cared.* They were concerned for their daughter. And not even in an unhealthy way—they just wanted her to survive, wasn't that the goal? And what if something bad *had* come from the food labs? I had used to work there. It was only a remote possibility, I told myself – so much that the Lab Heads were justified in saying it was impossible. There was no way this had happened to their daughter. So why were they thinking of it?

Because they were predisposed negatively towards the food labs? Sure sounded like it. They hated the place where all our food for the survival of everyone was made and grown.

But... I kind of did too. Hated working there, anyway.

But that is just the way life is. Nothing anybody can do about it. They were talking the way Detractors would talk. They deserved one negative mark; perhaps they would learn from it. I wasn't hurting them, I told myself. They wouldn't be brought up for review unless they had many violations.

I pushed down my feelings and gave them a violation.

There was an indoor pool on the tenth floor of the Central building.

"You need to learn how to swim," said Cam.

For the life of me, I couldn't imagine why. In all my time in the Settlement I hadn't encountered any body of water larger than a bathtub. The very existence of a pool was an unbelievable luxury.

He gave me two separate days to go down and "learn how to swim," and when, on the third day, I still reported no success, he came down to "teach me how to swim." He came out of the men's locker with a pair of loose shorts and a white towel.

I had my hair pulled back in a slick ponytail and stood barefoot on the edge of the pool. "Okay… show me," I said, skeptical that he'd be able to show me anything that I hadn't already tried.

He responded by pushing hard with both hands against my back.

In an instant, my feet were out from under me. I landed in the deep end with a hard *smack* and flailed about wildly. Water was all around me and under me. So much water. Within a moment, it was on top of me too—the world submerged into deep echoes. My eyes squeezed shut by reflex. There was water in my nose—in my mouth, as I had tried to scream. I clamped my lips together, but the chlorinated pool water burned my throat and lungs, and I found myself trying to cough only to gulp more. It had only been seconds, but I was drowning. Oh, Earth, I was drowning. I kept flailing, but I was sinking—sinking—I was going to drown in water barely higher than my head. Ridiculous, but my feet were the wrong way around.

One of my hands, trying desperately to grab anything, hit something solid.

It was Cam.

He was in the water too, and he righted me by the arms until he'd pulled me up to the surface.

I hated him.

My sinuses were still burning as I coughed and desperately tried to use what air was left in my lungs to expel the water. I breathed in raggedly a few times, then coughed some more. "I hate you."

"Good. Great. Whatever." Cam was treading water. "I thought you might just be afraid of the water. That wasn't so bad, now, was it?"

"Are you kidding me? That was f__ing terrible."

He was holding on to me by the shoulders to keep me afloat, and I was weighing him low in the water. I resented the fact that he was touching me, but I also knew that if he let go of my arms, I'd be headed straight to the bottom.

"Well, you can talk now, so you must be all right. I'll bet if I did it again, you'd handle it a bit differently, huh?"

"Screw you." I splashed water in his face.

We spent the rest of the day learning how to swim.

The pool still unnerved me. The bottom looked close, but it was so far away. I could drown. *Die.* I knew Cam would save me if it came close to that, but he didn't exactly give off a reliable bedside manner.

After we got out of the pool room, and I was back in my normal clothes, my hair drying off, Cam came back from the men's locker, now in a white shirt. "I know you're angry," he said.

I gave him a dry look.

"That's not surprising. Go ahead and hit me."

"What? Come on." I was bemused. I might have been angry, but even in the water, I hadn't been inclined to do anything more than splash him.

He spread his arms. "Well, go on. Do it. Punch me in the face. It's the perfect time. You won't get another chance like this."

I was once again speechless. I dropped the towel I'd been using for my hair. "Are you serious?"

"I am, actually. You've never punched anyone in the face before, have you?"

"No."

"That's why DYNTEC wants you to do it. Gotta have a first time."

I curled my fingers experimentally into a fist, feeling a prickle along my arms that caused me to flinch. "You want me to hit you… because DYNTEC wants me to be able to hit you."

"You have a mental block. How are you going to learn fighting skills if you don't overcome it?"

"Fine," I sighed. If DYNTEC wanted it, I might as well get it over with. I walked up to him and gave my fist a test swing for trajectory. Cam appeared to brace himself but didn't move.

I moved again slowly through the swing. Yeah, that would do it. I held my hand right up to his jaw. I began again, but despite having a good start, something inside me made me stop inches away from his face.

"What's the matter?" he asked.

I swallowed. "I don't want to hurt you," I said.

"It's only fair," said Cam. "What I did to you today was worse, and I'm going to do worse than that to you in the future. Don't feel bad about it. It's a part of your training."

The near-drowning had been a part of my training too. I'd learned how to swim. It had worked. I tried to bring back the anger of a few minutes ago, but it wouldn't come.

Mildly and unenthusiastically, I punched Cam in the jaw.

I could tell that I had still made a little bit of a dent, but he at least had the decency not to act like he was in pain. "That was pathetic," he laughed, after getting himself to rights. But he didn't ask me to try again, and I caught him rubbing his chin when he thought I wasn't looking.

That night I went home even more sore than I had been after the weight training. I rubbed my arms and legs all the way down to the first floor and through the sublevels until I reached my own tenement building.

Chapter Seven

Detractive Impulses

My Profile was clean because the juvenile records were sealed, not because I was never disciplined in school.

I was passive and compliant enough, but I couldn't read minds like everybody else seemed to be able to do. It was hard, sometimes, to anticipate what they wanted. It was hard to choose language intentionally. It was hard to avoid pissing off the Educators.

"Now then," said Jordan, passing around small squares of synth-paper, "as I taught the class last period, everyone has Detractive impulses. For this exercise, you are going to think of a Detractive impulse that you've had and write it down on this piece of paper that I am giving you."

I stared at the paper. I twirled my pen, but my mind was as blank as the sheet. I always wanted to do what I was told. Surely that had to count for something. It wasn't like I'd never done anything wrong in my life, but it didn't feel right to name any of the incidents. Letting go of my mother's hand and running off in the Sublevels—daydreaming in class—none of that was motivated by *Detractiveness.* Not as he'd described it yesterday.

Maybe I just didn't understand what a Detractive impulse *was*. Maybe if I had a few *examples—*

"You haven't written anything," said Jordan, walking by my desk.

"I don't… understand," I ventured.

"What's not to understand? Just write down a Detractive impulse that you have. Any one will do."

"What if I don't have any?"

"You do," he said firmly. "Everyone does."

I put my pencil to the paper, but I felt paralyzed. I was afraid of delaying any longer, afraid of resisting him, but I was also afraid that my answer wasn't going to be good enough and he'd accuse me of avoiding the question.

"B…but what if I don't? I can't think of anything."

He put his finger on my paper square. "Contradicting your Educator is a Detractive impulse. Write that down."

***

I was the last one to turn in my paper. Jordan collected them all, shuffled them, then to most of the students' dismay, he started pinning them up on the board in front of the class.

We didn't know whose was whose (except for mine, of course), but it was clear that most weren't meant to be seen. It didn't matter to Jordan.

"Now you see, kids." He waved at the papers and read off a few. "I want to eat too much dessert— there you go. I want to go outside—there's a good one. Or a bad one, should I say. Some of you have got the point of this more than others."

He turned from the board back to the class. "I think I've proved my point. Every one of you has Detractive impulses. But these are things that, with training, you can learn to curb. To change the way that you act, speak, and even think."

I couldn't contradict him, because it was then that I understood the purpose of the assignment. The Settlement could see guilt within us, even if we ourselves could not see it. As such, it was up to the Settlement to decide whether to absolve or to condemn.

❋

Chapter Eight

I Don't Want to Shoot You

I learned to shoot a gun from the ground up.

Cam wasn't always alone in teaching me this; there were other instructors. One of them was a burly Sergeant named Jesse. He was a man in his forties with a receding hairline and a perpetual frown. I respected him, because he was the one who stopped me when I was making ridiculous mistakes. Cam never did that.

Cam's idea of "teaching me to shoot" was all about being a fast and accurate draw.

Jesse put the horse more in front of the cart.

"A gun is force," he said. "Deadly force. The power to kill. You're goin' to respect that. You respect anything with the power to kill ya."

I nodded.

We practiced at first in DYNTEC's indoor range. The first time he saw me holding the gun with the barrel pointed towards myself, he grabbed it and wrenched it out of my hand.

"Keep your finger off the trigger," he said. He had to get on me about that one several times.

"But it's unloaded!"

"It's always loaded."

"But I just unloaded it. You watched me."

Jesse said it again, rougher and more serious. "*It's always loaded.* Even if it's unloaded, it's loaded. You get my drift?"

I did; this form of rhetorical contradiction was not unfamiliar to me. I slapped myself mentally for questioning him. But he surprised me by restating himself in plain terms.

"You never point that thing at anything you're not willing to destroy. Never at anyone you're not willin' to kill."

I knew Cam could hear, but he wasn't listening. Now every time he moved his pistol, I imagined a laser pointer coming from the end, and it moved around the room wildly, glancing across me a few times.

We were dressed the same, Cam and I, at least during work hours. We usually wore black or gray shirts, like the other DYNTEC agents, long pants, and jackets with long puffy sleeves when we had to be outdoors.

I turned out to be a fairly accurate shot. Jesse nodded in approval once he was sure I had the basics down.

"If you can pass the advanced course," he said, "You can go on to Level Two."

"Level Two?" Was he saying what I thought he was saying?

"Yes. A real, certified Level Two."

It must have been the discontent part of me, the part that could never sit still, that spoke next. "I want to do it," I said.

***

The advanced shooting range was outdoors. That surprised me, because not many things were held outdoors in the Settlement. This was mostly due to lack of space. The city was tightly packed. It had to be, in order to fit the entire world's population of fifteen million into an area of twenty by twenty miles. In effect, this meant that within the walls of the city, there was little but city.

The range was comparatively a very generous space, on the outer edge of the 1st Southwest District, directly next to the Wall. The three hundred-foot high outer wall of the Settlement was used as a backstop for some of the targets. I noticed that out here by the Wall, the air smelled a little different. Moist, perhaps. There was a wind blowing inward. I worried about toxins from the outside. The air outdoors was often unsafe to breathe, but we would have been warned if it was a bad day for air quality, so I was forced to shrug it off.

Jesse ran the training course today.

First, we went through a series of simulations. The simulations were rather rudimentary, in fact. I was made to hold my hands in ice water until they were numb, then try to load the rifle with stiff and shaking fingers as the clock ticked. I barely hit the targets; my accuracy suffered.

"When you're in a real situation," said Jesse, "adrenaline will make it harder to fire. Trust me, I know."

There were a few other strange ones. The range did have a small building to accompany it; only two stories tall. After our short break, I walked out from the upper story onto a balcony overlooking the targets. They were out there on the gravel yard with sandbags behind them. There was also a crate down below, about twenty yards from the targets, with a rifle on it. Jesse followed me out.

"Your next test is timed," he said. "On start, you'll go down there, pick up the rifle, and shoot the targets."

I eyed the stairs that led from the balcony to the ground. "Okay." It seemed simple enough.

Jesse stepped back. That should have been my first warning.

He blew the whistle, and at the same time the floor dropped out from under me.

There was a foam bag down there, and I fell into it with a *splat*. I hadn't been prepared for that at all—as was certainly the intention. I struggled to sort out my head from my feet. I'd landed on my bottom and luckily didn't seem to be injured.

The target! I was timed.

I rolled off the cushion and onto the ground, then stood up from my hands and knees. I ran to the rifle, loaded it, and fired five shots, one into each target.

"Nice work," said Jesse, a rare compliment. I flushed. "Stay down there."

I looked back, and noticed he was coming down with Cam. What could he want me to do that required both of them? Cam hadn't been involved before. He'd been off doing other exercises at the far end of the range.

Now he and Jesse approached me.

"Your last test today is to shoot the targets again," said Jesse handing me more rounds, "but this time, Cam and I will be standing on either side of the target."

At first I couldn't believe what I was hearing. I laughed nervously, but my laughter died as I realized he wasn't joking. Jesse was giving me a look that indicated that he was absolutely serious.

"Is… is that really…"

"It is necessary. There *will* be times when you'll need to aim at targets near other human beings. I don't want you hesitating. You need to be confident."

This seemed to fly straight in the face of everything he had said before about not pointing the barrel of a gun in the direction of a person, but I didn't dare question it any further.

He and Cam moved down range.

"Cam," I asked tremulously. "aren't you scared that I'm going to hit you?"

He smirked. "Come on, Alex. I've seen your spreads. I know how accurate you are. You can do this."

I clicked the cartridge into place. "What happens if I do hit you?"

Jesse looked at Cam.

"I'd do anything for the Settlement, same as you, Alex. It's okay. Just do it."

They were standing confidently now on either side of the target, about fifteen feet apart from each other, feet planted, arms crossed on their chests.

"Ready," said Jesse.

I took aim. I had broken out in a cold sweat. *Don't let my hands shake now.*

"Fire at will."

I couldn't say it out loud now, but I found myself whispering "*I don't want to shoot you...*" under my breath.

I fired into the target dead center. One, two, three, four, five.

I lowered the rifle, weak with relief.

Cam was already at my side, perhaps as eager to be out of there as I was to be done. He gave me a shrug and a fake punch in the shoulder. "See? I knew you could do it."

By now I'd realized that "being strangely open with physical contact", though sometimes required for training, wasn't a DYNTEC thing.

It was just a Cam thing.

Jesse raised an eyebrow as he strode back up range. "It's good to be alive. Congratulations, you graduated to Level Two." Then he turned to Cam. "Good job with your first trainee. That makes you two equal for now."

The first? Cam had never mentioned this before.

Jesse turned back to me. "That means he's not your boss anymore."

I allowed myself a small smug smile.

In spite of his dry humor, Jesse was, as always, stone-faced. "You're ready to start prep for your first mission."

❖

Chapter Nine

Detention

I had detention only once.

One of my classmates was named Morgan. She was a short girl with shoulder-length auburn ringlets and a double chin. I liked her, though I had never spent any particular amount of time with her, nor any of my peers, due to the anti-clique protocol. There were forty of us to a classroom, and we sat two to a table on a rotating schedule so that everybody sat an equal amount of time with everybody else. This was to make sure that nobody would be any more isolated than anybody else.

During lunch period one day, I noticed that Morgan hadn't taken a bite of her cheese sandwich, which had been specifically released for her at the food dispensers.

"Are you going to eat that?" I asked.

She pushed it away. "I don't want to. It makes my tummy hurt."

"You can have my sandwich if I can have your sandwich," I said. Mine was peanut butter and jelly.

"Okay," she said.

I managed to finish her cheese sandwich before the Educator (the assistant Educator, really, we had two per classroom) turned around.

Morgan was still halfway through mine. The assistant Educator, whose name was Payton, had unusually keen eyes, and somehow she noticed that the sandwich Morgan was eating was the wrong color.

"Morgan!" she exclaimed, panicked. "Is that Alex's sandwich?"

Morgan's eyes went round. She looked at me.

"Alex, is that your sandwich?"

I nodded, truthful as always.

"N—" she snatched the PB&J out of Morgan's hand, and let it drop like it was radioactive. "No! Morgan, no! That is unacceptable! Alex, that is unacceptable! Alex, did you eat her food?"

I hesitated, then nodded again, but smaller this time. She was so tall, about twice my height.

"You know you're not allowed to trade food! People can't switch food! *People have to eat what gets assigned to them!*" She sounded quite breathless; her voice had risen quite significantly in pitch and volume. I couldn't understand what had made her so upset.

Maybe if she understood why I had done it, she wouldn't be so upset.

"But," I said in a tiny voice, "if she didn't eat my sandwich, she wouldn't have any food."

"She has her own food! Her own food, all right? The dispenser gave Morgan her own food, you know that! Everybody gets food based on their own nutritional needs, you can't change that!"

"But," I said, "it makes her feel sick."

"*Food doesn't do that!*" yelled Payton. "That's not true, that doesn't happen! I don't want to hear you say anything like that ever again! You either, Morgan! Do you want to be Detractors when you grow up? I'm going to have to put you both under detention."

The entire classroom was staring at us now, and I could tell they were all annoyed with me for making Payton yell. If I hadn't argued back, this wouldn't be happening. Even Morgan was looking at me as if to say, *stop talking. Don't defend me anymore. You'll only make it worse.*

I stopped.

The sentence of detention had been decided, there was nothing else to do but wait for it. I was terrified.

When Ellison, our primary Educator came back to the room, Payton went to him behind his desk and explained what had happened, including the extent of my rebelliousness.

I strained my ears to listen as Ellison calmed down his assistant. "I'm going to waive her detention," he said, and I was stricken with relief. Then, "But the other one, the argumentative one—no, that's not acceptable. She needs to learn that won't be tolerated. You can remove her from class now."

So, I was removed. Payton grabbed me by the arm and pulled me from the classroom. Tears leaked from my eyes involuntarily. "You won't manipulate me with a performance like that," Payton snarled.

At the end of the hallway was a dark closet.

I remained there without visitation for the next two hours.

During that time, I finished crying, and tried to wait patiently for my release. It was dark. I felt insistently that I'd been wronged. I felt my way to the back of the closet, sat down on a box, and despite my emotions, became bored.

When Payton returned, the flood of light was blinding.

"Alex! I know you're in there."

I crawled forth from the back of the closet and stood up. I had done my time.

"Can I come out now?" I asked.

"Not until you say you're sorry."

"I'm sorry," I said, not sorry.

"You're only saying that because you want me to let you out."

Now I was just confused. *Well… duh?*

"No, I'm not," I said. "I really am sorry." I was well past my natural truthful impulse and ready to say whatever she wanted to hear.

"For what?"

"For… um… well… um… for arguing with you."

"You don't mean it. I'll come back later."

"No!" I rushed toward the door and the light, which was closing into a narrow slit. "No, no! Wait!"

She left anyway, though. The light vanished, leaving me only the small crack under the door.

I was dumbfounded. She couldn't just leave me here forever… could she? My heart went cold. Maybe she could. The Educators, as the Settlement's primary caregivers for children, had total power over every facet of my existence.

I supposed they probably weren't allowed to kill me.

I had a long time to sit and think about why I ought to be sorry. It was clear that Payton could see through my limited eleven-year-old powers of deception. I couldn't convince her that I was sorry until I was actually sorry.

I was already sorry that I'd talked back to her. That hadn't helped anyone, even Morgan. If I hadn't done it, I wouldn't be here. I tried to think on what she had said about the food. I thought about the sandwiches. Maybe she was right, and it was more important not to switch food. I could try to be sorry.

"I'm sorry that I gave Morgan my sandwich," I said when she opened the door again. It was later, a very long time later—by the closed doors down the hall, I could tell it was the end of the school day.

"Why?"

"Because everybody is supposed to eat their own food, and I knew that."

"And?"

I panicked internally. *And? And what?*

"...and I should do what you say?"

"That's right. Now come out of there; it's time to go home."

I went home very silently.

When I got home, I let myself in at the sublevel door. My father was sitting at the kitchen table, scrolling through something on the surface.

"Today I got detention at school," I said blandly.

"Oh?" he didn't look up. "What did you do?"

"I... I gave somebody my sandwich," I said, kind of regretting bringing it up.

"And? Don't expect any sympathy from me. You broke the rules."

"I know," I said. "I wasn't."

"Wasn't what?"

"Expecting any sympathy."

"Then why did you tell me about it?"

I faltered. "I don't know." I put my chin down and went to my room.

That night I had a stomachache.

Chapter Ten

White Lies

"Alex." Cam moved only his eyes as he spoke to me from his desk. His tone was unusual, a little quiet, as though he didn't want to be overheard, but deliberately nonchalant. I moved closer.

He continued. "Just a bit of a heads-up." His fingers kept moving on the keyboard. "The Administrators are going to want to see you in person about your first mission."

"In person?" I echoed. "Where?"

"Their lower lounge on the fiftieth floor of the Central tower." Something did seem to be eating him, I thought, though I wasn't sure what it could be. "It's a big one, very secret."

"Oh? Really?" I wasn't keen on meeting any Administrator again, let alone more than one, but if he was going to tell me in advance, I'd get all the information out of him that I could.

"Yeah, really." He shifted uncomfortably.

"Am I in trouble?"

"No… no, of course not. Alex…" He stopped typing and actually turned to look at me this time. "What would you say if I told you there were people living outside the Settlement?"

I laughed in his face.

He swiveled his chair, crossed his legs, and leaned back, elbows on the armrests, fingers steepled at his chin.

I eventually stopped laughing. He was staring at me rather drily.

"Oh… what, you're serious?" I kept smiling.

He closed his eyes.

"No. No way. I mean, this is a test. Right? You're testing me. Well, I'm not falling for it." I fell back into my own chair.

"I'm just trying to prepare you a little in advance," said Cam slowly. I don't want you to be too shocked."

I wasn't capable of believing it. Not yet. "Look," I said, "even if there were, hypothetically, people living outside the Settlement—which is such a really obscure fringe idea, it's almost Detractive—heck, it *is* Detractive—even if there were, I don't see how they'd survive out there without any food or clean water. Plus, I don't see how you'd know about it. You've never been outside the Wall."

He just gave me a knowing look.

I was shocked. "You've never been outside the Wall, have you? Cam, you've never been outside the Wall?"

"No, I haven't," he said, and I was relieved for inexplicable reasons. "But there are other ways of knowing," he said.

"Like what?" I asked.

"Never mind," he said. "It's all classified anyways. You'll find out when the Administrators tell you."

***

When talking with superiors, it is usually advisable to put on the blankest face you possibly can, so that you can't be accused of thinking anything.

I kept a poker face all the way up to the meeting room, trying to remember that I wasn't in trouble.

The meeting room was above the one where I'd met the previous Administrator. That had been Floor 30, the lowest of the Administration levels in the Central tower. Floor 30 was a general-access area where members of the public were allowed to meet with these top-ranking officials. Anyone could go, but people seldom went without invitation.

I was headed to Floor 50, which was off-limits to the public. It was yet another windowless area.

I was surprised when I was ushered into a room less like the empty conference room from my original meeting with the woman Administrator, and more like a DYNTEC lounge. That meant faux leather furniture and blocky stone coffee tables for the most part. There were three Administrators here, but one of them was at a reception-style desk, one of them was on a couch reading from a handheld screen, and only one of them was talking to me.

It may have been casual for them, but I was tense, not knowing what to expect.

"You can have a seat," said this Administrator. I sat on one of the smooth cushioned chairs. It wasn't the same woman from before—what had been her name? Morris-Fletcher? This one was a man in smart business casual. He was nearly nondescript in every way; smooth-faced, Caucasian, good-looking but unmemorable, like a walking photo composite.

"Alexandra," he said to me, using my full given name, which rang oddly in my ears. "Do you believe in white lies?"

The unexpectedness of the question startled me. "Yes," I said. "Of course."

He picked up a white cup of coffee from the side-table and stirred it with a small stick. "Then you understand that it is sometimes necessary for an organization like DYNTEC to lie to the public."

"Of course," I said. "They're an intelligence and military corporation. That's simply the nature of the kind of organization it is."

"Indeed, but what about their nature requires them to lie to the public?" he asked.

I struggled. I had never been good with the *open-ended* question-and-answer format; it was hard to tell what the correct thing to say was.

"Well," I said, "security… security reasons. They—we—are responsible for taking down organized threats to society. When something threatens the world, you can't always be open about that. You have to take care of threats with some prudence. If you announce your intentions, your enemy will get the first move."

"That's a good answer," said the Administrator, whose name, according to a nearby desk plaque, was Jamison.

"Tell me," said Jamison placidly, "are you loyal to the Settlement?"

This question had been asked of me from time to time, and usually it was asked in a tone of accusation. I jumped fervently to my own defense.

"I love the Settlement," I said. "I'd do anything for the Settlement."

Anything? I chided myself. Strong words for someone like me. Yet, I thought, I did love the Settlement. It was the same sentiment that had caused me to trade sandwiches with Morgan, even if it had been somewhat misguided at the time. While it was true that the good of the Settlement had been better served by everyone sticking to protocol, the desire to help other citizens of the Settlement was fundamentally good.

Still, deep in my heart I remembered begging to be reassigned from the food labs. I remembered being willing to say anything Payton asked me to when she had me over a barrel.

"…that I can," I finished, less strongly.

He sipped his coffee. "Would your answer change if there were people living outside of the Settlement?"

I tensed. "No, not at all."

"Then I have some news for you."

The enormous, unspoken implications sat in the air between us for a long moment.

"Now that we've established that there are such things as beneficent lies," said Administrator Jamison, "I must tell you a top-secret truth. You understand it is a vital matter of national security that no one becomes aware that there are people living outside of the Settlement."

"I understand," I said, and I did understand. "I presume they are enemies of the Settlement?"

"Very much so." Jamison paused, took a last drink, and then set his cup back down with his fingers spread around the rim delicately.

"There is a cult located about seventy miles out from the Wall. We discovered them some time ago with our sat-cams. We believe they may be the descendants of Detractors who either left voluntarily or were exiled some generations ago."

Seeing my questioning gaze, he added, "Yes, exile used to be a punishment used by the Settlement. We don't do it anymore, for obvious reasons. Simply put, it's too important not to have people running about compromising the purity of Gaia. That's where you come in. We've got to bring them in. We want you to find out what their society is like. We need to know how many of them there are, what sort of weapons they have, and more information on their culture and beliefs. We have some limited information, but we need to know if it's possible for them to be successfully reintegrated into the Settlement. The adults may prove too difficult, but we have hope for the children."

"They have children out there?" I said, horrified.

"Yes, I know. And what's more, their parents brainwash them to believe horrible things."

People living outside the Settlement!

Something about the way he had said it (so different from the way Cam had said it) made me feel, instead of bewildered and skeptical, special and a little smug. It was real, and I was in on the secret.

But the *implications*.

My heart ached imagining innocent children forced to grow up outside the safety of the Settlement, in a toxic wasteland, in unimaginably harsh conditions, without proper education, being abused and brainwashed by their parents. It was a strange idea; my own parents had never attempted to interfere in my education. Outside of the Settlement, they weren't even connected to the sublevels, so kids would have to stay in one building all the time. It sounded awful.

"So. Will you do it?"

A request from an Administrator was a command I dared not refuse. However, I was surprised to realize that I was truly interested in doing this.

"Yes," I said.

"Good," said Jamison. "Cam will be working with you on this. He won't be infiltrating the cult with you, but he'll be your point of contact, and Jesse will supervise you both. Good luck."

Chapter Eleven

Cats and Dogmas

"They call themselves the Kingdom of Heaven," said Cam, reading from the screen.

I was nonplussed. "As in 'castle in the sky'?"

Cam shrugged. "I really don't know that much more than you do. I've known about the existence of people outside the Settlement for a few years now. DYNTEC has been keeping an eye on them for a while. But we only have a couple… sources of information. Our satellite imagery gave us a rough estimate of their population, somewhere between two hundred and three hundred people. But we couldn't get closer images. We weren't able to fly a drone anywhere within a mile of their location."

"Why not?" I asked.

"Well… I'm not sure, to be honest." Cam scratched the back of his head. "They just disappear, from what I'm told. They all end up crashed and wrecked. If you can find out what type of anti-drone technology they're using, that's another big item."

"Okay." I made a mental note.

"They also refer to each other as *the children of god.*"

"The children of god," I echoed. "They believe they're descended from a god?"

Cam shifted in his seat. "Well, presumably. I think they believe they were created by this god."

I took interest. "Like, a god created them specifically? Or their ancestors?"

"Well, their ancestors. And everybody else. And the whole world, I think."

"The whole world? That's weird." I smiled bemusedly and shook my head. "I've never seen anything that tempted me to believe it was created by a god. I mean, everything in the Settlement was created by humans, that's a fact."

Cam raised an eyebrow, but didn't say anything.

"What kind of god?" I asked, now very curious.

Unfortunately, it was not until this moment that I picked up on Cam's signals of obvious discomfort. He huffed. "What kind of god? What does it matter what kind of god? You say the darndest things, Alex."

I couldn't understand what had bothered him so much. It couldn't be anything *I* had said. "Well, I am supposed to be learning more about their culture, right?"

"I said, I don't know much more than you do. Ask them what kind of god when you get there."

I decided to leave well enough alone. "All right. How am I going to blend in, though?"

"You're not," he said, and smirked—back on comfortable footing, clearly. "You're posing as someone who's on the run from the Settlement. You're supposed to know next to nothing about these people."

"Oh." I puckered up my face. "Well then, what's the point of the briefing? Can't I act ignorant better if I'm really ignorant?"

Cam's smirk became even more dry. "Well, actually… Now that you mention it, I might as well tell you. The briefing is less about getting information and more about making sure you have some necessary skills before you go in there."

I nodded slowly. Yes, this was serious business… I was wishing again that I could have stayed at a desk job. They should have kept me as a Level One.

No! I slapped myself mentally. *You agreed to this. The children. Just go in there, get information, and get extracted. You can do it.*

"You need to be able to resist brainwashing," said Cam.

"Oh." I became more afraid.

"There's going to be a seminar," he said, and my fear morphed into boredom.

***

The lights were dim, and the screen behind Administrator Jamison gave an occasional flicker, backlighting him in pinks and purples from a visually uninspired lecture slide. We were in DYNTEC headquarters, only half a block from the Central Tower, located in upper South Central.

The room had about twenty of us in it. Everybody had looked over their shoulder when I came in. I was the face of the mission, as the one infiltrating the cult. And I was a sight different from most of them—young, female, allegedly pretty according to Cam, green eyes, red hair. Seeing the difference, it was less of a wonder to me that I'd been chosen, or that my physical regimen was less rigorous than theirs. I didn't look like a DYNTEC agent was supposed to look.

"When a person is in a cult," said Jamison, "they don't know they're in a cult. They're simply conditioned to believe that all of the backwards things that happen in the cult are normal."

The slide changed to a picture of an animal—a cat, I recognized this one.

"Take, for example: killing animals. These people kill animals regularly, and not only do they kill them, but they also eat their flesh."

They have animals?

I leaned forward, riveted despite the disgusting topic. Would I have to eat animals in order to blend in with the cult?

"Cults have what are called, 'dogmas,'" said Jamison, pointing at the word on the screen. "A dogma is a rigid belief that cannot be questioned. Manipulative tactics and threats are used to keep people following the rules and to make them feel bad about themselves if they even think the wrong way."

He looked over the room. "Dogmas are one of the great evils of religion. Of course, we have no problem with religion here in the Settlement, provided that it is a private matter kept purely to the self. The public discussion of religion gives rise to groups, subcultures, and ultimately the social evils endemic in cults, such as dogmas."

He changed the slide to a color-enhanced photograph of fire. The red and orange light rippled over his face. "One example of a dogma is the religious belief in 'hell.' Cults such as the Kingdom of Heaven will threaten their adherents with being sent to a place called 'hell,' an archaic notion of a place where people are tortured with fire for eternity."

Eternity? For eternity? My skin crawled. Who would wish that on anyone? Surely he was right; these people were evil.

But yet, I reminded myself, even Jamison had said that maybe their children stood a chance of being rehabilitated.

After the seminar, Jamison came to me. This was what I'd been worried about.

"Walk with me," he said, and I followed him down one of the hallways. "We have some more work to do. You will be the only person actually having face-to-face contact with the cult members. We need to know you can resist their brainwashing."

"I am loyal," I said. "What do they do to brainwash people?"

"Talk, mostly," said Jamison. "But talk is subtle and insidious, especially when you're not used to it. They'll use words like 'freedom,' and 'privacy'. But what they really mean is the freedom to do evil, the privacy to keep that evil secret."

I nodded.

"You do understand?"

"I understand."

"They'll also talk about something called rights. I want you to understand something very well, Alex: when they talk about rights, they mean the right to do things that harm the world as a whole, and those rights don't exist. Nobody has those rights."

"I understand."

"In fact, they may and almost certainly will attempt to level accusations at the Settlement, and even at us, the Administrators. You must understand that everything we do is for the good of the Settlement. The Settlement is the last hope of humanity—"

I could almost recite this part.

"We saved mankind from extinction caused by their own greed and selfishness. The Settlement has both the right and need to exercise total control over everyone, because we won't be able to save humanity unless every single person is working together as hard as possible in every possible way. People have no right to anything that detracts from this goal."

"I understand," I said.

"Good," said Jamison.

We had walked so far in the halls we had nearly come back around the full circuit to the conference room.

"So, to return to the question at hand: How do you resist their brainwashing? And the answer is simple. Just don't listen to them. Why should you give evil people a hearing? They don't deserve it. You already know everything they're going to say is wrong. Why should you let their ideas into your head?" He tapped his head. "What's the point in that?"

Somehow, I needed help rationalizing this. "But," I said. "How are we going to convince *them?* That they're wrong, I mean. You said we were going to try and rehabilitate them. How can I do that if I don't listen?"

"Look," said Jamison, seeming a little put out, "if they're not convinced when they see our superior technology, morals, and mode of living, they're probably hopeless. That's just how it is. But if you can convey any ideas to them, great. Just don't let them radicalize you. Detractors are full of talk, but if you don't let it get into your head, it's only noise. Simply remember what you've been taught."

With that he looked around to make sure the conference room was empty, turned off the light, and closed and locked the door. We stood outside.

"That is not by any means all you have to learn about resistance," he said. "Go back to Cam and Jesse. I have instructed them to provide you with a program on deception and noncompliance."

�֍

Chapter Twelve

Deception and Noncompliance

I was back in the curved plastic chair surrounded by desks: the one in which Cam had first reprogrammed my Biometric.

Today, the Biometric was the star of the show once again.

Cam leaned in toward one of the screens. "So, this test works the same way as what they used to call a polygraph. The Biometric measures your heart rate and breathing rate, just like it does all the time. We watch that during the test." His lips quirked. "Bet you didn't know; that's actually the function it was named after, and why it kept the name 'biometric'. It literally means 'biological measurement'."

I didn't care at all, but didn't want to be rude.

Cam rolled his chair back and pointed to the blue bars and graphs on the screen. "I've got your heart rate and breathing rate showing right now, as well as skin conductivity, which is an indicator of perspiration. Now, is all of that an indicator of whether you're lying? No. Obviously. But it *is* a really good indicator of stress."

"And lying causes stress," I said.

"Right. So does being under the interview process in the first place." He gave a short laugh. "So, the first thing we—or they, or anybody who can access your Biometric—is going to do is ask you some introductory questions. Some of the questions are normal, boring questions like 'what did you have for breakfast this morning?' I'm sure you can answer that."

"I had grain flakes," I said.

"Yep, that's a truth," said Cam. "Barely any change at all."

"It changed though?" I was confused.

"Well, yeah. Normally just about any question elicits a little stress. But certain types of questions stress people out more. For example, have you ever stolen anything? Ever?"

I couldn't believe he was actually asking me this on record, with my Biometric hooked up to the computers. "No," I said quickly.

"Right," said Cam, and examined my results. "Then after the initial questions we start asking the real questions."

"And you compare the graph to the introductory questions?"

Cam laughed. "Haha, no. We throw the truths out."

"Huh?" I shook my head, confused. "I thought you'd compare my answers to see if they match a truthful pattern—"

"Nope." He grinned. "The stealing question? I presumed you would lie about that."

I didn't say anything; I *had* lied but didn't feel inclined to offer any further details.

"Basically," said Cam, "we use small lies for a baseline. Any question that gets a milder reaction than your presumed small lies is considered to be truth."

"And vice versa?" I asked.

"Yes. Any reaction that gets an equal or greater reaction than your presumed lies is considered false."

"That's very cynical," I said. "I mean, what if I was telling the truth when I said I'd never stolen anything?"

"Were you?"

I gave him a dry look, rebuffed.

He laughed a little. "You see. But anyway, that would mess it all up. Not that it would help you. Telling the truth on the small lie questions actually biases the test against you. Because your threshold for stress is lower, you're more likely to get a false positive. That's why, if you really want to beat a Biometric analysis, you should just work yourself up as much as possible during the baseline phase, definitely tell some lies, and then calm down later when they get to the real questions."

I was thoroughly confused now. "Okay," I said. "Just maybe write all that down, and I'll read it again later."

"You got it," said Cam. "Just remember, a Biometric analysis is pretty easy to beat."

"You think they're gonna do that to me?"

"Maybe. They're going to suspect you based on where you're from. They'll almost certainly have some kind of initiation rite or test."

The idea of an initiation rite did worry me. I'd thought of backing out of this whole scheme a couple times already since signing on, but it was too late now. I was simply going wherever the Settlement sent me. *Maybe I could have just said no.* The thought passed across my mind like a cloud.

For the rest of the afternoon, Cam worked with me until I could fool the Biometric analysis easily.

***

Jesse and Cam both greeted me at work the next day. I had known there would be a second training program, but I was surprised that they had both come to my 'bland desk' in the Central Tower 11th floor instead of meeting me at the training gym. I had been granted assigned hours in one of the little office rooms in the Central Tower, which was where I had been doing the profile checks. The room was used by others intermittently, and it never really felt like my own.

Today they slipped in through the frosted glass door, Jesse in the lead. Cam shut the door behind them.

"It's time for you t' learn noncompliance," said Jesse. He pushed the rolling table that I'd been using as a desk off to the side of the room.

I stood up and blinked, perplexed. "Why would DYNTEC want me to learn that? Isn't compliance a good thing?"

"Normally is," said Jesse. "Not when yer dealin' with a cult, though. Y'already know that. You gotta be prepared to… not do things they ask ya to."

"Like what?" I asked, nervous. "I'm blending in, right? That… that means complying with them, or at least I'd assume so."

Cam stood behind Jesse, leaning one shoulder against the wall, not looking at me. He seemed quiet today, and I thought this was odd, as he was usually quite talkative.

"'S'right," said Jesse. "You try. But what if you get caught?"

"I don't want to get *caught*," I said, troubled.

"I hope," he said quietly, "for your own sake, that'cha don't. How-ever. If they did, which is possible—they might hurt'cha."

"I don't—" I backed up a step, bringing me away from Jesse and closer to Cam. I didn't like where this was going. I directed my plea to Cam, as Jesse was unassailable. "I don't want them to hurt me, Cam. I don't want them to hurt me."

Cam was silent, and his face was troublingly blank.

"I understand," said Jesse. "People 'round here never learn to resist anything. Noncompliance never gets rewarded. There's good reasons fer that. But that's why you have to learn now. Because this is one of the rare cases where, in real life… it matters. That's why you're goin' t' learn it here first," he said.

"Learn?" I repeated. "I… I don't understand. How do you *teach* someone noncompliance?"

"It's more of a practical lesson," said Jesse, and while I was distracted, looking at him, Cam grabbed me from behind.

Before I realized what was happening, Cam had me in a lock. He had grasped my arm and twisted it behind my back. He was in a strong, wide-legged stance, and I struggled to keep my balance.

"Whoa, what are you doing?" I burst out, too surprised to resist. "What's going on? Hey—hey— let go of me. Cam—ow—Cam that hurts, let go of me. What are you doing?"

"You are talking to *me*," said Jesse, "not him. He is not here. He only does what I tell him to. If you say, 'I'm a spy,' Cam will let you go."

Cam twisted my arm again a little bit. "Ow!" I said. "I'm a spy."

He dropped my arms, and I stumbled forward, trying to get my dignity back.

"Let me just be perfectly clear," said Jesse. "That is not what you are supposed to do."

And suddenly Cam grabbed me again. This time I struggled reflexively, but he was too strong. I felt a surge of low-grade but building panic.

Wait a second. Are they trying to teach me to resist torture?

I considered telling him that I was scared but changed my mind. What did I expect to get out of that? If I didn't sound scared enough while saying it, he might think that I was trying to manipulate him, but if I did sound scared while saying it, he might grow offended by my refusal to control my emotions while speaking to him. Either way, he'd probably find me a coward.

"Are you a spy?" asked Jesse.

"No—" I said, and Cam twisted my arm. I went up on my toes, and then down. "No, no—" He twisted harder. I gasped air reflexively. "That's what I'm supposed to say, right?"

"If you say it, he will let you go," said Jesse.

I felt my bones grind.

"I'm a spy!"

He dropped me, and I fell to my knees.

"Incorrect," said Jesse.

"I don't understand," I said, wrapping my arms in front of me in an attempt to delay any further arrest. I tried to stop the tears from coming to my eyes. "How is…is… this productive? This doesn't make sense."

Jesse had a mildly disgusted look on his face. "You're right about one thing," he said. "This really *is* pathetic. The Settlement produces such weak-willed citizens."

I was hurt by the insult, as well as by the pains that still shot from wrist to elbow. And yet, I still managed to register confusion at his willingness to criticize the Settlement in such an undisguised manner.

Jesse's frown deepened. "But we can do better than this."

I yelped as Cam grabbed me again by force. The pain lanced up my arm again under his iron grip.

What could I do? This had to be the last time. I couldn't keep doing this. I would try to hold out as long as Jesse wanted me to.

"Say it."

"No!" I tried to sound determinate.

There were seconds. Maybe minutes. I gasped harder, and the tears sprang to my eyes this time.

"Say it."

I felt my bones grind against each other. This couldn't be good for me. Had anyone thought about that? I couldn't go into this mission injured.

"Cam, really—!" The word trailed off into a yelp.

I seemed to have gotten through to him; he finally spoke. "Sorry, Alex. It's for your own good."

He *had* taught me how to swim. But this was so different…

"I told you I'd end up doing worse," he whispered low enough that only I could hear. There was a trace of guilt in his voice. "You should have socked me when you had the chance."

I struggled uselessly. Pulling away only made it hurt more. I didn't want to be fair. I just wanted him to be nice to me.

"Cut the chatter," said Jesse. He walked from side to side, looking at me. Then he looked at Cam. "More."

Cam was squeezing so hard I thought I could feel the small bones in my wrist shift, but at this I could swear he relaxed a fraction. I couldn't see his face, but his voice was neutral, almost casual. "Any more and I'm going to break her arm."

"Did I stutter?" Jesse raised an eyebrow.

Cam's grip tightened, but he hesitated.

I was, at this point, making a rather irritating noise.

"Cam."

More hesitation.

"Do I have to say it again."

"No!" I yelled at him. Tears rolled down my cheeks. "No, no, nonono…" I wasn't sure if I was giving Jesse the answer he wanted or begging Cam not to break my arm.

Cam twisted more.

I screamed.

Without warning I was dropped.

Jesse was holding up a hand. "That's enough," I heard his voice say, from my position on the floor.

I had gone to my knees immediately, nursing my wrist. It felt awful, like something in it had been sprained, perhaps. But my arm wasn't broken, most likely. I caught deep breaths, trying to silence myself.

"I think we've all learned something today," said Jesse. "Report to medical at first convenience," he told me.

I continued to sit, legs folded under me, not looking up, until both of them had left the room.

What *had* I learned? Noncompliance? I'd complied with Jesse's instructions on noncompliance. The thought disturbed me.

I wasn't learning anything, I thought. When "yes" and "no" were both wrong answers, what could you learn? I wasn't sure. I wondered if that was because there was something wrong with me or if there was something wrong with them. I even, in the depths of my own mind, below my willingness for worded thoughts, despised the entire "program". All I was learning was that they could and would hurt me and were willing to hurt me for no clear benefit.

Maybe someday some benefit would come out of this. But Jesse's eyes had been so cold and Cam's, after he dropped me, had looked so guilty.

Things cooled down between Cam and me for a while after that.

Chapter Thirteen

Gaia

It was the day before I was to leave the Settlement for the mission.

The elevator rose quickly and smoothly towards the top of the Central tower. I didn't know why I'd been summoned.

I'd never been to the top before. The tower narrowed, but at its top was a wider floor like a flat disc. This was (or so I'd heard) where the Administrators retreated when they wished to convene.

Civilians *never* came here.

It frightened me.

The doors slid open at the top. I took in the room. The wide, empty space was not unexpected. A core pillar rose through the center of the room, made of stainless steel, but it was unassuming. Around the edges, there were red chairs and couches, spaced generously. Several Administrators lounged on them, sipping wine or other beverages out of glass. Strangely, the couches were facing *outwards*.

The walls of the room were paneled in glass, but instead of being the usual one-way, the glass was covered by cloth screens. Windows. A faint daylight glow came from the edges. There were windows up here? That didn't seem right. This was the 150th floor. It was the tallest building in the Settlement.

They were covered, and no one was looking out of them, at least for the moment. Perhaps nothing to see, after all. But I was seized by an intractable curiosity.

I could not give it any attention, for Dana Morris-Fletcher was walking towards me. Her business heels were almost hidden under the flared legs of her gray pantsuit.

"You've made it," she said, and, "Thank you for coming," which surprised me, but not unpleasantly. She wished me to perceive myself as an insider, at least, if not an equal.

I nodded.

"I'm sure you're wondering why I've called you here," said the woman. Her eyes skirted across me for a moment, and I remembered why they made me so uncomfortable; the intensity never abated for a second. "I have a couple of things to show you before you leave," she said. "In the interest of preparedness."

I nodded again. Hadn't I been shown enough already?

"I'm aware you've already received most of the mission briefing information," she said, with an air of careful word choice. "There is, however, a certain… sensitivity…" I was grateful that she had turned away, though she was now beckoning me to follow her. "Well, better to just show you. Come."

She went to the core in the center of the room.

As she approached, a piece of the metal slid away, revealing a small, lighted compartment. Inside, there was a plant.

I could see its slender, green stem, curling up along a thin support rod. It coiled like a small, tender worm would grasp a branch. Its leaves were large and arrow-shaped.

I leaned in, despite myself.

"This is a real bean plant," said Morris-Fletcher, "hatched from a bean sprout."

My fingers crept forward.

I could hear the warning on her voice. "Look, but do not touch. The oils on your fingers will damage the leaves."

I withdrew my hand quickly, but continued to fill my eyes. It was a lovely being. There was even a small pod on it, near the top of the stem.

"While under ordinary circumstances it would be considered unethical to keep a plant inside of the Settlement, this one is for demonstration purposes only. We need to understand what it is that we're protecting. Don't you agree, Alex?"

"Certainly," I said, a bit startled.

However, my mind went to *conservatory.* I wondered if that had been a real place after all. I'd never seen it anywhere on the maps.

"Humans pollute everything. We maim, kill, and destroy. That is why we quarantine ourselves in the Settlement. We must protect Gaia from our evil at all costs."

I nodded.

Gaia wasn't precisely a god to us, since a god is a supernatural being. Gaia was nature itself. Gaia had no magical attributes, but could be understood purely by science and logic—or so it was said. I'd studied cell division, the water cycle, and photosynthesis. I'd memorized chemical formulas for proteins.

In my mind, I had always pictured Gaia as a sort of tree. A tree like in pictures, but bigger and more living. I even harbored a secret fantasy that maybe when I was young, I had *seen* Gaia in the form of that little tree.

"However," said Morris-Fletcher. "For the greater good, it is not only possible, but in fact certain that you will be required to commit certain offenses against

Gaia. I regret it, but it is inevitable since you will be trespassing into her domain to stop other trespassers."

I waited, puzzling. I wasn't sure what she was getting at.

"It is time you knew." Her words were spoken louder, the tension reaching a crescendo. "This is a closely-guarded secret, but at this point in our development, Gaia is nearly healed from her devastation. What you are about to see… may shock you."

With her final words, the curtains began to rise on slow, automated rollers. Light began to pour in, light of the sun, almost painfully white.

I squinted through my fingers, then took my hands away.

I saw green.

With the large windows open on all sides, the room had become open, airy, almost like we were flying over the world. I could see past the city, which looked like a gray mass of rooftops and fog, and out over the wall.

It was a sea of green. I couldn't process the visual information, at first. Then I began to pick out in the nearer distance what I thought might be individual trees. The sky was blue and so, so big. In the distance were mountains.

I was overcome immediately with a sort of fear that I'd never experienced before. I fell down on my knees.

"Oh, Earth," I said. And it was.

Dana Morris-Fletcher allowed a small smile to steal across her lips. And strangely enough, I thought it was genuine.

"I never imagined…" I mumbled. "It's so big. I didn't realize how big it was. It's so beautiful. It's so much prettier than anything in this dirty old city." Then I was immediately embarrassed, and a little frightened. I'd lost control of my tongue. That was potentially Detractive, and I had just said it in front of an Administrator, and not just any Administrator, but the Chief Executive of DYNTEC.

But she just sighed, wistfully. Her back was toward me as she looked out over the Earth. "I feel the same way. Do you see it? Pristine. Sacred. Holy. Untouched by the ugliness and evils of man." There was a sincere emotion in her voice that was more cutting than any of her masks had been. "That is why we must keep it that way."

I wasn't sure what to say. I just kept looking. I had never seen anything like this before and I felt as though I had to absorb it all now, in this minute, or I'd never see it again.

"Hence, our hands-off policy. Gaia is perfect. She has no sin or flaw. Humankind is the aberration. We are the bastard children of Gaia, the one animal capable of killing its mother. Our basest urge is to consume her until she is no more.

"It's a sad fact of the human condition, we have no limits to our greed. No limits to expansion. We can't resist the urge to rape the earth. In a darker age, all people used to do as the cultists do now. They bred uncontrollably and indiscriminately, spreading out over land until no place on the face of the Earth was untainted by their mark. Our species once had cities all over the entire planet. Now the Settlement is the only one —thank Gaia. The population of our species used to be over eight billion. Now we are down to fifteen million, all within the Settlement. But we can do better. We can. That's why we're always walling off parts of the Settlement that are no longer needed and returning them to the Earth."

I had never in my life imagined that so many trees could *exist,* let alone be seen all at the same time.

"Here in the Settlement, we understand our own nature," she continued. "If people knew about this—if they knew—they would want it all for themselves. It would ruin our centuries of progress. People would want to go out and ruin her all over again. They'd defile everything, put their dirty little fingers all over every leaf and tree. Can you imagine?"

She looked at me, and I looked back blankly, unable to imagine.

"It is only we, those few who are intelligent enough to rise above and subjugate our baser instincts, who are fit to make decisions about the future of human life. There is nothing good we can do for the Earth. Our every touch kills. If you love Gaia, you must let her go."

All I could think about was how I'd been told all my life that this didn't exist. I hadn't just been told the Earth was a barren wasteland. I'd been told that anyone who said otherwise was an evil, malicious Detractor.

In my heart, a small and suppressed but real flame of anger was kindled against Dana Morris-Fletcher.

Chapter Fourteen

Plastered

That night I couldn't sleep. Tomorrow I was going outside the wall and into that great unknown.

I struggled within myself. Surely my angry reaction meant that she was *right*—to feel that I deserved to access Gaia proved that I was simply one of the unwashed masses incapable of respecting the Earth. But what did I want from Gaia anyway? When had I ever desired any resource from the Earth? We were a closed system. I had never lacked for food, water, or energy.

Yet, she claimed, when I was let out of the Settlement, I would develop a greed for those things. I was only human, after all.

But what if I could control my greed? She had said some people knew better.

But I wasn't one of her sage elite. I wasn't even a person. I was "people". At least, I had been all my life up until the moment Dana Morris-Fletcher had declared otherwise.

My parents would never see the sight that I had seen today. Would their lives have been different if they had?

To soothe my fears and calm my mind, I messaged Cam on the Profile. We didn't usually communicate with each other this way; our DYNTEC contracts forbade discussion of classified business through this insecure medium. But we still had tensions after the other day's training, and I wanted to make peace with him before the mission started.

How are you tonight? I asked.

Trying to relax, he said.

Then a couple minutes later, *at 10th and 3rd North. You're free to join me.*

I'll be there, I said.

It was a speedy affair to hop on the bullet train that ran below my building. I got out on 10th and walked below the streets until I reached the intersection at the edge of the 3rd North District. There was a bar on the corner.

It was a chain establishment, of course—perfectly above board, full of cameras.

Regardless, when I found Cam, he was sitting in the back of an alcove, half-shielded behind a venetian screen. Whoever was on staff tonight must have been at least a little negligent, because he was absolutely plastered.

His cheeks and nose were flushed pink, and there were four empty bottles in front of him. A fifth was open on the table. He gave me a lopsided smile.

"Cam, what are you doing?" I chided him. "You'll be hung over tomorrow!"

"F___ this mission."

I gaped at him, appalled. "What? What do you mean?"

"F___ DYNTEC." He grinned again, but its usual ironic dryness was a little bit broken.

I slid into the booth opposite him. "What?! Cam, no!" I leaned over, my voice lowered into a hiss. "That's *Detractive!* They'll *hear* you! Cam, I've given people *violations* for that. This is why it's a bad idea to get drunk, I always say. People say crazy things, things they don't mean. Cam, you have to put that away."

I grabbed the bottle's neck to take it, but he grabbed it by the bottom and held it down.

I pulled. He continued to hold. I glared.

"No. Just let me have this," he slurred, then with an effort seemed to pull himself together. "Not tonight. I need it tonight."

I sighed in resignation. "Cam. Why."

"Come on*nnn*. I thought you just wanted to come drink with me. Not babysit me."

"I don't drink," I said, unamused. "I thought *you'd* be the one reassuring *me* about tomorrow."

He laughed a little too hard, and his laughter brought on a bout of the hiccups. He took a sip from his bottle.

I sat there with him for a few minutes before he seemed to have any idea what to say next.

"Remem…ember when you asked me how we know… things… about their culture?"

He meant the cult. I leaned forward on the table. "Yeah."

"Well. Ahahaa." His laughter was messy, unfocused. "We caught one of them. Back when we first discovered them. He was wandering… walking…" he gestured wildly, almost hitting me in the face. I leaned back again.

"A few miles out from their place. We brought him in. I told you the truth. I never went—" –he hiccupped again— "outside the Wall. But I was there. When they brought him in. They ordered me to interrogate him. Me and some of the guys."

I grimaced. "You?"

"It wasn't my first time. I've tortured political prisoners before." He somehow managed to say the words without stumbling this time.

My eyes widened. "You what? You did what?"

"You know. They're bad guys, you know. Real scum, usually. The worst of the worst. And we need to know" —Hiccup— "what they know. For the greater good. They curse us to burn in hell, and they fight us, and they hate us. You can feel it. But… this one. There was something different about him."

I leaned forward again against my will, not wanting to miss a word. My fingers gripped the table so hard they were white.

"He didn't seem afraid of me. Even after we broke him, he'd beg for mercy, not from us, but from his god."

He just sat there for a minute.

"He got sent back to us after being interviewed by the Administrators. I don't know what he said to them, but whatever it was, it must've really pissed them off. He's dead now."

I was silent for a long time, and Cam was silent too, running his finger around the rim of the bottle.

I didn't end up getting very much sleep that night.

Chapter Fifteen

Wounded Gazelle

Cam was heavily hung over the next day.

I was just exhausted, but shrugged it off with a caffeine brew. Not exactly the best way to go into a mission, but I would have to make do.

We arrived at the Wall at around nine A.M. I'd been instructed to wear civilian clothes. The same was not true of Cam or the other DYNTEC agents on the job today. They all had on black combat fatigues and waterproof boots and various belts and straps. All were heavily armed.

As far as I'd been aware up until now, there was only one gate in the wall. It was the big ceremonial gate, the one two hundred feet high that was supposed to remain shut until the day when humanity could finally return to the Earth.

But, as I'd discovered various times over the last few days, I'd been misinformed. There *was* a second gate. It was a bit smaller, and it was at a totally different place in the wall, hidden by a concrete building adjacent to the wall. The building itself was covered in signs reading, "NO TRESPASSING", "KEEP OUT", and "DYNTEC PROPERTY".

Inside, there was something resembling a large garage door. Parked in front of it was a jeep. It was a large, box-shaped vehicle, with seats open to the air. I'd never seen anything like it before, and I hung back, afraid to touch.

Jesse was the driver. "Get in," he said. He seemed to have finished growing a handlebar moustache specifically for this mission. I took the passenger seat.

Cam and two other men jumped up. They were expected to cling on to the back and side rails while standing. I hoped Cam wouldn't fall off. He had dark circles under his eyes.

"All right," said Jesse into his Biometric. "Operation Wounded Gazelle is a go."

The garage door slowly began to rise. Through it I saw more concrete walls, though dirtier—what looked to me at first blush like more city.

The jeep revved, and we trundled forward into the unknown.

***

For a few hours we were silent. It was still morning, after all, and we were tired. But mostly, we were entranced.

Over the last several hundred years, green things had encroached all the way up to the Wall of the Settlement. Technically we were, even now, still driving through a lost district. This place had once been like the city inside. Broken roads spread out under us, and there were abandoned buildings for miles. But there were also plants. Even trees. They came out from everywhere, from the holes in the concrete, from the windows of buildings (and strangely shaped buildings they were), and from the skeletal shells of cars.

Plants had consumed this city like spores of the edible fungus in the food labs that grows to the shape of its mesh. They filled and spilled from everything.

My senses were overwhelmed with green.

Besides all of this, there was a strange, recurring, high-pitched noise, the origin of which I could not quite discern. It continued, growing only occasionally louder and then quieter, as we traveled.

The air smelled different out here, too. It revitalized me almost instantly. I thought I could never breathe enough of it. And to think I'd been told that whenever the air blew in from over the wall, it was toxic. I looked up at Cam, wondering if he was having the same experience. I couldn't read him.

Jesse did not stop.

The building corpses grew smaller, into the ruins of single-dwelling houses and two-lane roads. I knew he'd said fifty miles, but I had still been picturing the Kingdom of Heaven as some kind of poverty-stricken slum-like outgrowth of the Settlement, just beyond the wall. When we eventually left behind any signs of civilization other than the remnants of the road, I slowly began to realize that this was not the case.

We continued using the road until the ground began to slope and the concrete became too broken to drive on. Jesse was using a screen on the jeep's dashboard to navigate. I examined it, but it showed only a topographical map, with GPS coordinates and elevation defined by contour.

We drove across a space filled with dense, lush grass. It was unspeakably luxuriant compared to the spare, weedy blades that used to come up in the Settlement. Finally, we parked between two small hills. There were trees visible from here too, some tall thin dark ones away on the hills. More trees were ahead— we couldn't go on, at least not in the jeep.

"We're here," said Jesse.

"Where are we?" I asked.

He looked me directly in the eye. "The place where you get out."

Cam and the boys had jumped down onto the grass.

I was hesitant at first to put my feet, wearing plastic-soled shoes, down on the grass in full weight. I thought, perhaps, it might be more respectful to take my shoes off.

So I did. Jesse didn't stop me. Then I carefully slipped down. My feet touched grass. I was sure that I was still damaging it. The blades were so soft. And they tickled, too. There seemed to be a hundred itchy things in the grass.

I put my socks back on. That was all right, and then my socks were suddenly wet through. I grimaced and put my shoes back on.

"Necessary evils," said Jesse, giving me the side-eye.

"Right," I said.

"I've got a map for you," he said.

"Are you guys leaving? Now?" I felt a little panicked.

"Yes. We're driving back to the Settlement. As you've been told, Cam is your contact..." Jesse gave Cam a thump on the back, and he jumped to alert.

"That means he's going to be driving out regularly to meet with you. Now take this." He handed me a piece of synth-paper. I'd hardly used this stuff since elementary school. I unfolded it gingerly.

"It should be water-resistant."

It was a topographical map similar to what Jesse had been looking at on the Land Rover. There was a red X marked on it, and a blue dot on the opposite corner of the paper.

"The dot is where we are now. The X is your destination."

There was also a green triangle, and curving streaks of blue. I wasn't sure what they meant. "What does—" I started, but Jesse had already gotten back into the jeep and started it. I ran toward him. "Hey, what—"

He started backing up, ignoring me deliberately.

Everybody was on board, but Cam sat in the passenger seat now. They were leaving. I couldn't believe it. I took a few more steps after the vehicle, but faltered.

The jeep got smaller in the distance, until it went around the edge of the hill and disappeared.

I stared after it for a long time.

Chapter Sixteen

Starvation

Never in my life had I been so far from another human being.

And yet, somehow, I felt less alone than I had in the Settlement. I wasn't sure what it was. Maybe being alone, really alone, made my own company more enjoyable. Or perhaps it was the echoing whistles from the branches of the trees.

I eventually gave in and stroked the rough bark as I wandered in the direction of the red X. I picked my way through the woods. I wasn't glad I'd gone barefoot earlier, as my socks were still wet and squelched inside my shoes.

The ground underfoot was brown and crunchy. Lots of small, sharp, spiky things covered the earth, and it took me a while before I realized they were from the tree branches, which had some type of green fur instead of leaves.

The trees eventually gave way to more grass. It was a field much wider and broader than the one the jeep had stopped in. I had to pause and take a breath. I wasn't tired yet, just overwhelmed.

The scenery varied so much, and every new type of plant was unfamiliar. I heard those high whistles again, and when one sounded from directly overhead, I looked up to see a dark object swoop by. A closer look showed a creature—an animal! It was a bird, in fact. I had never known they made noises like that. These small animals continued to fly overhead from time to time, no longer having the roar of the jeep to frighten them away.

I continued trekking across the level plain, but it soon became clear the distance was much greater than I'd anticipated. I began to re-examine the scale of the map. Surely they hadn't meant to drop me off this far from the cult. It was even farther than walking fully from one end of the Settlement to the other. I thought, perhaps, I could do it in one day, but I was glad it was morning.

I wandered for the rest of the day, wading through the fields of grass and flowers. I was distracted by every little thing, like a child. There were buzzing insects, and small arthropods and gastropods everywhere. I stooped down close to the ground to examine one such creature climbing a sort of fungus, which had taken on a tubular shape in the absence of a structure to conform to.

Everything I encountered seemed improbably big. The field stretched on forever. There were mountains, distant, but they drew me to them by the way they faded into blue. It was impossible for me to gauge their size. I had never imagined anything could be so far away.

In fact, prior to my experience at the Central Tower, I didn't believe I'd ever seen the horizon before.

The green, yes, the green. But more than green. The red, yellow, the blue. The different shades of green, dark and wet, almost black and slick with mud, to the light and dry grass gold with sun. The semi-transparency of leaves.

The *clouds,* clouds that I had scarce looked at because I never saw the sky as a child. It felt as though in the Settlement the sky was always overcast, a uniform gray, and obscured by the buildings. But now, the patterns of clouds and their colors flourished before me. Pink, purple. The way they retreated in converging parallel lines off toward the mountains, tempting me to imagine what could be there, so far away. To imagine flying into a golden blaze of light. And the edges of the clouds; mountainous masses that terrified me with their volume.

And then there was the rain. In the Settlement it had sometimes rained, but it seemed to be always a weak drizzle that never had a true beginning or end.

Here, when it did rain, it rained for real: fiercely, wetly, and broke from the sky with a loud and laughing thunder. The world was instantly soaked. Water swirled through the dirt, and tiny rivers appeared from nowhere down gullies and rocks. And as quickly as it had started, it was over, and the sun came down in full brightness like some benevolent deity.

If this was for what they worshipped Gaia, I understood.

I had come to believe that nothing existed larger than the Settlement, that the Settlement was the beginning and end of all life, that nothing was outside its power or beyond its ability to control.

Now I felt the dawning sense of something much vaster and deeper, something that mocked us and our pitiful pretense at power.

Eventually, my stomach began to growl.

I had assumed I would reach the cult before it was time to eat. Now I'd been walking nearly all day, and I was hungry. But I hadn't brought any food. I was thirsty, too. Luckily, I could drink anything. The only thing in my pocket was a straw – a filtration straw, capable of filtering pathogens out of water.

Finding water was the next order of business. Looking again at the map, I realized what those blue spots were. I oriented myself in the direction of the nearest one.

Before long I found myself climbing uphill. I had re-entered the pine forest, and the ground sometimes slipped under my feet. There was occasional dark undergrowth; strange feather-shaped plants.

I hadn't eaten any food or drunk any water all day since the coffee, and I was beginning to feel dizzy. When I reached the water at last, it wasn't even the large body I'd seen on the map. It was a tiny thin line painted across the page that I could only see if I squinted, and in real life, it looked like a thin white stream that leaped across smooth rocks. It was about the width of my hand.

I dipped the straw into a stiller part and drank. It was ice-cold and tasted good.

And suddenly, I felt it. The greed that the Administrator had described. Here I was, consuming nature, and enjoying it.

But it was only water! And I drank water all the time. But I wasn't in the closed system anymore. And I knew she was right about one thing: this was only my first baby step into the world of exploiting Gaia. There was still food to be had. I wasn't sure how I was going to clear that emotional hurdle. I had neither the knowhow nor desire to kill an animal, and no idea what plants were edible.

Now that I had reached the stream, I was able to orient myself better on the map. I was still so far from the cult! How would I ever get there? Why had they left me so far away?

The stream made a clear path of white stones through the woods, easier to walk on than grass. There was another line of blue on my map. It was much wider, and the red X was close to it, further down the river.

If I reached that river, I thought, perhaps I could easily find my way to the cult without getting lost. I jumped over the small stream and kept going.

More terrifyingly, it was starting to get dark. I didn't know how I could sleep out here. It was getting colder, too, and what if there were animals? Some animals could be dangerous to humans. I knew that. Now I began to imagine that I could see them moving in the shadows. The woods were a scarier place at night.

Then, suddenly, it started raining again.

Well, that was it. I couldn't go on tonight. Not like this. I stopped under a tree. Rain fell around me, dripping softly through the branches. I was at least mostly dry here. My stomach kept making noises.

I was cold. I pulled my light jacket tighter around me. They should have dressed me better, I thought.

Across from me, there was a broken tree, with its trunk lying diagonal to the ground. Perhaps, I thought, if I crawled under there—simply breaking off some branches to lay across it—I could have better shelter from the rain.

There it was again. The primitive urge to exploit the earth. I was in despair. How could I even live without altering my surroundings in some way?

I steeled myself and broke down some small branches. They cracked loudly in a way that made me wince. I crawled beneath the makeshift shelter. It was still cold. Very cold. My teeth clacked together. If only I had some kind of space heater. But where would I even plug it in?

***

If I had fallen asleep there, I probably would have frozen to death.

But as Earth would have it, I was thirsty once again. When my bones themselves began to stiffen from the cold ground, I got up. Lying there, I had begun to hear a deep, low sound that made me realize that perhaps I wasn't so far from the water after all.

I stumbled blindly and weakly toward it in the dark. My hair was matted now from lying on the leaves, with dirt in it that I couldn't get out with my dirty fingers. I found this appallingly difficult to tolerate, as I loathed dirt and seldom made contact with it in the Settlement.

I did eventually find the river. I could barely make it out. A faint light rippled on the water, but clouds covered the sky, and it was still raining heavily. The drops pierced my clothing like bullets, and as soon as I left the tree cover, I was instantly soaked to the skin. This had been a mistake. I should have stayed in my shelter.

There was a steep slope down to the bank. I gingerly started down. But I was not practiced on this sort of terrain. Unexpectedly, my feet slipped out from under me, and I found myself sliding— sliding— I tried to catch myself, but my shoes drove through the mud.

I splashed into the river.

The cold shock that hit me seized my lungs. This was nothing like the pool.

So this is why you learned to swim.

But it wasn't easy to swim here, even though I knew how. I paddled hard, keeping my head above water, and coughing out some of the water washing into my mouth. The world was a whirl of black now, and I could scarcely tell if my eyes were open or shut. *Cold. Cold. Cold.* My feet dragged the bottom, and then I was pushed up again and pulled toward the center of the river.

No. I had to get back to the bank. But the river was much bigger and wider than I'd expected, and moving rapidly. I hadn't been able to tell its breadth from the shore. It swept me along, dozens of feet, maybe hundreds. There was a downward tilt in the land. The river suddenly grew deeper.

I was moving fast, so fast. I took a deep breath, feeling a downward pull. The next thing I knew, I was fully under, tumbling and spinning. Swimming meant nothing here. It was the water that was in control.

I was going to die.

Just as I felt I couldn't hold my breath any longer, my head came back up again. I sucked in a lungful of air and droplets. I opened my eyes and found my hands and wiped my hair out of my face. In the one moment I could see, a split-second lightning flash lit up the world. If I hadn't already been frozen to the bone, what I saw would have made my blood run cold. The white glare flickered off the white drops of the leaping rapids, and the slick surfaces of tall, monolithic rocks, like embedded spikes.

I had no time to escape. I wrapped my arms around my head and hoped for the best.

That was the last thing I remembered.

Chapter Seventeen
Binding the Broken

With my eyes still shut, I could feel the position of my own bedroom around me. My fluffy pillows, bundled up under my head. A heavy blanket on top of me. The nightstand to the right and the wall to the left. It wasn't until I tried to move and excruciating pain flared through my arms and stomach that I realized something was wrong.

My eyes snapped open and my entire world reoriented.

I *was* in a bedroom.

It wasn't any place I had ever been before.

The cult.

I had almost died in the rapids. How had I *not* died? Somewhere in the back of my mind, I reserved the possibility that I had, in fact, died. However, for the moment I was willing to assume that I was alive. My body hurt too much to be dead. Unless this was hell, but I didn't think they gave out fuzzy blankets in hell.

My arms were lying on top of the blankets. They were wrapped in white strips of cloth. My fingers poked out the ends of the wraps. It hurt to breathe. I didn't try to move.

The room I was lying in was dim, appropriate to the fact that I had been sleeping.

It is important for me now to emphasize that while I recognized many of the objects and shapes of my surroundings, something felt different. I didn't contemplate it in my state at the time, but I wasn't sure what they were *made* of. They were all of an interesting brown color and rough texture. There was a window at the far end, but it was covered with a thick curtain.

A little light was instead coming from the dresser next to the bed. Sitting on the dresser, on top of a plate, was a pale lump of wet-looking stuff like melted plastic. There was a little pinprick of light dancing on top of it—a pale orange dot, as if out of nowhere. I stared at the light for a much longer time than was reasonable given the circumstances. It was mesmerizing. It never stayed still for a second, but kept shifting, getting taller, shorter, waving back and forth in the air. It tinted red, sometimes even blue as it shrank and grew again.

I tore my attention away from the dot as a new light source flooded the room.

The door was opening.

Brilliant daylight pierced through the crack, and there were quick footsteps, but I couldn't see anyone, until–

"Ma! Mama! She's awake! Ma!"

There was a *child* in here, a *baby* practically. I could see only the top of a head of brown hair bobbing around down there, and then a tiny nose peeped over the side of the bed. There was a tug on the blankets and I feared they'd slide off of me altogether.

"Jeremiah! Come out of there." And then a woman stepped into the doorway. I saw only her shadow at first.

"Leave the poor lady alone. Thank you. Yes, she needs to rest. Go play."

The child's footsteps ran off.

The woman, the first cultist I was to meet, came into the room. She sat down beside me in a chair.

She had a face that in the Settlement would have been described as "once beautiful," but it occurred to me at the moment that it was still beautiful. She had lines at the corners of her eyes, around her mouth, and across her forehead. Her hair was a sun-bleached blonde and put up behind her head. She was wearing a long, draped cloth about her waist.

I lay still, as if frozen.

"How are you feeling now?" she asked. "Does anything hurt?"

I had not expected this to be the first question to come out of her mouth, but I did my best to answer. "Yeah." In her eyes I was surprised to see no skepticism or suspicion—nothing but concern for my well-being.

"Where does it hurt? Are your arms comfortable?"

"My right arm," I said.

"That doesn't surprise me. It *is* broken." Her hands hovered over me, and I tensed painfully, fearing she would touch it. She restrained herself.

"You have one broken arm, lacerations on the other one, lacerations across your stomach and back, and possibly other internal injuries that I'm not aware of. You're lucky to be alive; those rapids have been known to kill people."

I coughed and groaned a little bit. The blankets were check-patterned and rough, although the ones under me were a bit smoother. The bed also had a prominent headboard and a smaller footboard.

"You can call me Mrs. Jones," she said, standing up to go through a cupboard affixed higher on the wall.

"Thank you, Misses Jones," I said, mildly confused about whether "Misses" was a first name, but now was not the time to question it.

"Thank my son. He's the one who found you on the rocks by the river."

"Jeremiah?" I said, forgetting my reservations. "The baby?"

"No, my other son, Samuel. He's fourteen." She withdrew some white cloth from the cupboard and looked at me again.

Now I saw not only empathy, but also a trace of pity enter her eyes. I felt for a second almost as though I was one of her children, which was strange, because I was a full-grown adult.

"I can't believe you made it this far away from the city on your own," she said. "Poor thing, it's no wonder that you're in this condition. Of course, the river probably has something to do with both."

That was when I realized. Of course DYNTEC had dropped me off miles and miles from the Kingdom without any food or supplies. Arriving bedraggled and half-starved was the only way to keep my arrival from being suspicious. If I wasn't fully satisfied with that arrangement, I could at least try to understand. The rapids were obviously not part of the plan.

I wondered if Cam had known about this plan. Did he know that he was leaving me in danger of my life? Yeah, probably.

"Well, a blessing in disguise, as we say around here." She pulled the chair around the other side and sat down. "I'm just going to have to change the bandage on that arm if you don't mind."

It was the non-broken arm, so I didn't object, and indeed I didn't dare.

She paused reaching for it, and looked me in the eyes again expectantly. "If you don't mind."

She was, in fact, looking for my explicit consent. I gave a tiny nod, although tears of fright leaked out of the corners of my eyes. This was going to hurt a lot.

"You were unconscious," she said. "Half drowned. We thought at first you might be dead. But after we got the water out of your lungs and warmed you up, you were visibly breathing again. You know what they say."

I didn't know what they said.

"Nobody's dead until they're warm and dead." She was unwrapping the bandage, and slowly uncovering my wounds. I tried to close my eyes, but I couldn't help myself. *Just one peek.* I saw a long, jagged wound running lengthwise almost from elbow to wrist, a sickening dark red gorge surrounded by pale, puckered white flesh. The rest of the arm was pink inflammation. My stomach flipped, and I closed my eyes tightly again.

Her touch was very light. I felt a faint soreness, like a sunburn, but other than that, nothing she did hurt me. The new bandage wrapped over my hand like a boxer's binding, and then up again to the elbow.

"You can open your eyes now," Mrs. Jones said, slightly amused.

I did. It was all right.

I knew where I was, but I wasn't supposed to know, and I felt as though I had to make sure. "Where am I?" I asked.

"You're in the village of Hock," said Mrs. Jones, surprising me. "We have two villages, Hock and Hanfell. Together we call them the Kingdom of Heaven." She smiled, as though this too was somewhat amusing.

She threw the old bandage into a… bucket. I knew that. It was strange, nothing here was plastic.

"What is that?" I decided to ask.

"What is what?" She tilted her head.

"The…" I changed my mind. "Well, everything. What's it made of?"

She seemed utterly perplexed by my question. "How do you mean?"

"Like what is your house built out of?" The walls had rounded shapes in them. Suddenly I remembered breaking branches off the tree. *No… it couldn't be.*

"It's a log house," said Mrs. Jones carefully. "All of the furniture is made out of wood."

I again silenced myself in fear. Houses built out of trees? The very concept was almost as shocking as a house made of human bones. Maybe more so, I contemplated, because a tree has to be killed in order to use its parts. Most humans would consider it an honor to have their bodies used efficiently after death.

She must have sensed that something was wrong, or that I was experiencing some sort of culture shock, because she said mildly, "I'll let you have a little bit of privacy, I think. Try to get some more sleep, now," and saw herself out of the room.

I was left alone with my thoughts and fears. My Biometric was under the wrapping on the broken arm. I couldn't get to it at the moment, and I'd never felt so helpless. I tried to go back to sleep.

❀

Chapter Eighteen

The Ritual

When I woke again, I was still in the cultists' house.

I was also very, very hungry. I supposed this was probably the longest I'd ever gone without food in my entire life—I'd gone all day yesterday without food and hadn't eaten anything yet today, and it had to be afternoon.

In the Settlement I gave scarcely a thought to my next meal, and it hadn't occurred to me to bring anything along for my trek. Food was provided wherever I went (not as a courtesy, I did have to pay for it) by the ubiquitous dispensaries. It didn't take much labor to heat or prep a meal that was grown in the food labs, and I could order anything that was on the menu for my health classifications. Adults at least had that much control over their diet.

Now I wasn't sure where anything was going to come from.

When I sat up, my midsection lit up as though on fire. I grimaced, waiting for it to subside.

My bare feet touched the boards. I was frightened—a little frightened to walk on wood, but that compunction was rather short lived. I didn't know whether it was a crime against Gaia, but Jamison had told me about necessary evils and all that.

I still was frightened to speak to the cultists again, despite all my training. I was in a vulnerable state. My entire body hurt, and my feet and legs were bruised with small bandages on them. Some smaller scrapes went without.

I must have looked a bloody mess when they found me at the river. I wasn't even wearing my Settlement clothes, but instead, a white loose shirt with a folded-down collar and one button. It came down to about my mid-thigh.

Unfortunately, I had no pants. The rocks must have shredded my old ones beyond repair. For the first time I began to wonder about how much work Mrs. Jones (alone?) had gone through to patch me up. Surely she couldn't be the worst of the cultists. We'd have to find a way to save her. I owed her my life.

Eventually I began to poke slowly around the room, looking for pants. In the dresser drawer, I found nothing but more shirts and some blankets. There was a standing closet where I found some more of those loose draping garments like what Mrs. Jones had been wearing. I realized after a moment's hesitation that this must be what people of the Kingdom wore instead of pants. I chose a plain-looking brown one. I was afraid to put it on without her permission, but more afraid of appearing in public naked.

When I hiked it up, I found that there were two long ribbons, evidently meant to secure the garment more tightly around the waist. I tied them in a knot in the front, rather like a necktie, unsure if this was proper form. It was very difficult, since I could only use one hand and my other elbow to brace the ribbon.

Though it was strange to be wearing such a loose garment, it was just as well, since it didn't irritate the abrasions on my legs.

Finally I noticed something laid on the chair Mrs. Jones had been sitting on—a loop of fabric that was probably a sling, and if it was not, it could at least function as one. I slipped my right arm into it. That at least gave me a little support and eased the pain of hanging my arm down.

Better.

Now that my Biometric was swaddled along with my right arm, I struggled to pull it toward the door. I waited for it to activate, but nothing happened, and I felt stupid.

I pulled the door open with my good hand. It had a handle and latch made of wood. I took a moment to mentally brace myself. Then I stepped out into a flood of brilliant light.

I was standing in the kitchen. Most of the windows were set high on the wall, but they were open. They were glass-free, with double-shutters: outer ones made of wood slats and inner ones with paper screens. There was a (very) long dark wood table down the center of the room, and ten chairs, four of which were occupied by children.

They all twisted around to look at me. There was Jeremiah, the little one I had seen before, and two others, a boy and a girl, who were perhaps eight and ten.

The front door of the house was beyond them, and on the right, a part of the same open room, was a living room with a couch made of wood and small cushions, chairs, and a rug.

Mrs. Jones was leaning over a black box, out of which came a burning smell, which was not unpleasant.

I wasn't sure what to say, but that was all right, because she stood up and noticed me first.

"Our traveler from the city is awake," she said to me. "And dressed, I see."

"Sorry," I said. "I didn't want to bother you. I don't want to get blood on your clothes, either. I'll wear whatever you want."

"No, it's all right. I was going to offer those to you," she said. "Your own clothes were badly damaged, I'm afraid. They can possibly be mended, but not right now. Don't worry about it. I suppose you must be hungry."

I nodded vigorously.

"Then sit down at the table. I'll have something out in a moment."

As I moved toward a chair, she said, "Oh by the way, that skirt ties in back, dear."

My hand went to the laces.

"No, don't. You can't reach with your arms like that. Come here."

It occurred to me that the boy children were wearing tiny pants. So, they did *have* them.

I was limp as Mrs. Jones turned me around and repositioned my skirt, retying it in the back. "Now," she said, "you've met Jeremiah, but I don't think you've met John and Eva yet." John and Eva waved to me dutifully from the table.

I took a seat across from them, a little ways down the table. The chair was a light-colored wood and felt solid.

"I'm John," said John. "That's the same name as my daddy. What's your name?"

I smiled at him cautiously. "My name's Alex."

"Hi Miss Alex."

To be quite honest, the honorific didn't register in my mind at the time, so I didn't correct him. Instead, I just kind of shrugged with a small "hi" and watched Mrs. Jones some more.

She was pulling something out of the box, which had more of the dancing lights in it. I couldn't stop myself from asking about it.

"Is that fire?" I asked. I had not seen it except in diagrams, and hadn't recognized it immediately.

"It is," she said. "Mr. Smith made us a stove. It's much more convenient than cooking outside." She came over holding a plate with some form of meat on it that was not recognizable to me.

Animal flesh.

Administrator Jamison said you would have to do this.

I tried to hide my distaste.

"It's chicken," said Mrs. Jones. "I understand you don't have chickens in the city."

"We do not," I said.

"Well, that's too bad. You should try some; perhaps you'll like it."

It did smell good.

"But if you're not well enough to stomach it, those are beets and carrots on the side."

Ah, the red and orange things. Plants were hard enough to deal with, but it was better than the animal.

She put down a plate in front of me and three more for the children. I also received a fork. I cautiously put some carrots and beets on my plate. It was strange to imagine that this was a real Carrot, the one upon which the faux-carrots we just called "carrots" were based. It was sort of like seeing a mythical creature in which I had long ago ceased to believe. They were soft when I cut into them. I cautiously ate some.

They tasted very much like the faux-carrots and beets from the Settlement, although those were usually cut into much tinier, harder cubes. These were more flavorful, though, and more tender.

I ate the rest of them. I was still hungry, but not quite ready to eat the chicken.

Mrs. Jones sat down last. "You may be wondering where my husband is," she said. I hadn't been, but nodded politely.

"He's off hunting with the other menfolk of Hock. It's their seasonal expedition. But don't worry—the men of Hanfell are still around in case something happens. They trade off." She cut herself a slice of chicken with a large and terrifying-looking knife, then licked her fingers. "My eldest son Mark is with them this year," she said. "It's his first time now that he's sixteen. I do worry about him, but they are all together, so I'm sure it will be okay. I'm sure the Lord will protect them."

They had a lord. *Feudalism?* I wondered.

I had so many questions and was not sure what order to ask them in. "How many children do you *have?*" It was the first thing that came to mind, and I only realized afterwards it might sound rude.

"Eight," she said. "Rachel is down for a nap. The other three are at the Bakers' house."

I was just amazed that one woman could even give birth so many times.

"How does the stove work?" I asked.

"It's a wood-burning stove," she said. She seemed content to let me ask the questions for now, which was good.

I didn't dare balk at the desecration of wood, since it was clearly one of their cultish dogmas, but I knew how damaging fire and all sorts of fuel-burning were to Gaia. This was exactly the sort of thing that the Administrators were targeting them for. They *had* to stop using fire. "We don't have stoves in the Settlement," I said.

It was eight-year old John who responded next. "How do you cook your food?" he asked loudly.

"We don't... cook our food," I said.

"You eat it RAW?!" He stuck his tongue out. "EWWW."

"No, no, no." I shook my head, embarrassed to be embarrassed by a child. "We don't eat food that needs to be cooked."

"What do you eat?" he asked.

Microstructured mycelium genetically engineered to synthesize vitamins, minerals, complete proteins, and phytochemicals. I wasn't sure how to explain it to him. I waved my hand. "Bread. Vegetables. Ice cream. You know, stuff." I was supposed to be winning them over to our superior ways, but somehow I just felt ridiculous.

"I wanna eat ice cream," said John, effectively derailed. "Mom, they have ice cream in the city. When she goes home, can I go with her? I wanna get some ice cream."

"She's not going home, dear," said Mrs. Jones.

There was a mutually awkward silence for a long moment between the woman and myself.

She looked at her plate. "We must thank the Lord for what we have eaten."

At first I was uncertain what she meant, but then they all closed their eyes and bowed their heads. I felt odd looking around at them like this, so I shrank and squinted.

It was my first experience with a cultish ritual, but it was not to be the last.

"We thank you, Lord," she said, "for the fruits of the Earth that you have given to us, and we thank you that Alex has made it to us alive. We ask you for her swift recovery. Amen."

Chapter Nineteen

Triage

"Now," said Mrs. Jones to me directly. "we need to talk." Her demeanor seemed to shift a little toward the sober. She looked me in the eye, and I looked back. Her presence exuded power in a way like—and yet totally unlike—Dana Morris-Fletcher. I detected no pretension or waver; she was queen here and her word was law.

"Follow me." She beckoned me back into the bedroom where I had slept. I went with her, frightened again out of my mind. She had been kind so far, but perhaps something just now had tipped her off, and I was about to be murdered and skinned like the chicken, or thrown back into the river, or at least turned back out to the woods.

Mrs. Jones shut the door behind us. Her hand stayed on the door, preventing my exit. "No one has come out of the Settlement since my parents were young."

I wasn't sure how to respond to this. She was still looking me up and down.

"A man," she said, "when my father was a child. He said that he had escaped. No one ever left because no one was allowed to leave."

I nodded with a tiny twitch of my chin, eyes wide.

"That in the years since our ancestors left the Settlement, it became a terrible place where people live and work underground. Inside the Settlement, they believe the world is a wasteland, and there is no other life on earth."

I nodded again, in admission.

"But he and he alone found a way out. Unfortunately, he was never able to tell us what it was. He died less than a day after reaching the Kingdom."

I swallowed.

"How did you…?"

I reached for my prepared story. "Under the wall," I said. "There is a way under the wall."

"How did you know about us?" she asked.

"I didn't," I said. "I just ran because—because I am a criminal there. They would have killed me. I fell in the river. I guess you found me by luck."

"A criminal?" she raised her eyebrows. "What did you do?"

"I was what they call a Detractor. I spoke against the… the Settlement." I was supposed to say that I had been convicted of larceny, but I suddenly found myself caring what she thought of me, and changed the story a bit. "In public," I added quickly, not wanting to characterize the Settlement as overly extreme. "I don't think it would have been as many violations if I had done it… privately…"

Her hand slipped from the door. "All right," she said, gently, and relaxed in relief. "You're a refugee. It must have been God who brought you here alive. Try not to die on us, all right?" She smiled warmly. "We would like to know more."

Of course. They wanted information. The Settlement wanted information. Everybody wanted information.

"When my husband returns," said Mrs. Jones, "I'm sure he'll have more questions for you."

I tried not to show how this was making me break out in a cold sweat.

"At any rate, here's what I came back here to tell you. There's bad news, and there's good news. The bad news is that you can't leave."

I kept my face carefully still.

She matched my expression. "Ever."

I took a shaky breath. It was probably a good look for the situation, but I wasn't even acting.

"The good news is that this is your home now. And we welcome you to it. But you are committed. You were committed when you left the Settlement and arrived in the Kingdom of Heaven. You cannot go back there. You could strike off on your own into the wilderness; but until we trust you, we can't let you do that either. There is no returning to your old life. We cannot allow word of our villages to reach the city. They would destroy us."

I chewed my lips.

"You know this."

I did.

"I understand," I said.

"Good," she said. "Then I'll just go back to the kitchen. I have cleaning up to do."

True to her word, Mrs. Jones did not inquire more about my past for the rest of the day. Nor did her children, and I began to suspect they had been instructed not to. They certainly seemed curious enough.

Within the hour, more children piled in through the front door. A six-year-old Mary and a twelve-year-old Grace showed up, both girls.

Upon their arrival, I realized the obvious: the fact that there were no sublevels here didn't stop them from going about. We were in a simple one-story wooden house that sat level atop the ground, not unlike some of the ruins I'd seen on the way here.

A fourteen-year-old had found me on the riverbank, but he wasn't the only child allowed to be out of doors. Most *all* of them were simply allowed to wander from place to place more or less unsupervised—and out here in the wild wilderness, too! This was so taboo in the Settlement it would be considered borderline neglect. It was extremely unsafe, and surely couldn't be good for their long-term development.

"Is she still here, Mama?" asked Grace, and then caught sight of me and fell silent and awkward, scurrying off to one of the back rooms.

The others didn't seem nearly as shy.

"This is Alex. She's from the city," said John to Mary, leading her up by the hand as though he was so much older than her, although he wasn't at all.

"What's the city?" asked Mary.

"It's like… I don't know." The eight-year-old boy gestured to me as if to say, *you tell her.*

I was momentarily dumbstruck.

"It's a place where a lot of people live all in one place," I said, though by the time I answered I'd lost her attention. Mary was more interested in touching my hair.

Following that, while Eva and Jeremiah rolled around on the floor like worms, Mary wanted to know why my hair was that color, and then she wanted to tell me about a frog that she had seen that day. I didn't know what a frog was, so I let her tell me everything.

I felt overwhelmed. There were so many of them, and they talked to me and to each other with shocking ease.

The amount of sheer joy I felt hanging around with the children was outrageous; it was as though every word any of them spoke to me added a day to my life. I was cautious, as I knew how easy it was to hurt them, but I determined to treat them in the best way possible. I was certain they could be… what was it Jamison had said? "Rehabilitated"? If anything bad happened to any of them, I swore I would riot.

***

On the second day, I sat at the table watching the kids show me pictures they drew. Eva and Grace had been working on handwriting instead, and I got to see their samples as well.

I was looking over these when Mrs. Jones opened the door to three women. They were wearing brightly colored skirts and dresses. I quickly excused myself and retreated around a corner before they could see me.

I could still hear their voices. "We heard about Samuel finding the Settlement girl. Everybody knows about it by now. We just wanted to see her. We just wanted to talk to her. We were wondering if she knows if… you know."

"She's not ready to talk yet," said Mrs. Jones.

"Ah, well, if that's the case. Here; we brought some pies."

"This one's rhubarb," said the other woman. "And that one's a meat pie. We thought with the extra work you were doing, especially with the menfolk away you could use some time without having to cook."

"Ah thank you. I'm very touched."

The door shut again.

Mrs. Jones knew exactly where I was hiding and came over to me.

"They brought these for you."

I was momentarily stunned. "For me?" It was an emotional blow for me. I'd been feeling appalling amounts of guilt and assumed it was misplaced anxiety related to my mission here at the Kingdom, but this was different.

"But why?" I asked, as my voice started to shake. "I don't even know them. I've never even met them?! I don't understand."

"They heard you were injured. They know I'm taking care of you. They wanted to make things a bit easier on us. They're also welcoming you to the town. We would do the same thing for them. That's how we do things around here."

I silenced myself, amazed but with darker thoughts brewing. So it was a sort of preemptive exchange system. Now Mrs. Jones would owe them favors, and by extension I did as well.

I was already in so much debt to these people, and I didn't have any idea how I'd ever get out of it. If I didn't live up to my end of the bargain, they'd be offended. They might never trust me. If I failed to obtain a good relationship with them, how could I ever win them over to Settlement values? And if I failed to win them over to Settlement values, they'd be destroyed. It was too much pressure. I felt worse all the time.

I was actually very hungry now, and needed something substantial. I was also afraid to spurn their gift. When Mrs. Jones cut into the meat pie, the smell that wafted out of it put me into an almost ravenous state. It had a pale golden crust.

She put a stack of plates on the table, and the seven kids currently present started grabbing one each. I watched her cut the pie for the babies, then I waited until she wasn't looking, and portioned a slice for myself. I stared at it for a minute. It was easier, perhaps, because I'd never seen the animal alive. And it didn't really look like an animal. It looked almost like the regular synth meat. I tried to imagine that, and took a bite.

It *tasted* different than regular meat. Better. I finished it quickly, and then felt guilty. That had been far too easy.

Detractor, my mind echoed. *Greed. Untamable human greed, the basest urge to exploit—*

Whose voice *was* that? It wasn't mine.

That was Morris-Fletcher.

Well, she was not here.

Mrs. Jones again completed a prayer ritual after the meal. They seemed to do this regularly. I had been astonished when I first realized that they were praying to their god on behalf of *me.* At first I was half frightened to have my name invoked in these sessions, but there did not seem to be any potential for harm in it.

If their god was not real, he could do nothing, and if he was real, at least they were asking for good things to happen. I was in tangles trying to figure out if they were praying to a man, a spirit, or something else, but I didn't dare ask. I wasn't ready. I felt I'd be chastised for questioning their beliefs.

I imagined how Jamison would react if he knew that I was seriously entertaining the possible existence of some kind of incorporeal spirit.

***

Over the next few days, I continued my recovery.

"Why don't you go outside and help feed the chickens?" suggested Mrs. Jones on the fourth day.

At first after arriving, I had wondered what the woman's occupation was, and then I observed how much work she was doing, constantly, all the time, and stopped wondering.

Not only did she cook and clean, but she constantly prepared every individual ingredient for food and life. I observed her churn butter, mend socks, sew shirts, spin wool, bring in milk (I hadn't figured out where it was coming from yet), teach the children their ABCs, read out loud to them from a book called *Mother Goose*, and scrub slates, beat rugs, and even make soap (a very stinky process). I couldn't make heads or tails of half of it. The children were involved in everything too. And I was sitting around not really doing anything—a huge taboo in the Settlement, let alone here.

So I jumped at the suggestion of anything I could do to help—but I'd have to be taught everything, which would make me even more of a drag.

I followed her outside into the bright sunlight and open air. There were trees around the house, a small meadow, and a trod-down dirt path from the door. This split off in two directions: down a hill, and around the back of the house. At the bottom of the hill was another house. Further away I could see several more houses, spaced out at a generous distance. They were all similar to the Jones's, made of wood and logs. So this was the village of Hock. It was so spread out—a wasteful use of precious land, it seemed. But I knew now that there was no shortage of land. As far as I knew, there was not a soul but the Settlement and the Kingdom on the entire earth.

If there was anyone else, the Settlement would know about them. Right?

For the first time I wondered if they had a king. If their lord was synonymous with their god, perhaps their king was somebody else, and it was actually a monarchy. Or maybe their god was a human being claiming supernatural powers who lived around here somewhere. That didn't seem improbable either, given that it was a cult.

We took the road that led around the back of the house. There I saw another wooden structure; it was a sort of open shed with stalls. Inside these stalls were animals.

I was astonished and impressed by their sheer size. They were enormous, four-legged beasts, and they looked powerful enough to trample me down without really trying. They stayed still in their stalls, chewing slowly and flicking their ears.

"What are those?" I asked, pointing.

"Ah, the dairy cows?" Mrs. Jones stopped. "Daffodil and Sunflower are their names. That's where our milk comes from. And half the milk for all of Hock, really."

Milk? Comes from animals? Like the kind of milk that you drink? I didn't dare ask. It grossed me out.

Up ahead was a slatted wooden fence about seven feet high. Mrs. Jones undid the latch on the gate, and we went in. There I jumped back in fright. A large bird about the height of my knee was strutting about on two legs. It glared at me with an empty gaze.

"Don't act afraid," said Mrs. Jones. "They will come to recognize you if you feed them, and they'll like you better too." She offered me the bucket she was carrying, which was full of dried seeds and corn. "Just throw some of this around on the ground."

I did as she told me, reaching in with my good hand, and watched as dozens of chickens came running from all corners of the enclosure. They pecked at the ground viciously. I was still frightened of the creatures. Their beaks looked sharp and powerful.

"Why do you keep them in here?" I asked.

"They belong to us," said Mrs. Jones simply. "We have chicks every year. We trade some and raise the others to eat. The hens lay eggs. It's a good food source, and providing food is one of the hardest things to do outside the city. It takes hard work from everyone."

"Do the animals know that they're going to be eaten?" I said, in a quieter voice. It seemed cruel to me to raise them as slaves only to kill and eat them later.

She laughed. It was friendly, however. "You haven't gotten to know any animals before, have you?" she said.

I shook my head.

"Well, don't worry. We can change that. They're not all as difficult as the chickens." She kept scattering the seed.

I became distressed. "Why are you doing all of this?" I asked.

"All of what?"

"Being so nice to me!"

Mrs. Jones stopped scattering the seed and looked at me. "What do you mean?"

"Like… like… saving my life…"

"You expected us to just let you die?"

"Well, no, but…" Earth help me, I'd insulted her.

"Well, I just sleep all day. And you put me in your bed and feed me even though you have to make all of the food yourself. And…" and everything that was too sensitive to mention. Helping me with the skirt despite my ignorance. Letting me wear her clothes, though they couldn't have been easy to come by. Choosing not to interrogate me right away. Protecting me from having to talk to the women. Being sensitive to my… food sensitivities. I couldn't even imagine why my life was worth saving.

"And… I'm being such a drain on your resources. I don't know how to pay you back, since I'm not doing anything. I had a hard enough time not being a burden on the Settlement, and they have an economy with millions of people to absorb it. But you have so little to spare, and I'm pulling you all down. In the Settlement, I wouldn't even be allowed to live."

"Alex!" She put her chin down and lifted my own chin up gently with her fingers. "We don't think like that. That's terrible."

"But…" Tears came to my eyes. "It's called triage. More people survive on average when they aren't draining resources. I'm killing all of you."

It was more literal than she knew.

Mrs. Jones looked sad. "Listen, Alex. Out here we know more than anybody about limited resources. But we believe that every person is made in the image of God. You have value even if you can't do work right now. Our God loves all of us, and we have to share that love with others. That's why we always help each other out when we need it."

"But how?" I asked. "Who plans it? How do you keep track? How do you decide whose turn it is?"

She shook her head. "We don't plan or force other people to do anything. We just do it because we love each other."

Something about this statement was hitting a disconnect with me. Perhaps it was the overly bold use of the word "love." This is a word that people are frightened to use even in the most intimate of relationships, for fear that it might not be reciprocated, that it might be seen as a burdensome expectation on the recipient. I hadn't done anything to earn their love. It was too much for me, I wasn't sure I even wanted it. I felt overwhelmed.

"Okay," I said, quietly, and followed her back into the house.

*

Chapter Twenty

Way of Life

After about a week, the left arm bandage came off permanently. My right arm was still healing. My minor wounds and scrapes were mostly gone, but I had a wound on my stomach that was looking to become an ugly scar.

The next time the women came around, I was ready. I had gotten into a pink skirt and frilly blouse. It was fancier than anything I had ever worn, and being dressed like the other girls, I felt more feminine than before, though strangely without a male gaze as a point of reference—it was mere camaraderie.

"They want to meet you," said Mrs. Jones. "I think it would be good for you to meet them." I had agreed. I was on a mission after all, and I wouldn't be much good refusing to meet the rest of the cult.

"Hi," said the youngest of the three girls shyly. She had dark brown hair and was wearing a white cap tied under her chin. They all had on the white hats, which I found out were called bonnets. I thought it looked very strange but wasn't in a position to point it out.

"We're just going on a walk around the edge of the corn fields," said the oldest to Mrs. Jones. "We'll have her back here in a couple hours at the latest. We promise."

I left with them, and we started walking down the dirt road.

"What's your name?" the oldest one asked me.

"I'm Alex," I said.

"I'm Ruth," she said.

"I'm Sarah," said the second one.

"I'm Mrs. Baker," said the youngest one, and they all smirked.

"You have the same name as Mrs. Jones, then?" I asked.

"What? Ah no, her name is Grace. My name is Ann." She twirled her braid around her fingers.

"She's the new Mrs.," said Ruth, and Ann smiled looking at the ground. "She just likes the title."

"The title?"

They were all seemingly confused for a moment.

"Haven't you heard of an honorific?" asked Ruth.

"A what?"

"You know. It means she is married."

Ah, that explained why she was acting like that.

"The men have them too. We call them Mister, by their last name. Do they not use these in the Settlement?"

"No," I said. "We don't have titles. Even the people who have positions don't use them except when absolutely necessary to clarify them. We simply don't believe in honorifics. Everybody is equal."

Ruth walked along backwards, holding on to her bonnet. The wind blew about in her skirt and wrapped it around her legs. "How does that make people less equal?"

"Well, it makes one person more special than another, you know."

"How though? I mean they already have a specific role. How does the title make them more unequal than they already are?"

"Hmm." I considered this.

"If people have an honorable position, what's wrong with giving them an honorable title? It doesn't change their position; it is just a word to acknowledge what already exists. I don't see what is wrong with it."

I shrugged.

"Anyway," she said, "all three of us are married. My full name is Ruth Tiller."

There was an odd silence after this, but I couldn't understand why.

It was broken when she, still walking backwards, gave a yelp and jumped off to the side. "Ewww!"

It soon became clear that she had stepped in a large pile of dung.

"That's bear scat," said Sarah, sounding concerned.

"It's fresh," said Ann.

Ruth went a few feet away in the grass, trying to get it off of her shoes.

I couldn't figure out why they were all examining it. "What's a bear?" I asked.

They gave me a startled look, except for Ruth, who was still wiping her feet.

"Bad news," said Sarah. "They're huge, and they can kill people. We need to tell everyone about it when we get back to the village. If my husband weren't out hunting, I'm sure he would do something about it. I can't believe that they go miles out to find game, and then bears show up right here."

"All right then," said Ruth, who was coming back to the path. "As far as we know, there's only one bear. Let's get a move on."

"So you would be Mrs. Tiller," I said, when we had started walking again.

"That's right," she said. But she looked anxious. "This is one reason I've been impatient to speak with you, I confess. My husband, Paul Tiller, and I were married about three years ago. But it's been just over one year now since he went missing."

I wasn't sure, at first, what this had to do with me.

"He went on a hunting expedition," she continued, "near the edge of the Settlement. He was with a group of three men. The other two men on the expedition told me that when he was a ways off from their group, they saw a moving horseless vehicle, a self-propelled kind, making a loud noise? Do you know what I am talking about?" She gave me an anxious look.

I nodded.

"It was driving across a field. There were men in the vehicle, and when they saw him, they jumped out and grabbed him, and dragged him into the vehicle, and then they drove away back toward the Settlement."

I lowered my eyes.

"I'm sure he's in there somewhere, he's got to be. You have to tell me. Have you seen him? Is he all right?"

"I don't know," I said quietly. "I'm sorry. There are fifteen million people in the Settlement. I don't know all of them. Besides, we're not even supposed to know that there are people outside the Wall, so if somebody did come in from outside, they wouldn't tell us about it."

She seemed to accept this answer, though she was let down. She walked more quietly after that.

"That's why all the men go hunting together now," said Ann. "And they don't go towards the Settlement anymore. It is a shame because the game in that direction is very good, but it's just too dangerous."

I wasn't sure what to say.

***

When we got back to the Joneses' house, they dropped me off, Ann saying to me, "We'll come get you next time we go around!"

"Sure," I said weakly. "I'll come."

"Well, you should. We're going to be friends!"

We were?

Having met the girls, I reserved my judgment. The women of the cult might be nice to me, but the men were still away, and we would see the true nature of the Kingdom when *they* arrived.

"Mrs. Grace," said Ruth, speaking to the older woman, who was in the door behind me (and my head was once again spinning trying to decipher this new way of using titles), "Do be careful. There's a bear in the area. We found droppings on the path behind the field, near the edge of the woods."

Mrs. Jones narrowed her eyes. "Thank you for letting me know," she said. "We'll be extra careful."

When the front door was closed, she went to a closet in the hall. I watched as she opened it. Inside were guns. Long ones, short ones. There were at least twelve of the things. I couldn't stop my mouth from dropping open slightly. This was more guns than I'd imagined one household could ever own. Surely this must be the entire town's armory.

It was not quite as many as the case at DYNTEC, but still.

She pulled out a long rifle and a case of bullets and started to load it. "Samuel," she said.

The fourteen-year-old came to her.

"I want you to take this with you when you go out. Make sure your brothers and sisters stay close to the house until your father and brother return. It's only a couple more days until they're due back, and I'm sure they can take care of it."

He nodded, took the shotgun from her, and slung it on a strap over his shoulder before leaving the house. The barrel almost touched the ground on his small frame.

***

They were "schooling" today.

At least, Mrs. Jones called it schooling, although it didn't resemble any kind of school I knew of. John and

Eva's letter-writing on the kitchen table had been accomplished while Mrs. Jones worked, but evidently it was time now to get the older kids involved.

"Samuel," said Mrs. Jones. "Why don't you do the reading?"

The boy nodded and reached up to the top of the bookshelf. I supposed it was of necessity that all the books in the Kingdom were paper, as they had no screens, but it still surprised me that the family had so many in one place. They weren't in the best of condition.

The one that Samuel took down was of a bleached green color, fat, taped around the seams multiple times with some sort of cloth tape, and still looked as though it was about to fall apart.

He set it on the table and flipped very carefully. "Where we left off?" he asked.

"Yes dear… sit down Mary." Her name was the one most frequently uttered by her mother. "And you too, John. You know all the drawings you did of castles."

"Yes! Yes!" said Mary. "And princesses!"

"Yes, Samuel is going to read to us about the people who lived in castles."

I was surprised to hear real people ever lived in castles; I had thought they were only from fiction.

Eva was sitting cross-legged on the couch, and Grace the younger had come out of her room to listen but was concentrating on her knitting.

Samuel started. He was a competent reader. I knew fourteen-year-olds could *read,* even in the Settlement, but I was impressed by his confident tone.

"Master Tyndale happened to be in the company of a learned man, and in communing and disputing with him drove him to that issue that the learned man said, 'We were better without God's law than the pope's!' Master Tyndale, hearing that, answered him, 'I defy the pope and all his laws,' and said, 'If God spare my life ere many years, I will cause a boy that driveth the plough shall know more of the scripture than thou dost.'"

He began to read about a King, a king named Henry of a place called England, who seemed to be at odds with everyone. First some people, then others, seemingly concerned only with what he wanted, burning to death or beheading anyone who didn't please him.

But living in the same country were many other people who seemed heroic and admirable, minding their own business, and seeming to live in a similar way that the cultists lived.

I was astonished. "When did *this* happen?"

"The year 1523," said Samuel, pointing to the page.

"1523 what?"

They all looked at me.

"About six hundred years before the Settlement was founded," said Mrs. Jones.

"Six hundred years before the Establishment!" I hardly thought time went back that far. The Settlement said that very little was known about the world long prior to the Establishment. The people were primitive before they began to prepare the Settlement, and did not keep records.

But here was some kind of record of something, though I was hardly sure who the people were, when to place it—the timeline in my mind was blank—or where it had happened. Surely not here.

A voice floated to the front of my mind—not Jamison, no. This was further back than that. It was the voice of Jordan, my fourth grade Educator.

"The first smart and good people were the ones who started to build the Settlement. Anything that happened before that wouldn't be very important anyway even if we did know. Everyone back then was what would today be considered Detractors. You can't learn anything from Detractors."

***

That night Mrs. Jones shuttered all of the windows and locked them. It was very dark outside, like a wall of solid black, and cold. Summer was just starting to turn into autumn.

"Eva," said Mrs. Jones, "stoke the fire, won't you?"

The little girl stuffed more wood into the black box.

There were loud cracks and heat radiated outward.

"Don't you think," I ventured slightly, as though conversational, "that's a bit wasteful?"

"It's cold," said the woman. "We've got plenty of wood."

"It would be considered wasteful in the Settlement," I said. "Everything we do is very efficient."

"Whatever do you mean?" She turned to me now genuinely puzzled. "We hate waste here; we can't afford to waste anything."

"Well, that's not really what I mean," I said. "Think about the energy."

"I don't feel like I'm wasting energy."

"Well, you know. The energy in the wood."

"What better way to use the energy in the wood? It's keeping us all warm."

"Yes," I said, "but aren't there more efficient ways to do that?"

"Like what?"

"Well," I said, trying to explain something I didn't really understand myself, "In the Settlement, we use nuclear cold fusion. So much energy out of one atom."

Mrs. Jones pursed her lips. "Well, that's very nice, but it's just not practical for us. We simply don't have the means or ability to make that happen. And we're not about to move to that hellhole just to tap into it."

I thought about what she was saying. The proposition was that the inefficiency of wood burning was a small price to pay for their ability to remain separate from the Settlement, according to their preferred lifestyle.

If I was here to investigate their potential for rehabilitation, it only seemed clearer and clearer to me that these people would not likely welcome intervention.

And why should they?

***

It was the moment I'd been dreading.

Alone in the bedroom, in the half-dark, I started to unwind the bandage from my right arm. I pulled the white strips away until I could see a few bare inches of skin below the wrist.

No one knew the Biometric was there, of course, not even Mrs. Jones, who had dressed my wounds. It was invisible most of the time. However, at my touch, a bright blue pinprick of light shone up at me like a small, wicked eye embedded in my flesh.

Maybe it was the weeks I'd spent without using or needing it due to my broken arm and my cover, but for the first time in my life I had begun to feel dissociated from it, as though it were a foreign object.

A piece of the Settlement was with me. The presence of the Biometric seemed to expand until it filled the log room. At the same time, seeing it light up relieved a low-grade anxiety I'd been repressing. It was still here.

It *was* possible to use the Biometric without an attending screen as a visual medium, but the voice controls were a hassle, and people usually didn't bother.

"Biometric, activate voice controls," I whispered close to my arm.

Voice controls activated. I could hear the voice, but it was in my head only, routed through the auditory processing nerves in my brain. The wrist-centered biometric chip was only a central processor and a mechanism for the input and output of a full biological augmentation. There was nanotechnology embedded through various parts of my entire body, coordinated by the arm implant.

This was how voice calls worked. I didn't use them very much, since I thought the voice in my head was creepy. It was more secure than text-based communication through the Profile, though, at least since I'd been promoted through DYNTEC. It had been approved as our communication method for that reason, and also because there weren't any screens to type on out here, and I couldn't conceal any on my person without risk of the cultists finding out.

"Make voice call to Cam."

"Calling." I heard a series of soft beeps.

The beeps abruptly ended and Cam's voice came through. "Alex?" It sounded just as though he was standing next to me, speaking. "Are you there?"

"I'm here," I said.

"What took you so long?" I could hear his irritation and relief. "It's been over a week. I was starting to think they might've gotten to you."

"My arm is broken," I said.

There was a moment's silence. "How did that happen?"

"I fell in a river."

"I see. But you did make it to the cult, right? I mean, clearly, or you wouldn't be…"

"Yes, I'm here now."

"We need to talk in person. When can you find a chance to meet me?"

I leaned forward on the bed. "I don't know. Not yet. They'll never let me go out on my own in this state. Where are we supposed to meet?"

"You'll have to come to the green triangle on the map."

"Cam, I lost the map."

"You *lost* the map?" He sighed, exasperated.

"If it makes you feel any better, I almost died." I couldn't hold back the jab.

The map had been tucked into the meagre back pocket of my jeans before I fell in the river, but Mrs. Jones had not mentioned finding it, and I couldn't exactly ask.

There was silence again. "Sorry."

"It's not safe for me to talk here," I said. "If you don't know what you want from me, I have to go."

"Wait," he said. "The meeting place is going to be a mile outside of the cult, due south at the edge of the pine forest."

"I told you I can't leave," I said. "It's not just the injuries. They don't trust me enough."

"You can't make them trust you enough to let you get away for just a little bit? Long enough to walk one mile?"

"Not without being followed," I said. "I can find more privacy here in town though, and maybe we can talk longer."

"Not good enough," said Cam. "I need to see you face-to-face to know for sure they're not holding you captive and forcing you to say things to me."

I rolled my eyes, and I was sure he could hear it in my tone. "That's *not* going on, Cam."

"Prove it."

"Ugh, okay. But you have to give me time. This won't be easy."

✿

Chapter Twenty-One

Sand on the Scales

I was in the field doing my best to help Ruth, Sarah, and Ann with the harvest when the menfolk returned.

The carrots were ready, and I was kneeling in the dirt, pulling them with my good arm from the soft soil. The tops kept breaking off, which was quite frustrating to me.

"Make sure you grab all of the leaves and pull straight up," said Sarah.

There was dirt all over my hands, but it fell loosely off of my gray skirt, which was good. We'd all dressed more plainly today, as we didn't want to ruin bright clothes. I'd never had to think about that before—though we didn't often wear bright colors in the Settlement, laundering was nearly perfect. And in the rare occasions when it wasn't, clothes were practically disposable, and certainly interchangeable. I was used to wearing whatever I had whenever I wanted.

"It makes me feel bad," I said.

"What does?" asked Ann.

"Taking the carrots. In the Settlement I wouldn't be allowed to touch them, let alone steal them from the Earth and eat them."

"Stealing?" Ann paused, perplexed.

"Ah… yes. You see, in the Settlement we have what is called, 'The Closed System.'" I made air quotes. "Basically, this makes sure that nothing ever gets taken away from the earth. We don't take any energy input except sunlight. We don't put anything out, not even the carbon dioxide that we breathe. It's a net neutral; we are indoors most of the time and our exhalations are converted back into regular air components using photosynthetic carbon converters that mimic the operations of plants."

"But why?" asked Ann. "I mean, wouldn't it be a lot easier to just use real plants?"

"We don't have plants in there," I said.

Before she could ask why not, Ruth said, "It is sort of like a closed system out here, too."

"What do you mean?" I asked.

"You don't have to feel bad about taking the carrots," said Ruth. "The nutrients in them will go back to the soil soon anyways. Everything in nature works that way. The water that you drink doesn't disappear. The food that you eat doesn't disappear. The air that you breathe will be filtered by plants."

"I… guess?" I said. "But what if you use everything up too fast? Faster than the Earth can replenish it?"

"Then we'll grow more food," said Ruth. "More people means more food needed, but it also means more people to help grow food. We *have* to take good care of the earth. It's the only way to ensure a continuing supply. We put our food scraps back into the garden. Our children wear the clothes of their older siblings, and when they're too torn up to be worn any more, they get cut up and made into rags. When we want something to be permanent, we make it *well* and maintain it. That means we only have to do it once. Our children will live in these houses and inherit our furniture. We have to let the soil rest between planting it, or it gets used up and we won't get good crops. We have to take care of our animals and keep them from getting sick. Sick or unhealthy animals make bad food."

I was thinking about it. I really was.

It was at that moment that I saw the men. We were in Ann's backyard, but I could see around the front of the house and past, to where they were walking through the center of the town.

The "center of town" was actually only a few houses within a few hundred yards of each other, and a few non-residential buildings which I hadn't quite figured out the purpose of yet.

The men were there, walking down Hock's only road (in fact, it was also Hanfell's only road, as it connected the two villages). The other women jumped up.

There were approximately forty men, separated into two groups. They were bedraggled and dirty. Their eyes were bleary, and some of them were soaking wet or had ragged tears in their clothes. They had more of the long rifles on their backs—not a single person was unarmed. Between them they were dragging several animal carcasses, including an elk and a boar on a sledge. I didn't know at the time what an "elk" was, and thought perhaps it was a horse. The boar was enormous, with thick brown hair, not at all the way I'd pictured a pig to look.

They all had several weeks of beard growth, and even the ones who were too young for a full beard looked rather scruffy. I could practically smell them from this distance as well, but Ann did not seem to care a bit about that and ran to her husband. Sarah followed quickly after. Ruth hung back—I thought again about how she was a widow, although she didn't know it yet.

I watched as they started disappearing into the houses, along with much loud talking and laughing. Women came out briefly, and then went back inside. The townsfolk moved the animal carcasses into one of the smaller non-residential buildings.

I walked up the road, anxious to return to the Joneses' house, and tried to get ahead of the men walking that way. Who knew what life would be like for me from now on?

One thing I knew: I'd be giving up the bed, for starters.

***

Although John-Michael Jones and his eldest son Mark were back at home, I did not see much of them for the rest of the day. First they went to bathe (there were no showers here! Bathing was done in a wooden tub in the bathroom, as I had already had occasion to discover) and then they went straight to bed. As my presence had not yet been explained to the man of the house, I'd already been vacated from his bedroom.

I was surprised that he hadn't given me more than a sideways glance, but dressed as I was now like one of the cultists, perhaps he was used to Mrs. Jones's charity, or having strangers in the house. I wondered who he thought I was.

I slept on the couch that night.

The next day, the men were looking slightly more cleaned-up. The sixteen-year-old was smooth-faced again, and I noticed the menfolk were all wearing pants—so it *was* a gender thing.

That morning at breakfast, John-Michael Jones sat down heavily at the head of the table. There were eggs, bacon, and toast in front of him, at least twice as much as I could have eaten. He raised an eyebrow at me while taking a sip of black tea. "So. Who's this?" He had a rugged appearance; more so than Mrs. Jones, though he seemed only slightly older. His hair was mostly gray. He was in good shape for his age, but there was something a little tired in his dark eyes. He covered it well, though.

Was he the cult's leader? I wondered. Or was it someone else?

"That's Alex," said Mrs. Jones cheerfully. "We found her a couple weeks ago. The river spit her out after she went through the rapids. Samuel found her; thank the Lord he did. If he hadn't, she probably would have died."

"Hmmm." He continued to look at me pensively. "Alex. You're from the Settlement, I presume."

I began to sweat. I hoped he couldn't see how nervous I was. "Yes, Mr. Jones."

"How long have you been here?" he asked.

Agh. It was as Mrs. Jones had predicted.

"Couple weeks," I said.

He raised an eyebrow. *Still alive,* I was sure he was thinking. Unlike the other man. The one who died before they could get any information out of him.

"We haven't had anyone come by from there in quite a while." He stirred a bit of sugar into his tea. Despite his rough appearance, he had a quiet tone and an educated demeanor. It was unexpected. "Why did you leave?" he asked, cutting straight to the matter.

I began to repeat the story I had told Mrs. Jones.

"I had to run. They called me a Detractor. I would have been executed."

"A detractor." He tasted the word skeptically. "That's some sort of criminal?"

"Nothing that would alarm you," I said. "All kinds of things there are Detractive. We don't eat... plants. That would be Detractive to them."

"You don't eat plants."

"Well, I do now, of course," I said in a high-pitched tone. I waved my hands, trying to seem casual, but undoubtedly coming off ridiculous.

"How did you find out about us?" His eyes seemed to pierce me, but it was not him, it was only me, I thought, only the burning guilt in my soul as I struggled to lie to him.

"I didn't," I said. "I really thought I'd just... chance it. I was following the river, and then I slipped in by accident." Well, at least that last part was true.

He kept looking at me impassively. Did he suspect me?

"All right then," he said finally, and set down the mug with a *clack*. "You are welcome here. If my wife trusts you, I do as well. Everything we have is yours until we can find a way to settle you independently. But I do warn you, that may take a while."

Mrs. Jones leaned back against the counter, giving a wry smile while drying her hands on a dish rag.

"Thank you," I said. "I'm perfectly happy staying with you as long as you'll let me."

He turned back to his food.

The sixteen-year-old, Mark, continued watching me, perhaps a tad more suspicious, or not as good as concealing it as his father. He was remarkably tall and strongly-built for a boy of his age; boys in the Settlement were usually far more slim. In fact, Cam and Jesse and other DYNTEC operatives were unusual examples of their kind; most Settlement citizens weren't big on fitness. Nor had I been before joining DYNTEC, however.

"Tomorrow is Sunday," said Mr. Jones without preamble, "and we are going to church. The minister is back in town with us, and he says that he will be ready to preach."

"Oh, excellent," said Mrs. Jones. "We've missed him these last two Sundays. Alex hasn't been to church."

"I see," said Mr. Jones.

***

The next day I dressed in Mrs. Jones's second-best clothes. Everyone was looking sharp, even the babies. One-year-old Rachel was placed into a covered basket.

This is going to be the religious induction. Surely. I didn't know what it would entail, but I'd find out about it soon enough. In my mind I had images of hoods, chanting, maybe animal blood. I had to admit, I had a growing curiosity to learn more details about their god, since their day-to-day religious practice had been somewhat less terrifying than I'd expected. But I supposed it was too soon to be at ease— this *was* still a cult, and things could turn on a dime.

Mark saddled up two horses and pulled up in the front of the house with a wagon hitched. John-Michael Jones took the reins. "Climb in, everybody."

It took a long time for the children and babies to be loaded, but eventually we got moving. I sat in the back on the wagon bench and held down my bonnet whenever we went over a bump to keep it from flying off.

The church was midway between Hock and Hanfell, and it was several miles down the road. I had not seen the building before. It was a white painted house with wooden sideboards, and taller than any of the Kingdom buildings I'd seen so far. Its roof was steeply sloped, and there was a T-shaped symbol affixed to its peak, pointing up into the sky.

There were a large number of other wagons and horses drawn up around the church. Mr. Jones pulled up to the building and stopped the wagon. We got out and walked into the church while he went to hitch the horses.

When I followed Mrs. Jones and the family inside, the entire room was filled with people, all dressed in the common style. It seemed like every cultist in the entire town—probably both towns—must be here. I moved silently and stiffly, trying not to draw attention to myself. I was relieved that most of them seemed not to notice me, but I quickly located Ruth, Ann, and Sarah, who waved and smiled at me. I smiled back hesitantly and waved my fingers.

The building was full of long benches facing the front of the room. We filed into the rows. Mr. Jones joined us presently, and a round-faced man walked up to the front of the room.

"Please stand for worship," he said loudly.

A sound echoed from the front of the room. I could easily see over the heads of the people in front of me, and I saw that another man was sitting on a chair nearby, and he held an unfamiliar wooden device which was producing this sound.

I recognized it.

Music.

At the sound of the music, the cultists began to sing. They had no books and no prompters, but they seemed to have the song committed to memory and to recognize it immediately.

O Lord my God
When I in awesome wonder
Consider all
The worlds thy hands have made
I see the stars
I hear the rolling thunder
Thy pow'r throughout
The universe displayed
Then sings my soul, my savior, God, to thee:
How great thou art
How great thou art
Then sings my soul, my savior, God, to thee:
How great thou art
How great thou art.

Music in the Settlement was a private matter.

When I listened to music, it was only through my audio implants, where nobody else could hear it. If I sang, it was in the shower or very quietly, alone in my house. I would have felt mortified for anyone to witness such an expression; and to be quite honest I didn't have a clue what music anybody else liked, or whether my preferences were considered acceptable or irritating.

Because most people didn't know or talk about each other's music preferences, the taboos against noise imposition were strong, and so music was seldom played out loud. If two people wished, they could attune their audio implants to the same channel. I'd been told this caused a striking rapport between two people, but I'd never experienced it, since I'd never been that close with someone before.

But this music wasn't coming from an implant. That thing the man was holding on the stage was an actual instrument, such as wasn't used in the Settlement any longer, since we could synthesize any sound perfectly.

Or so I'd believed.

But compared to the implant, this sound was transcendent. Maybe it was something about the space that we occupied, but it seemed to echo from everywhere at once, filling the church. The voices of the people merged together in an imperfect harmony of various pitches and tones that somehow averaged into a pleasant, joyous, sound.

I could not sing. Not here. Not with these people. But the sound filled my chest cavity and sank down into my bones.

"You may be seated," said the Minister loudly.

I heard the rustling of everyone in the church sitting down at once.

"I regret," said the Minister, "that I have not been able to prepare a sermon this week due to my recent return from our hunting trip. Instead, I shall give a reading from the Book of Isaiah. Please open your Bibles to Isaiah 40."

Some others around me had this book. Mr. Jones had one, and the family crowded around him closely to read over his shoulder. Similar huddles were happening around the room.

The Minister began to read.

"Surely the nations are like a drop in a bucket;
they are regarded as dust on the scales;
he weighs the islands as though they were fine
dust.
Lebanon is not sufficient for altar fires,
nor its animals enough for burnt offerings.
Before him all the nations are as nothing;

they are regarded by him as worthless
and less than nothing."

What book was this? The words astonished me. He continued reading.

"Do you not know?
Have you not heard?
Has it not been told you from the beginning?
Have you not understood since the earth was founded?
He sits enthroned above the circle of the earth,
and its people are like grasshoppers.
He stretches out the heavens like a canopy,
and spreads them out like a tent to live in.
He brings princes to naught
and reduces the rulers of this world to nothing.
No sooner are they planted,
no sooner are they sown,
no sooner do they take root in the ground,
than he blows on them and they wither,
and a whirlwind sweeps them away like chaff.

"To whom will you compare me?
Or who is my equal?" says the Holy One.
Lift up your eyes and look to the heavens:
Who created all these?
He who brings out the starry host one by one
and calls forth each of them by name.

Because of his great power and mighty strength,
 not one of them is missing."

I was amazed. This God was not Gaia. He was nothing like Gaia. Yet he seemed to account for everything I had witnessed so far. I thought (while smacking myself for having such detractive thoughts) that this was a kind of God whose existence might not be so far-fetched.

I thought of this God looking down on the Administrators of the Settlement, feeling not at all threatened, but rather irritated. It was an amusing thought.

Perhaps I'd better take Cam up on his challenge to find out more about their deity. It would be good to report some real information back to him when we met up.

***

"Grace and peace to you…" the Minister finished reciting a blessing, and then said, "You may be dismissed."

Then the sound of talking gradually started and the service began to break up.

As the people started to disband, I slowly made my way toward the Minister, hanging back, afraid of being noticed.

He was talking to the other men, but there was a moment when his eyes latched on to me, and I knew that he knew who I was. The news had already gotten around, even to the men who had been absent during my arrival. In a community where everyone was known, I was easy to pick out.

"Good morning," said the Minister. "I understand that you're new around here."

I nodded. Finally, I was getting my chance to speak with the cult leader. If anyone was their leader, it had to be this man who stood at the front of the room during their religious services.

"I am interested in hearing more about your God," I said, cautiously.

"Well, that's a sentence I like to hear." He broke out in a wide grin, and I thought he was going to laugh, but he didn't.

"Follow me," he said.

I walked with him through a side door in the church and out into the long grass under the morning sun.

"We've had rumors and legends about the great oppression in the Settlement," said the Minister. "It has been some time since we've received a refugee, but we will do everything we can to help you. I'm very glad you found us."

You shouldn't be, I thought, and my stomach twisted bitterly. But I continued to walk with him. "Thank you," I said.

"What do you know of our God?" asked the Minister.

"Not very much," I admitted. "Until today I thought possibly that your God was a human being, and I just hadn't met him yet. But now I see that is not the case."

The minister smiled. "Perhaps you were more right than you think."

"What do you mean?" I asked.

The Minister started carefully.

"Our God," he said, "became a human being once."

"What? Really? When?"

He smiled.

I let him continue.

"It was a long time ago. We reckon it at twenty-six hundred years now, although we are aware the Settlement has different ways of accounting time."

"Five hundred since the Establishment," I said.

The Minister nodded, and then began to tell me the most outlandish story that I had ever heard in my life. We did not stop walking as I listened to him, and it took him some time to make his explanation.

"A very long time ago," he started, "a baby was born in a small village."

And so he went on, talking about histories and prophecies, and an ancient nation called the Hebrews, and miracles, and sacrifices, and death, and life.

It was a lot to take in.

We had made it some distance away from the church, turned around, and come halfway back to the building by the time he finished.

Eventually, I said, "So this God, he is all-powerful, yes?"

"Yes," said the Minister.

"And he knows everything, right?"

"M-hm."

"That sounds a lot like the Administrators of the Settlement." I was not entirely sure in what spirit I was saying this. At the time I told myself it was disdain, but perhaps it was a fear that this God and the Administrators were somehow the same.

"They enjoy playing God," said the Minister. "It is wrong of them."

"How is this different?" I asked. "You talked about obedience to God. In the Settlement, we comply with our Administrators in everything they require. This sounds just like that."

He shook his head. "No it's not. Compliance is passive. Compliance is a poor counterfeit for obeying someone you respect and trust. Obedience is something we do actively on purpose."

"Hmm." We were almost back at the church building now, and every wagon had gone except for the Joneses'.

I realized at this point he seemed to be expecting something, and I was afraid he might demand an immediate declaration of loyalty to his God. Of course, for the sake of the mission, I shouldn't have been afraid to do so, but my head was still turning over trying to even *understand* their religion. Additionally, I felt some vague fear about making any statements on the matter, either for or against.

"I will think about this," I said. "Really. I hope it's all right if I go now, I'm sure the Joneses will be looking for me."

"Of course," said the Minister. "No problem at all."

Chapter Twenty-Two

Break from the Fold

I found my chance to get away not long after that day. My arm bandages had come off at last, and I notified Cam privately that I was ready to meet.

After breakfast on Tuesday, the family had dispersed to do their chores. Mrs. Jones was outside feeding the chickens. The boys were cleaning out the cows' stalls. The girls were doing lessons. Mr. Jones was in the shed (which I'd only ever seen from the outside) apparently butchering a quarter of the boar, which had been divided by the men and stored in the village ice-house over the weekend. Something told me I wasn't going to see him for the rest of the day. And I probably didn't want to. I shuddered when my mind's eye gave me an image of the man covered head-to-toe in blood.

Since no one was watching me, I walked down to the road as casually as possible, then around the hillock, away from the view of the other houses. I began to walk round to the back of the nearest cornfield, which I'd learned belonged to the Smiths. I'd walked there before and no one would question why I was back there, but I'd have a good opportunity to make a break into the woods unseen. Surprisingly, this sort of thing was actually a lot easier out here than in the Settlement, where there were cameras everywhere.

Cam had said he would meet me at the edge of the pine forest. I walked through the trees for about half an hour.

The Settlement was twenty miles long, and usually that felt like a very long distance, because it was the sum total of everything that we knew. Everything I needed was close by, and I didn't usually need to walk more than a few minutes for any reason. If I had to go to another district, I would have taken the subway. Because my personal world had been so small, the Settlement had seemed large by comparison.

But measuring a mile by walking made me realize that a mile wasn't actually that far. Cam was coming dangerously close to the Kingdom.

When I reached the edge of the trees I saw the relative smoothness of the land that would permit a vehicle to come this far—perhaps it had been farmed once. It was no wonder this was his meeting place; but if anyone saw a vehicle parked out here there would be trouble for both of us.

Cam's voice came through my Biometric.

"I can see you up on the ridge. I've parked another mile off. I'm down in the grass; stay where you are."

I obeyed, watching, and eventually I spotted him, dressed in black clothes that covered his whole body to the neck and wrists. He was coming up out of the waving grasses to meet me.

"Alex!" He squinted at me. "What on earth are you wearing?"

"It's a dress," I said.

"Do they all wear that?" he asked.

"Just the women," I said, squinting back.

"You look a bit tan," said Cam.

"I've been spending time outside," I said. "Are you satisfied I'm not being threatened or manipulated?"

Cam had joined me on the ridge. He walked a circle around me. "Well, I can see you're physically well and you don't have a gun to your temple. Manipulation is a trickier beast. Why don't you tell me what you've learned about them?"

"I'm well because they've taken care of me," I said. "My arm's better now. I have… scars on my stomach, but that would be a bit inconvenient to show you now."

"That's all right," said Cam. "I don't fault you for taking so long to contact. Jesse and the Administrators are aware of your injuries." He squatted down on his heels.

I nodded, and sat down carefully in the short grass, folding my legs. "One of the women nursed me back to health. I owe her my life."

"*Owe* her?"

I shrugged a little.

"Oh boy," said Cam. "You don't owe anybody anything, Alex. She's a cultist."

"What difference does that make?"

"They're evil!" he protested, and made as if to stand.

I remembered his words in the bar. *Real scum, usually. The worst of the worst.*

"Every one of them is evil? And you are certain of this? Aren't I here to find out if they can be rehabilitated?"

His eyes narrowed.

But... this one. There was something different about him.

"The Administrators wouldn't have sent me to find out if they didn't think it might be possible. So even the Administrators wanted to give them a chance, but you can't even be that generous—"

Cam flinched. "Hey! I just said you don't *owe* her. Cults sometimes try to indebt you."

"I know," I said. "It was in the training. Just hear me out. They've got a sort of rudimentary society. They're doing their best. They produce only enough food to feed themselves, and they get it out of the dirt, by farming. It doesn't seem to be harming Gaia, as far as I can tell."

"Alex…"

"No, listen! They do a lot of domestic crafts and pretty much produce all their own products. And trade them with each other. They all know each other and are very friendly. They feed their animals and keep them healthy and the animals don't seem to mind their presence, usually. Their religion… they have daily prayer rituals after eating. Mostly they talk about love and… generosity and so forth, I don't really see any harm in it." I talked faster. "The children seem to be doing pretty well. They have lessons, they are able to read and write. I think if you were worried about their education, that's not really so much of a concern…"

"Alex." Cam's voice was grim. "Do you remember why you're here?"

"…yes?" I didn't dare to say no.

"Your job isn't to decide whether or not these people's lifestyle is acceptable. The Settlement has already decided that issue. You are here to provide us with information."

I lowered my eyes.

"The population and demographics of the cult?"

"They're divided into two villages," I told him, "Hock and Hanfell. It seems like they're mostly separated by family affiliation. There are thirty-eight men in Hock and forty-two in Hanfell, and another eighty women or so between both villages, and about two hundred children.”

“*Thank* you,” said Cam. “Now listen, it seems to me like you might be sympathizing with these cultists too much. I understand that you’re grateful to them, but you have a more… well… sentimental personality.” He shrugged. “You have to realize it’s probably more personal to you than it is to them. Anyway, I’m concerned. They’d turn on you in a heartbeat if they knew your loyalties were with outsiders. Just remember that. I’m concerned about you keeping sound judgment.”

“My judgment is as sound as it’s always been,” I said.

Cam studied me closely, and I noticed that he did seem legitimately worried for me, as much as he tried to disguise his emotions on the regular.

“Why did you ask to meet in person?” I folded my hands together.

It was his turn to get defensive. “I wanted to make sure you weren’t being held—”

“No, no.” I shook my head. “That’s not the real reason, is it?”

He looked sideways. “Out here we can talk without being overheard.”

“By…?”

"Anyone."

There was a moment's silence where I listened to the wind in the grass.

Cam started speaking fast, in a rushed way that seemed a little thrown, a little off-kilter. "I mean, Alex, this might be legitimately the only chance we'll have in our *lives* to talk to each other without being listened to."

"Don't be ridiculous," I said. Half of me didn't want to believe it, and the other half didn't want it to matter.

"I mean, like, if you wanted to be one hundred percent sure."

I stared at him challengingly. "Okay… and? What is it you are so desperate to say to me without being overheard?"

He seemed to clam up suddenly. "I…I don't know."

"What?"

"I guess I don't really know. Sorry. Forget I said anything."

I was still trying to look at him questioningly, but he went on to the mission briefing. "We'll meet again a week from today. You bring me some information on that anti-drone technology. I don't know how they're doing it, but it seems too advanced for what they should be capable of with the resources you've just described."

"I'll get it for you," I said, and nodded. A continuation of the assignment was what I needed. For a moment

I'd almost been afraid he'd pull me back to his jeep and drive off with me right there.

"Good. Stay in contact."

Chapter Twenty-Three

Gaia's Wrath

After Cam departed, I began to walk back to the Kingdom. I made a brisk walk through the forest. As I neared the edge of the woods, I kept a lookout in the near distance for the corn stalks that would indicate my return to the inhabited zone.

Somehow I didn't even see the bear until I was almost upon it. The brown of its coat camouflaged perfectly with the decomposing fallen leaves on the ground.

It stood there, stock-still. I froze as well, hardly daring to breathe.

The animal's ears flicked. It hadn't been hunting me, or following me, as far as I was aware. Perhaps it hadn't even smelled me coming. We had found each other in the woods and were almost equally surprised.

It turned its massive head on it sinewy neck and fixed its eyes on me. Its black, beady, vacant eyes. Its fur was a rough texture, and it filled the air with a rank scent.

The farm animals had scared me enough, and even they had stayed well away from me (except for the chickens). I had been frightened enough of the cows in the pasture even after the assurance that they weren't going to run up and attack me. This bear was so enormous it looked as though it could have fought one of those cows and come out the winner.

It was only about thirty or forty feet away.

I stumbled backwards through the leaves. My heart hammered inside my chest and throat. The bear was between me and the Kingdom.

I wanted to run, but I felt frozen. My feet would barely move. The bear started lumbering towards me on its massive paws. Its shoulders rippled as it walked.

I let out a short scream and started shuffling, trying to run without turning around. My foot caught on a root, and I tumbled face-first into the loam. I rolled over, and panicked as I tried to free my foot. The bear was only ten feet away now. I could see its white teeth in black gums.

Suddenly, a shot rang out through the woodlands, startling birds from the trees. A shiver went through the bear. Its ears flicked another direction. It recoiled on its hind legs, turned about, and then loped off through the forest.

Behind where it had been, I saw Mrs. Jones. She stood behind the scope of a long rifle. Her eyes fixed on me, and she lowered the gun. She frowned and beckoned to me.

I clambered to my feet and ran to her.

"Alex!" she started. "Are you all right?"

But I couldn't stop running.

I made it back to the edge of the corn field, and I kept running down the path towards the houses. Mrs. Jones adopted a quick but decisive stride in the same direction.

"This is why it's dangerous for you to go out on your own," she continued, calling after me. "You're fortunate. Samuel saw you go off in this direction. If I hadn't decided to go looking for you—" I could barely hear what she was saying; I was running too fast.

When we had slammed the door of the house behind the both of us, I pressed back against the wall, trying to catch my breath. "When you see a bear," Mrs. Jones told me, "you *don't* run."

John-Michael Jones stood up from the table. "A bear? Where is it?"

"It's gone," said Mrs. Jones.

Mr. Jones reached for the rifle, and she handed it over to him, with the point towards the ceiling.

"Did you kill it?" he asked.

"No. Definitely hit it, though. It's run off into the woods. I should have told you earlier. The girls spotted some droppings recently. We knew it was in the area."

"Then I have to go kill it."

"John! Are you sure? It ran away."

"Yes, I do." His voice was grim. "It's even more dangerous now that it's wounded. It won't leave the area. It will come back here, since it won't be able to hunt its normal prey. It will go after the livestock or even the kids."

Samuel and Mark immediately stood up. "Can I come?" "Yeah, can we come with you?" they asked at the same time.

"No!" said Mrs. Jones.

"No," said Mr. Jones, and both the children's faces fell as they sat back down slowly.

"I'll be back. Keep an eye out for me." He then slammed the door behind him.

The atmosphere in the house was tense. I couldn't help feeling as though this was somehow my fault. Of course, it wasn't my fault that the bear was there. But Mrs. Jones had wounded it trying to protect me. And now they had no choice but to kill the bear or it would kill a human.

The Administrators would have sacrificed many humans to save one bear.

The thought popped into my head before I could stop it. Hopefully no humans had to die today. I couldn't help it; I was biased in favor of the humans.

We tried to resume our activities. I started washing the dishes. Gracie and the babies started writing at the table again. Mrs. Jones picked up a broom and kept nervously sweeping the same area of the floor. Thirty minutes went by; an hour. Mrs. Jones kept going to the kitchen window, which was high, at her eye level, and peering through the shutter slats. I looked through after she moved away.

As the sun fell, a fog had begun rising lightly from the ground into the cold air, and now it rose around the distant trees. We could see a ways down the hill, to where the rooftops of two other houses peeked over the ridge.

An echoing gunshot cracked across the silence.

Mrs. Jones straightened up like a rod and raced to the back of the house. We followed her to the bedroom, where the window was much larger. She threw open the curtain, letting a flood of silver-gray light stream across the floor. Then she pulled up the inner shutters with the paper, and the outer slats let us see through.

There was a dark shape against the treeline. It staggered backwards. John-Michael Jones was standing nearby, with his rifle leveled at his shoulder.

The bear lunged forward. At the same instant, there was another loud *bang!*

The bear slumped to the ground.

I saw Mrs. Jones breathe a sigh of relief. The children crowded around the window. "Did he kill it?" "Dad killed the bear!"

I noticed, however, that she had not yet answered them. Mr. Jones cautiously closed the distance on the bear. He walked cautiously in his boots across the wet grass, extended his rifle barrel, and prodded it in the neck.

There was an instant that couldn't have been more than half a second, but seemed an eternity, where I couldn't guess what was going to happen next.

Then the bear lunged. Its paw swept out, knocking Mr. Jones off his feet. He tumbled into the wet grass. The bear's jaws yawned open, and Mrs. Jones gave a stifled scream.

Something happened very fast: a movement, a flash of metal. Then Mr. Jones was scrambling away from the bear, half crawling. There was a wide smear of blood—on his clothes, on the bear's mouth and fur—soaking into the grass. The bear dropped limp and its eyes closed.

Mrs. Jones had run to the front door and was already outside. The children and I watched at the window for her to appear.

She was visible a moment later, running out across the grass to her husband, who was now stumbling toward the house. She put her arm under him, supporting part of his weight, and he continued limping up the hill. They were saying things I couldn't hear.

We all gathered in the front room.

"What happened?" John asked me, tugging on my skirt. "Is he all right?"

"Are they coming back?" asked Eva.

I looked down at them, bewildered.

I had a sudden acute awareness of being the only adult in the room. I'd been an Educator once, assisting in the classroom management of Settlement children, but yet somehow, I felt like the children's respect for me was misplaced. These kids knew more about their environment than I did. I didn't even have any way to reassure them in a crisis. I hardly deserved to be called an adult.

Fortunately, the older boys seemed to have the situation well in hand. "Just wait," said Samuel.

"Don't crowd around the door," Mark said, and shuffled them off to the table. I backed away from the door, right about the same moment that it burst open.

Grace Jones supported John-Michael over the threshold. He limped inside with a loud grunt, and then into the living room, where he fell heavily onto the couch. His trousers were torn, and his leg was injured badly enough to scatter drops of blood across the floor.

"Stay there, I'll get a towel and the bandages." She ignored all of us and dashed for the cupboards.

"Dad, what happened?" asked little John. "Did you kill the bear?"

"Are you okay?" asked Eva anxiously. "It got your leg."

"It's dead, right?" said Mark, the eldest.

"It's dead this time." Mr. Jones grunted with a pant.

"How did you kill it?" asked little John.

"We all saw it get your leg," said Mark.

"Well, Mark," said Mr. Jones. "Maybe a while later you can go out there and bring back my hunting knife, the long one. It's still in that thing's throat."

I shuddered.

At that moment, Mrs. Jones arrived back with the bandages and shooed us all out of the room.

I couldn't help feeling that the bear attack was my fault. That it was because Gaia was angry. At me. I wasn't sure why. Perhaps it was because I was betraying Gaia, or because I had betrayed the Settlement to allow myself to be won over by these people. As much as I liked them personally, I simply couldn't let myself be taken in by their worldviews. My thoughts were all wrong, my head was all wrong. It was they who had to be corrected; surely Gaia was trying to punish us.

I went to sleep that night with my face toward the back of the couch, muddled and confused.

Chapter Twenty-Four
Flying Machines

Cam wanted me to get the information about the anti-drone technology, but I had no idea where to start. That day, however, I had plenty of time alone with the smaller children while Mrs. Jones watched over Mr. Jones and the older boys did the chores.

I got the sense that Mr. Jones was going to make a full recovery—his leg wasn't broken, and his wife had stopped the bleeding. Around midday, Mrs. Jones got back to doing the chores as well. But she didn't have time for schooling.

Gracie went off to her room as usual. Mark and Samuel went off to pay a visit to one of the neighbors—but didn't say which one. That left me with the responsibility of entertaining Eva, Little John, Mary, and Jeremiah until further notice.

We went outside, in front of the house, on the hillside, opposite from where the bear had been shot and its corpse was still lying. We couldn't see it, but the idea of it still being there haunted the back of my mind. The kids didn't seem to think of it; it was they who had insisted on going outside to begin with.

Jeremy, as his siblings called him, was playing with a large bowl. I watched as he pulled out grass by the fistful and dumped it into the bowl. He toddled over and grabbed some leaves from the nearby azalea bush and threw them into the bowl, with shreds of dandelion and clover.

Mary grabbed it from him possessively, put it in her lap, and started sprinkling in flower petals. The two of them got into a pulling match, Jeremy fell on his bottom and yelled a little bit, and then he ran and got a handful of dry dirt and threw it in. I cringed.

"Hey guys," I started, "what are you doing over there?"

Mary picked up another handful of dirt and sprinkled it finely over the concoction like it was a fine seasoning. "MAKING SOUP!" she yelled, and then brazenly, without a hint of hesitation, grabbed a fistful of the dirty leaves and grass and put them into her mouth.

I *screamed* and dove for the bowl.

They scattered like running spiders. I found myself holding a nearly empty bowl and nothing else—the 'soup' was spilled out.

The door burst open.

There was Mrs. Jones, looking a little panicked. She calmed down when she saw everyone playing calmly, except me, lying on the grass curled around a wooden bowl. I sat up.

"Alex! What is going on? I thought someone was hurt!"

"Mary was eating grass—and dirt!"

"Just—oh, come on. Just tell them to stop, they know better. They'll listen to you."

That she was not alarmed shocked me, but I nodded.

She looked at the girl. "Mary, don't eat the dirt."

"Okay…" said Mary, spitting out a leaf.

"Maybe you can think of something to entertain them," she said, "they're bored." And then she closed the door again.

It took me a few more minutes to come up with what I thought was a pretty good idea. I couldn't just start asking the adults questions about the anti-drone technology, and the older children might become suspicious. But maybe the little kids would be able to help me out.

"Hey Mary," I addressed the six-year-old.

"Yeah!" Mary jumped up off the ground.

"Have you ever seen… anything… in the sky?"

"Like a bird?" She tilted her head.

"No, like a machine. A flying machine."

"A machine," she repeated. I thought for a second she'd completely lost her train of thought, because she turned around and started walking away. Then she came back and leaned onto my lap, getting up in my face. "What are *you* talking about? Machines don't *fly.*"

"Yeah, they do," I said. "Some of them. They have little spinning blades like… bzzzz." I moved my finger in a circle. "You might not hear them though; they're pretty quiet."

"Bzzzzzzzzzzzzz," said four-year-old Jeremiah on the floor.

"What kind of machine?" Asked Eva. She was ten, and pretty smart. I was just glad Grace was busy right now. The twelve-year-old was quiet, but smart, and I sensed she would have been on to me, even if she kept it to herself.

"I was just wondering if you'd seen any," I dodged. "They have them in the Settlement where I come from."

"I don't think so," said Eva. "Why would they fly so far away from where they live?"

I didn't like the direction this was going. "Oh, you know," I said. "Just looking around. They do that."

"We only have flying birds," said Mary.

I nodded, disappointed, but willing to accept that they couldn't tell me anything.

It was several minutes later that a funny thought occurred to me. "Hey Eva," I said. "Your sister said you have flying birds. What does she mean? What kind of flying birds?"

"You know, like hawks and falcons. Hunting birds. Do they have those in the city?"

"No," I said. "We don't have animals in the city."

"Well, the Falconers have them. They live in Hanfell."

"That's cool," I said. "I've never seen a falcon. Maybe sometime soon you can show me the birds."

"I wanna go see the birds!" Mary jumped up onto the porch and ran to the front door.

When I looked over my shoulder, I saw that she was gone, but I heard her voice from inside. "Mama! Can Alex take us up to see the Falconers? Pleeeeease?"

"I..." Mrs. Jones sounded stressed. "Now?"

She came out to look at us, wiping her hands on her apron. "I...I do feel a bit nervous about it, but I don't suppose there are any more bears around. Not likely. Alex, do you want to? It would help me out for the moment."

"Yes!" I said, decisively. I was a bit excited, and I let her see it. I stepped up to the doorway.

"Good, I suppose. Just take… just take the gun with you, and Rachel and Jeremy are not coming. Grace!"

"Yes, Mama," I heard her dully from the back.

"Jeremy is with you now."

"Yes, Mama."

I stood in the doorway as Mrs. Jones opened the closet, removed one of the rifles, and handed it to me. I took it gingerly.

"Stay on the road between here and Hanfell. Be safe."

"We'll be safe," I assured her. "If I see a bear, I'll shoot it." I smiled a little. "Twice."

As I turned around, Mark was there in the doorway, as though to come into the house. He looked up and down at me, holding the rifle, and he seemed almost affronted. I stared back, but could not tell what he was thinking. There was a momentary awkward silence, and then I slipped past him.

***

We walked the dirt road; myself, John, Eva, and Mary. It was a bright, sunny day, and the hillside was clear and grassy, leaving me an unobstructed view of any approaching bears.

No danger of any kind appeared, however. We soon passed out of Hock, and into the empty space between towns, then the church, which stood uninhabited for the time being. I saw one far-off man walking towards us, and tensed as he approached, but he merely nodded and tipped his hat to us as he walked past, and the children greeted him by name as Mr. Smith.

We entered Hanfell before an hour had passed. The first signs of the other village were the sprawling fences, and the sheep and grazing cows on the hills.

"The Falconers live over there!" Eva shouted into the wind and pointed. There was another log farmhouse a ways off. Somebody was already outside. He was standing out in the field, a roughly-trimmed pasture with a goat chewing on some grass away at the far edge.

Eva climbed up and leaned over the wooden fence rail. "Hey!"

The man turned toward us. He was young, perhaps in his twenties. His arm was raised. On his hand he wore a thick, heavy glove, and perched on the glove was a bird.

This bird was nothing like the little sparrows in the field. It was the largest bird I had ever seen— it looked even bigger than the chickens, though perhaps that was an illusion. It preened with its beak, and then spread its wings wide. They unfolded to a span of several feet. The animal launched itself into the air with a mighty thrust.

I watched it flap up into the sky, where it circled around the house calmly.

"Hey! Looks like the Joneses came to visit! Eva? Mary? John? And…" the young man gave me a quizzical look as he quickened his step towards us.

"Alex wanted to see the flying birdies!" shouted Mary.

"Hi," I said. "My name's Alex."

"Ah, right. I think I saw you at church. Sorry about that."

"No worries," I said.

"Did you need something?"

"Just taking the kids out… of Mrs. Jones's hair," I said. Then I jumped, and the kids screamed and flinched as the bird swooped in again and landed on his glove with enough force to nearly push him back.

"Well, hi. My name's Matt. This is Russell."

"Russell?"

"He's a fishing eagle." Matt smiled. "And a very good hunter, too, aren't you boy?"

"Does he catch fish?" I asked.

"We eat a lot of salmon around here," nodded Matt.

"He's so big," I marveled.

"Very intelligent, too. We train him for a lot of things. Of course, for messages, we have the pigeons, but when you want to hunt or attack, this is the bird for the job."

"Cool." We then watched the bird fly again at Matt's command and listened to a long explanation of his eating habits and care that was probably more interesting to Matt than it was to me.

I was careful not to say anything else about flying machines, but I was pretty sure I now had a pretty good idea of what was going on.

***

When we arrived back at the house, the kids all dispersed and settled in. I started washing the clothes in a tub for Mrs. Jones, and then pinning them up on a line out back. I hadn't been at it more than an hour when the Joneses' eldest son, Mark, found me.

"You're back," he said.

I paused to take a clothespin out of my mouth, waiting for him to continue.

"You'll never guess what I've found," he said.

"What?" I asked.

"Come with me!" He started off toward the shed.

I didn't follow, at first. "What Is it?"

"It's a surprise, you'll just have to come along and see."

Somehow, with my mind so fixated on drones and birds, I didn't suspect anything. I half wondered if maybe he'd found a drone, or maybe it was just another new animal that I'd never seen before. I dropped the shirt back into the tub and went after him.

"Come on," said Mark urgently. He started off towards the shed. I followed him inside.

The shed was a dark, musty place built of unpainted wooden planks, with knots and holes in the wood. The floor was covered with straw. The only things I could see inside were some shovels, a rake, and a workbench with hammers, nails, and a saw. There were hooks hanging from the ceiling where Mr. Jones had been working on the boar carcass. That was gone now, however, leaving only a little blood on the mostly-fresh straw.

Mark brushed aside the straw with his foot, revealing a wooden, square-shaped trapdoor.

He pried open the door with some effort. It squeaked rustily. I looked down into the gloom. I couldn't see anything except for the top of a wooden ladder.

"It's down there," he said.

"Down there?"

"In the storm cellar."

I nodded and waited for him to go down first. When he was at the bottom, I could see the top of his head, so I gathered my skirt carefully around my legs and descended the five or six steps to the bottom, then stepped off the ladder. The storm cellar smelled damp and earthy. I was standing with only one layer of wooden planks between me and the moist earth.

I turned around, examining the cramped space. "Is there a light down here? I don't see anyth—"

I cut myself off. Mark was gone. His boots were already withdrawing into the light above. I grabbed the ladder. "Wait! What are you doing? What's going on—"

My words were cut off by the sound of the trapdoor slamming loudly shut. The light source was cut off, and I was suddenly immersed in total darkness.

I was alarmed, but even still, at first I didn't understand why he'd done this.

I started trying to climb up the ladder immediately, but I could only pound on the underside of the door. There was the loud grinding noise of something heavy sliding over the trapdoor.

I banged on the underside. "Hey! What are you doing? Let me out!"

There was a clack of boots on board as he stepped down toward the hatch. His voice was smooth, casual, like nothing was wrong. "I was walking a couple miles up the river," he said. "I found it there. You'll never guess what it was."

"Huh?" I didn't understand. What was this, some kind of bizarre prank? I tried to backtrack in my mind, allaying some of the panic. He was only a kid. I didn't know what was going on. "No," I said impatiently, "I'm sure I'll never guess."

"I found a piece of paper. Do you want to tell me where it came from?"

I realized, with a sinking feeling, that I'd been had. I knew what he was talking about. My panic started building again. He was on to me. Everything was broken. But I could fix it—okay maybe not, but the only proof he had was this paper.

"How should I know where it came from?" I demanded. "Probably one of you guys dropped it." I wondered if he could hear my breathing, faster and faster.

My denial didn't land. "This isn't like normal paper. I found it on the riverbank, lying half in the water, but when I took it out, it wasn't even wet."

It was. There was no getting around it now.

"Do you know what's printed on it?"

"No," I said. "I told you, I don't know what you're talking about." I didn't even know what I hoped to gain from keeping up the pretense, but I had to, I *had to*. I didn't want it to be true. I wanted to keep living the lie— No! I wanted the lie to become the truth. I wished I was an innocent refugee. But I wasn't. Oh, Gaia, I wasn't.

"It's a map," he said. "You didn't find us by accident. You came here on purpose."

"Maybe, but—"

"Maybe?"

"Yes, okay, but…" I cast about desperately. My voice wavered. "I knew there were people, yes, but I was trying to escape…"

"Then why did you lie about it?" I could hear the note of satisfaction in his tone.

That silenced me. I pulled my hands back from the door.

"You didn't escape at all, did you?"

Chapter Twenty-Five

I Am a Traitor

Mark's voice faded, his steps passed from the floorboards, and I knew that he had gone. He was telling his parents about me. About the map. My lies. The truth.

Could I escape? *Should* I escape? I continued pounding on the underside of the trapdoor in panic, but then, fearing to have it opened while I stood on the ladder, I backed down and kept touch on the ladder with my fingers, trying to stay grounded in the consuming darkness.

I could not.

They're going to kill me.

The thought floated in on the waves of void. I was surprised by it, and surprised that I was surprised.

DYNTEC warned you about this. The Administrators warned you about this. This is the part where they torture you for information and then kill you. They can. You know he could. The man killed a bear. Your training means nothing.

Still I waited, stiff with fear.

I didn't know what they were doing up there, but every moment of deliberation was worse and worse.

I can't tell them anything. My training… my training. If I do, the Settlement… I struggled to think. *The Settlement will kill me. Oh Earth, I'm going to die one way or another.*

I continued to think, and my thoughts came with increasing clarity as though the light and color of the Kingdom, which I was so unused to, had overwhelmed me before and blocked them out.

John-Michael Jones was coming to the storm basement to kill me, and it was better for me to die at his hand than face what the Settlement would do to me if they found out I'd failed my task. But if he did, Cam would move in on the hitherto unsuspecting Kingdom with fire and fury. I couldn't let that happen. They were all going to die, and it was going to be my fault.

It felt like it had been hours. No one was there to provoke me, but alone in the darkness of the storm cellar I suffered torments as dreadful as anything the Settlement could have devised, as terrible as anything I imagined the cult could do to me. I was crushed under my sense of guilt. John-Michael Jones could kill me, and he'd be right to do so.

So would the Settlement. I'd been false to both of them.

But the Settlement had ordered me to betray the Kingdom.

How can both of them be right?

The answer was obvious. They couldn't.

A strange moment came over me then, like the moment when a vase becomes two faces. Nothing had changed, yet somehow everything had changed. There was only one person in this town caught in the grip of an evil cult, and I knew that person was me.

Truly, the Settlement was a sequestered backwater, and this, *this* was the real world. I had lived all my life inside of an illusion, a dim façade, trapped in the screen of a small black and white television.

But why? Why did we live this a way? It was the trees, the sky, the fire, the stars that were real.

The moment Dana Morris-Fletcher had shown me the true state of the Earth from the top of her tower, a core dogma of the Settlement had taken a fatal blow.

None of this was necessary. None of this was life-or-death. The Administrators were lying, and they knew they were lying. We had spent five hundred years trapped inside the Wall for *no good reason.*

The Administrators' iron grip over every resource, every drop of water, every breath of air, every second of work and energy expended, every word and waking thought of every person, it was for *no good reason.*

The designation and punishment of Detractors—it was for *no good reason.*

And I—I had been sent out here to shatter the lives of innocent people and drag them back with me to the murky depths of a living lie, for *no good reason.*

After what seemed like an eternity, there was a rattling sound above and I heard the work bench being removed from the trap door. My heart leapt and caught in my throat so sharply that I felt a physical pain; my heart fluttered and I could swear the blood had drained from every part of my body. I thought that I was likely as not to faint.

The light poured in. Before I had remembered the inside of the shed being dim, but now what I saw above was almost blinding. John-Michael Jones came slowly and carefully down the ladder.

He turned around. There was a lantern in his hand. He held it out, illuminating me, huddled in a dark corner of the room.

"Alex," he said in his gruff voice.

I quavered.

"Alex?" He took a half-step toward me.

I do not know how I did it, but I somehow peeled my gaze off the floor like lifting the weight of a heavy beam.

"Who are you, really?"

I broke.

Once the tears had started coming, they wouldn't stop coming. "I'm a traitor," I said.

"Alex…"

"I'm a traitor," I sobbed again, in desperation. I fell onto my knees. "The Settlement sent me here to collect information about you. I've been in communication with them. I went to see a man from the Settlement once, but I don't have to go that far in order to talk with them. I have the… the… a Biometric implanted in my body. It's a communication device and a tracker. I'm supposed to go back to them eventually. I have no choice."

"What?" his voice was soft, but a little surprised. He slowly got down onto one knee in front of me, to be more at my level.

"They know where I am. They'll come here, and they'll kill all of you. You don't understand," I pleaded.

"Here? When?"

"When I come back. Or when I don't come back." I had to explain it to him. "You don't understand how much they hate you. You can't reason with them. Individually, maybe—but not as a group. Not as an entity. People… people can be saved, but not DYNTEC. Not the Settlement. You can't imagine their power. There's nothing I can do. Just the fact that I'm here is the end for you." I clung to his arm. "I'm so sorry. Please forgive me."

"Alex," said Mr. Jones again softly. "What have they done to you?"

I cried for a little while longer, and he wrapped his arms around me. He didn't even seem angry. I couldn't feel safe. Not from the Settlement. But it was comforting anyways. I didn't understand his reaction, not at all. But I was willing to let him do it.

"It's a long story," I said.

"We need to hear it," he said.

I nodded, leaning back and wiping tears from my cheeks with my palms. "Please don't kill me," I said. "I'll tell you everything you want to know. I know I deserve it, but if you kill me, the Settlement will destroy you immediately."

"We're not going to *kill* you, Alex," said Mr. Jones. "You asked for me to forgive you, and I do."

I nodded. It was very hard to get my mind around the forgiveness, but I could at least understand that he wasn't going to kill me.

He stood up. "Let's not talk anymore here. Please come back to the house."

❁

Chapter Twenty-Six

Untangled Web

Once I was back in the house, still shaking but taking slow breaths to try and calm myself, I sat down on the couch in the living room. Mr. Jones brought me a cup of tea.

I started crying again.

"Why are you crying?" asked Mary, climbing up next to me and trying to wipe the tears off of my face. I cried harder.

"Leave her alone, Mary," said Mr. Jones gently. The little girl slid down to the floor.

They waited until I had regained my composure. In truth, I wasn't crying because of the bad things that had happened to me. I was crying because they were very good people, and I was a very bad person.

"Alex," said Mr. Jones eventually, leaning forward in his chair, with his elbows on his knees, "tell me more about the Settlement. We need to know what we're facing. How did you get to be here? Start at the beginning."

So I told him everything.

The family members had slowly gathered in the living room, none of them wanting to miss anything. Mrs. Jones stood behind me in the kitchen, looking over the back of the couch, surveying her family as the children crawled in and settled themselves on the rug.

I started with my childhood, and with details as they came to mind: the tree, my education, the general disinterest of my parents.

"Children weren't allowed to go outside?" repeated Samuel in disbelief.

"Don't interrupt," started Mrs. Jones.

"It's fine," I said. "You would be allowed to at fifteen. But there's not a lot to do out there anyway. Everything is under the ground."

I knew he must be having trouble picturing it, but I almost didn't want them to know what it was like, even if only by proxy. How could I explain that crippling depression in words? It was far more horrible to imagine that it would soon be inflicted on him in reality.

"In the food labs, I spent ten hours per day painting food-growth cultures on to hosting plates…." I continued as the night fell outside, retracing my ill-fated career path.

"Anyway, after all of my failed jobs, I was sent to the Administrators, and as a last resort, they assigned me to DYNTEC. I guess you could say I failed my way to the top. I had never thought seriously about working for DYNTEC before, and I was already growing nervous again after my initial relief. They were all about saving the world and stopping crime and all that. Those were high stakes. High stakes, big guns, cool tech…"

I started running through the various parts of my training. I had briefly mentioned the age at which I had received the Biometric, which earned me some raised eyebrows, but I had yet to describe its functions in full.

Now I did my best to explain.

"So you're telling me," said Mr. Jones, "That this device," he held his own wrist, "which is in your body, constantly transmits your location to people at DYNTEC."

"That's correct." I nodded.

"And that it controls—what did you call it? Nano-technology? In your ears? That allows you to communicate with them at will."

"Well, the auditory nerves, so more like in my brain, really. But yeah. And a lot of other stuff, too, like security clearance scans, unlocking doors, basic ident-ification, access to all my computer accounts, access to my money, buying and selling, and so forth. I couldn't function in the Settlement without it."

He pinched his nose and exchanged a look with Mrs. Jones. "All right." He waved me on. "You were saying."

"Right. So they adjusted my Biometric to give me DYNTEC clearance. After that I was able to check out guns, and they taught me all kinds of things, like how to swim. Which came in handy later. As you know. And how to lie, with the Biometric."

"With the Biometric."

"Yes, because it can provide vital signs, it can be used to determine whether someone is lying. But they taught me how to beat the test. And how to resist torture."

"They did what?" said Mrs. Jones loudly.

I was uncomfortable. "It wasn't really anything serious," I mumbled.

"How can it not be?" She was astonished.

"Well it was just, you know. He twisted my arm or whatever." I felt mortified saying it. I was simultaneously afraid that I had misrepresented the encounter and was eliciting far more pity than was warranted, and also realizing that it sounded a lot worse when I said it out loud.

Mr. Jones's eyes registered something deep and hard, and I realized that I'd never actually seen him angry before.

"Horrible people," muttered Mark.

I frowned, not sure what to think. "…Hey." Cam was the best friend I'd had in the Settlement. "They're not horrible. They're just…" I was going to say, "like me," but then I was cut off by the realization that being like me didn't preclude them from being horrible.

Mrs. Jones placed a hand on my shoulder. "I understand," she murmured. "It's all right."

Mr. Jones once again moved us on from the uncomfortable topic. "And after the training?"

"They told me lies about you. All kinds of lies. They told me you were an evil cult that wanted people from the Settlement to go to hell, and would threaten to send people there."

Everyone in room made a different face at that. I looked around.

"They think we *want* them to go to hell?" asked Mrs. Jones.

"Yes—well… I don't know what the Administrators really believe; and most people don't know you exist, but that is what they told us."

"That's absurd," said Mrs. Jones. Then she stopped herself. "Sorry. Not angry at *you*. Just…" she shook her head.

"But you do believe in… it," I clarified.

"We believe in it because it's real and dangerous. It's too horrible to wish on anyone, even if we had the ability to 'send people there', which we don't. We don't have any control over that, except possibly to steer people away from it, but the real work is done by God, and all we can do is preach the Word that gives life.”

“We can’t *make* anyone believe,” added Mr. Jones. “And we certainly can’t *prevent* them from doing so, and if we could, we wouldn’t.”

“You can lead a horse to water, but you can’t make it drink,” said his wife. “But if we knew any way to reach the people inside the Settlement, we would do it immediately. There are millions of lost souls in there who do not know what they are doing, who do not even know their right hand from their left. We are so few out here. We pray for them every day, in tears sometimes. We only know of one person who did make it inside, and he didn’t even go on purpose. We don’t know what happened to him.”

At this point I had to break my silence on the matter.

“He’s dead,” I said. “They killed him.”

Mrs. Jones closed her eyes. Mr. Jones sighed very quietly and pinched his nose again. The younger kids just looked confused, but the older ones’ eyes widened.

There was a very long moment.

Mr. Jones opened his eyes again. “And you know this because…”

“A member of DYNTEC described him to me and told me that he had been killed,” I said.

They all sighed again, and the kids were starting to get antsy with all of the silence.

"So how did you come to be here?" Mr. Jones asked.

"Well, the last thing that happened before the mission was when they took me to the top of the Central Tower. That was when I found out about the plants."

"What plants?" said Grace.

I waved my hand around. "All of the plants. Like, in general."

"What do you mean?"

"We didn't know there were plants. I never saw any inside the Settlement."

I could tell that fell on their ears very oddly.

"I mean," I said. "I did see one *once*. And I knew what plants *were* before coming out here." I was getting a little embarrassed again and decided not to linger. "So we got in a jeep—a vehicle—and drove out miles and miles past the edges of the ruins, to a grassy place between two small hills, where the woods start."

Mr. Jones nodded.

"She's talking about the lower end of the south pine wood area," said Mark.

"Right. And they left me there. I had nothing with me except... well, you know." I blushed.

"The map! And I found it earlier today."

Of course he had. I hunched and looked down.

Mark's proud face dropped into a slight awkwardness.

"So I walked from there," I said.

"But that's twenty miles away," said Mark. "I mean, you can't be telling me that you—no offense, but *you* walked all that way by yourself. With nothing except a paper map."

"I…" I smirked a little bit. "I didn't walk."

"We found her half-drowned, washed up on the riverbank," provided Mrs. Jones. "It made more sense when you told me you were a refugee. Why didn't they give you any food? A tent? Water, at least?"

"So that you would believe I was a refugee," I said. "I think I was supposed to show up half dead, though I didn't know it at the time."

"That's cruel," said Mrs. Jones.

"No!" I said, feeling some deep-seated need to defend Cam. "He wasn't being cruel to me. You don't understand. It was for the greater good."

"The greater good," repeated Mr. Jones.

"You really think that goal was good?" asked his wife to me.

"He thought it was."

"Which completely justifies being reckless with a person's life."

"Well…" For some reason I had never considered how I might view the situation if it had happened to another person besides myself. "I don't know. I fell in the river, and ended up here, and now you know the whole story. The point is, they sent me here so that I could find out whether you could be rehabilitated."

Mrs. Jones looked down at me apprehensively. "What does that mean?"

"I think what that really means is they want to know if you can be taken alive."

"Absolutely not," said Mark grimly, crossing his arms over his chest.

I looked up pleadingly at the two Joneses. "Please. You have to come, or they'll kill you. I know you have a lot out here, but is it worth your life?"

Her mouth opened, but I didn't let her answer.

"Please," I begged. "I'll just go back there and tell them that you're totally curable." I didn't like what I was saying, but I had no choice. My face twisted against my will and my eyes leaked. I wiped at them with my sleeves. Their lives were at stake. I kept my voice from breaking by forcing it into a quick, flat tone. "You can get a house in the Settlement. Maybe two houses because I don't know if any of them are big enough for this many people. And all get the Biometric…" I could taste bitter despair. "And then you just try to keep your head down and don't make posts on the Profile, that wouldn't go too well. I don't know what kind of job you'd get assigned or how you would make enough money to pay for eight kids, but I guess Mark is almost old enough to work."

Slowly, Mr. Jones stood up from his chair. Everyone looked at him, waiting.

"We are not going to the Settlement," he said.

My heart seemed to stop.

"But we can't stay here, either. We have to move."

All the children scrambled from the floor. "What?!" There was a chorus of surprise and dismay.

"Not just us," he said. "Everyone in Hock and Hanfell has to be warned. We all need to move."

"How?" Mrs. Jones asked him, slack-jawed. "Where? Is there enough time?"

"I don't know," he said, "but we have to get started as soon as possible."

Chapter Twenty-Seven
War Council

The next morning, the church bells chimed out slow and rhythmic for a meeting of the elders. This was a rather broad word, as Mr. Jones had tried to explain to me: a generic elder versus a designated Elder. I wasn't sure I understood either concept.

The Minister was already here with us, but he was sitting in the very back of the room, at the wall, silent, just watching, turning his black hat over and over in his hands.

Mr. Jones leaned back on the pulpit, on top of the dais. His arms were crossed high on his chest, and his legs too were crossed, with one boot-heel dug into the edge of the stage. He watched as the townsfolk filed in, responding to his summons.

I sat on the far corner of the dais, trying to be as close to Mr. Jones as possible without drawing attention to myself. I kept my head down and folded my arms across my stomach as though I had a stomachache. The platform was only a few inches tall, and my knees came up high. I glanced only sparingly at the people coming in.

Some of them I recognized from the church services. Others I did not, although they could have been there and simply escaped my notice. There was a tall and stout man with a hat similar to the Minister's, a thin man who I recognized from church as the father in-law of Ann Baker, someone who looked like an older version of Matt Falconer, and an elderly couple who sat near the back. These were maybe the oldest people I'd ever seen; they walked slow and stooped over. The man had a cane. I found their appearance mildly frightening, for reasons I couldn't quite explain or control. Their skin looked like wax melting off a candle. There weren't very many old people in the Settlement, and certainly none who looked like this. I tried to make sense of it in my mind and calm myself. This was normal, right? How did they live so long out here? I would have thought the roughness of this life would kill them early.

"Why have you gathered us?" asked the stout man, striding up the aisle unabashed and looking Mr. Jones directly in the eye.

"Morning, Mason," said Jones. "Men, it's unfortunate news that I have." His posture was no longer full confident, and he was doing his best to appear apologetic. He grasped the top of the pulpit with his right hand. "The Settlement has found us. And they mean to come here." His eyes strayed to me, though he put them back on his audience right away. "I am reliably informed they intend to come in military force and kill anyone they cannot capture alive."

The room was only momentarily stunned.

Then a barrage of questions burst forth. "How do you know?" "When?" "Who told you?"

"It was her," I heard the old woman say quietly to her husband, "She's the one from the Settlement."

I cringed lower, hands on top of my head.

"How does she know?" Baker asked, taking a step forward. "Is it because she was—"

"This isn't about her," Jones said firmly.

"But it is. At least partly. You can't ignore that."

The chattering grew louder.

"Send her back, I say!" Baker continued. "Perhaps they won't have a reason to attack if we're not holding their spy."

"We need her," said Falconer. "She might have more information that could help us prepare for the attack."

The others nodded, humming their agreement. They seemed to find this reasonable.

"Aye, but afterward we send her back; she could persuade them to leave off."

"Pass on a nice message too," said one of the men in the back. "Tell 'em where to shove it."

"Now then," said Falconer, "we don't want to invite aggression."

This had gone on long enough. Jones raised his hands and spoke over them. "Gentlemen, you don't understand. It's too late. Sending her back won't change anything. Once they learn we'll resist being brought in, they're liable to shoot first and ask questions later."

"All right then," said Falconer. "But we still need information. When are they coming? How many men are they bringing with them, and what kind of weapons do they have?"

"Five days from now, next Tuesday, is her next scheduled meeting with the Settlement operatives. It could well be her last meeting. She could be extracted, and we have to assume they could attack the same day. So we have to be ready by Tuesday."

The old woman behind me inhaled softly. "Tuesday."

"But if she fails to report, we'll have the same problem. Either way, there's no getting around it. As for numbers, all I know for sure is that they have got more men than we have."

"What difference does that make?" said Mason. "I sure ain't goin' with 'em. We have weapons enough here for everyone. We'll organize a fighting force."

I could see some dismay on Jones's face. "Gentlemen, listen! I'm not for going with them any more than you are. But we're overpowered. There's only one solution here. We must flee."

"What? Flee?" Mason pulled his hat down and slapped it against his thigh. "You must be joking. I've never known you to be a coward, Jones."

"I—" Jones took a step back.

"Leave our homes? Pick up our families and abandon everything we've ever worked for? Our families worked for generations to reach this standard of living and give us everything we have. Now you think we should flee? Into the wild? When winter is coming? To risk the elements, and leave our crops rotting in the field? We'll die! Our children will starve!"

Many people from the assembly echoed strong agreement, though some remained silent and troubled.

My illusion of Jones's authority in this place faded somewhat as I realized he was being strongly overruled.

"We'll stand together," said Falconer. "Show them we won't go down without a fight. We're tougher than we look, and maybe it will scare them off."

"Aye," said another voice. "They can't take us all."

"Yes, they can," I said. I raised my head, my eyes puffy.

They turned to look at me. I'd had no input at all until now.

"They absolutely can and will take you all," I deadpanned. "At the same time. And win. Ten times over. You don't understand. They could wipe you out with the push of a button."

Some of the people shifted uneasily.

I set my elbow up on my knee and put my chin in my hand.

"You can't fight them. They're too powerful."

"You're just saying that because you don't want us to hurt your friends," Mason accused me.

"No, I'm saying it because they're too powerful. Also," I continued in a sullen tone, "they're not my friends."

They waited as if to hear me say something else, but I had nothing else to say.

"You've heard it," said Jones desperately. "Who's with me?"

"Stay here if you're with him," said Mason. "If you're with me, come outside. We'll make plans for the defense of the towns."

He walked down the aisle and out the door, and most of the room followed him.

There were a few left standing in the church, but not many. The Minister was still there, as were the Smiths, and a man I didn't recognize.

"Ah," said Jones, sliding down to sit next to me on the dais, "Doc Brown. At least we've got you."

The man didn't reply, just sat down with us in one of the pews wearily.

The Minister was getting up tiredly to close the doors. "Not the result you had hoped for, I take it."

"That went about as badly as it could possibly go," said Jones.

"I'm not sure about that," said the Minister. "I've seen people do worse. They could have turned on *her*."

"I suppose."

"You at least believe I'm right, then," I said desperately to the Minister.

"Yes," he said somberly. "But there's nothing I can do."

"You can't persuade them? You can't speak to them? You do it every week!"

"They'd see it as an abuse of my authority. They're only using this building because it's convenient," said the Minister. "I don't rule them."

"What are you going to do?" I asked Mr. Jones. "Are you still going to run?"

He was silent for a moment. "This is a disaster," he said, finally. "I won't see my family killed or turn them over to the Settlement, of course. But I saw them when they took Paul Tiller away in that machine, and I believe what you say. I must try to speak with the men individually. Maybe they will see reason when they aren't having an ego-measuring contest." But he shook his head, and his face was full of lines.

Doc Brown and the four or five others who had stayed went to confer with Jones.

I slipped out through the side door, back onto the path I'd once walked with the Minister.

Now seemed like as good a time as any to walk it again. I picked my way along through the long grasses, my long skirt billowing in the wind and folding around my legs. I threw off the bonnet, undid my braid, and shook out my hair.

I was alone, finally, to think out some of this mess.

How could the Joneses forgive me for all of this? I could tell, in part, they pitied me and viewed me as a victim of the Settlement. But that was only partly true. And their losses were going to be steep.

It was because forgiveness was a part of their religion, wasn't it? I had been thinking over whether I believed in their God. There *was* someone running the universe, but I knew now that it couldn't be the Settlement or Gaia. It was Him.

But I figured I couldn't exactly be in good with Him at this point. I felt like he, not Gaia, was angry with me.

As I was pondering this dilemma, I heard rustling behind me. I turned around, and saw something moving, disappearing behind a rock.

I was not alone.

"I know you're there," I said, loudly.

Ruth Tiller came out disappointedly from behind the boulder that lay alongside the path in the field. She hung her head. "Bother."

"What are you doing?" I asked.

"My father-in-law asked me to follow you."

"To keep me from going anywhere?"

She nodded, blushing.

"I understand," I said.

"I guess I'm not a very good spy," said Ruth.

"Well," I said, "I'm not either."

I could see the red rings around her eyes where she had been crying. "I just have to ask," she said in a low, controlled voice. "Is it true? What you told Sarah Jones."

I cocked my head a fraction of an angle.

"Is he really dead?"

Oh. Of course.

"Yes," I said. "I'm sorry."

"Oh."

There was a long pause.

"You're absolutely certain?"

"I'm sorry," I said again. "I found out while in the service of DYNTEC. I heard a story of a man who'd been brought in. I know it was him. That sort of thing doesn't happen very often. I should have told you earlier, but I… I didn't."

"Why not?"

She made large steps toward me over the grass.

"I guess I still believed them," I said. "A bit."

"About what?"

We walked along together.

"About you guys. Being evil."

"You don't think that anymore, do you?"

"No," I said.

"What do you think, then?"

"I think I need help," I said.

"Alex," Ruth asked me with an emotion that was difficult to peg. It was some mix of hesitancy, surprise, and hope. "Are you ready to believe in Christ?"

There it was, laid out in the open, the ultimatum I had been afraid of. I was still afraid of it. But I knew what the right answer was.

"I think so," I said.

"Let me pray with you," she said.

And so we did, sitting down in the grass in the sun, with our skirts puffing around our crossed knees.

Chapter Twenty-Eight

The Biometric

When we finally stood up, I felt better than I had in as long as I could remember.

"Do you know what baptism is?" said Ruth.

I shook my head.

"Our Lord commanded that everyone who becomes a Christian should be baptized. It is a symbol, an outward sign that points to inward faith."

A ritual, I thought, but I didn't feel bad about it. "All right," I said.

"Come. We must talk to the Minister about it. There may not be very much time."

We headed back to the church.

I found the Minister sitting on one of the wooden benches. He was reading the book all the families had, the one called the Bible. He seemed to be deep in thought.

He wasn't startled at being approached, however. "What can I do for you?" he said at last in a friendly manner, closing the book.

After we had talked with him, he nodded.

"I think you are right," he said, when we were finished talking. "You are ready. We will hold it on Sunday, by the river."

This seemed appropriate to me. Every moment I felt we were in more danger. On Tuesday the Settlement would be here, and I didn't know what was going to happen to me after that.

***

Through Friday, the Joneses and the few other families who were with them made preparations to flee. It was hard to imagine that any preparations would be adequate, as indeed, Mason from the meeting had made valid points. How well could they really survive out in the wilderness? For how long? Where would they settle?

They had, nonetheless, prepared bags of necessities they could carry with them, and loaded more into the wagon, though it was unclear how much notice they'd have, or if a wagon would travel fast enough to take them away from this place in time.

Mrs. Jones and the girls had been busy most of the day preparing rations. Mr. Jones had done the same, trying to smoke and dry as much meat as possible over the last few days. Then we had a hasty dinner of eggs and toast.

"Listen," I said, as we finished dinner. It was a difficult conversation to have, but easier than some of the other ones I'd been forced to have recently. "Once you are ready to leave, I should go back to the Settlement."

Mrs. Jones craned her neck and looked at me like I'd grown two heads. "You *want* us to send you back to them?"

"Well, no…" I stuttered. "But… I have to. It's better to let you get as much of a head start as possible before I go, because once I report back to them, they will definitely come here."

"You could come with us," said little John.

I looked into his big, earnest eyes. He really did want me to come.

His parents looked at each other, in a moment deciding they would not rebuke the child for the offer—it would stand. Mr. Jones nodded.

But my heart sank bitterly.

"I can't," I said. "My Biometric. They'll follow me anywhere I go. I would give away your location."

"Hmph," said Mr. Jones. "Look. We won't force you to come with us. You can choose to go back to the Settlement if that's what you really want. But I don't think you do. If they'll follow you anywhere, what you need is to get rid of that tracker."

He was right. I didn't *want* to go back to the Settlement. I didn't want to leave the Joneses. I wanted to stay and be a part of their family. *I would rather die than let anything happen to these people,* I thought, and it was not an idle thought.

"All right," I said, though my voice was hollow with fear. "You can try to remove the Biometric if you want. But it's not that simple."

***

Doctor Brown's place in Hanfell was clean and well-lit. We were not in his house proper, but a room built off to the side, which he called a patient care room. I was familiar with the concept, of course, but any procedure like this done in the Settlement—if it were done—would have been performed in a place far more clinically sterile, and it would have been done under anesthesia.

I didn't figure they had anything like that, but I brought it up to him anyways.

"Sorry," said Doc Brown. "This ain't no hospital. I'd love t' give ya whiskey, but I cain't even do that. You'd bleed out."

We had discussed the problem and its risks a great deal, and waited as long as we felt we could. It was now Saturday. Mr. Jones said that his family would start out no later than Monday morning. The Smiths and some of the others were claiming they'd be ready at the same time. Mrs. Jones said she wanted me to be healthy and rested, ready to move by then. And this, just as soon as my bone had fully healed. I winced remembering it.

The room had carefully placed stone tile floors, glass in the ceiling to let in sunlight, and few surfaces for dust to collect on. In the middle of the room there was a single reclined chair.

This was unquestionably the best the Kingdom could offer for medical care. I'd already seen Doc Brown once, said Mrs. Jones. He had made a house call to attend my broken bone and give advice.

I tugged experimentally at the cloth binding my arms to the chair.

"You're going to have to tie me a bit tighter than that." My voice wavered. "No offense, but I… I don't think I'm going to be able to sit still for this." I felt quite light-headed. For the last day or so I had kept on trying to forget what was about to happen, but wasn't able. I had come very near to telling them I had changed my mind on at least three occasions and was nearly at that point again. I hoped weakly that if I did blurt out something to that effect, they would be smart enough not to listen.

Doc Brown pulled the cloths tighter and doubled up the knots again. This time I was sure I would not be able to move.

There was a tourniquet on my upper arm as well, ostensibly to slow the bleeding, although Doc Brown believed he would be able to avoid the major artery that ran through the wrist.

Next to him, on a stool with his hands folded, waiting awkwardly, was Mark. I had recently learned the sixteen-year-old was the Kingdom's *only* expert on electronic devices, and though his knowledge did not extend to the kinds of computing technology used by the Settlement, he would be able to understand a circuit. I wasn't even sure that *I* properly understood a circuit; the actual education received in the Settlement was somewhat lacking outside our general social conditioning and career-focused hyper-specialization.

Both of the adult Joneses had also wanted to be around to "support" me; Doc Brown had actually had to shoo them out. "No more people in the room than strictly necessary, please," he said, and then, "that means all'a ya 'cept Mark."

It was just as well. The last thing I wanted was for more people to be around to see me break down. I was not a strong person. DYNTEC had done their best to change that, and when they couldn't change it, to make me forget what I was. But ultimately, I knew that slick operative image was not me, and everyone was about to find out.

The problem as I had explained it to Doc Brown was thus:

While the external interface of the Biometric was close to the skin, in fact, barely below the surface, that was not the only part of the machine. The wrist implant managed a computing network for the various types of nanotech embedded in my body and functioned as its central processor. This nanotech was powered by a constant feed of bioelectricity in my bloodstream, but the wrist processor itself was too energy-intensive to run on merely passive bioelectricity and needed to charge itself during dormant periods, such as while I was sleeping. That energy went into a capacitor. While many of the nanotech particles were used for various health-related purposes, there was one particular health function of the Biometric that was going to be a problem.

When a citizen of the Settlement suffered un-expected heart failure, I had explained, the Biometric's capacitor could release a high-energy charge into two small leads connected to their heart, which could also be used as a pacemaker if necessary. For most people, it went unused and never noticed.

As it happened, it was also capable of stopping my heart at the Settlement's whim or in the case of tampering with the device.

Mrs. Jones's reaction had been one of horror. "They can just kill you?"

I nodded.

"And no one would know if it was the Settlement or natural causes?"

I cringed into a tight smile. "The Administrators don't usually own up about ordering someone's death, unless that person committed an especially egregious crime. Sometimes they will deny it in specific cases, such as if the person who died was well-known or politically powerful. But usually they don't bother. We know it happens, and they want us to know. We are allowed to talk about Detractors being killed, as long as we say they deserved it. After all, if we didn't believe at some level that those deaths were linked to the Administrators, how could they keep people in line? But there is always a bit of doubt. Too much doubt to make a direct accusation."

I had lived with this knowledge since the age of twelve. It had troubled me then, but since no one around me dared to complain about it, I gradually did what every individual must do and accepted it as a fact of life. There was no way to cope with this knowledge except to make yourself believe that the Administrators only killed people who deserved to die. There was no way to lessen this anxiety except to tell yourself that if you were a good citizen, you would live.

At any rate, we needed more than a doctor. In order to safely remove the Biometric, we would need an electrician. And so… Mark was there.

"Take this," said Doc Brown, and I knew he was trying to help. "Don't hurt yourself." He put a small piece of rag in my mouth. I accepted it and chewed it anxiously.

He swabbed my right forearm with alcohol. I felt the cold air brush my skin, and a shudder went through my entire body. I closed my eyes in a hurry before I could have a chance to see him pick up anything.

My heart stilled mysteriously, at least for a moment.

While this scenario easily competed with anything I had imagined suffering at the hands of the Administrators, something was remarkably different today. Today, I was going to be free.

I was not with enemies, and this was not a punishment. I had chosen this because there were people that loved me and wanted me to come with them. I was afraid, yes, but less than I had thought I would be. Something had restrained me from panicking, and I thought it was probably God. What else could do that?

Still, when I felt his fingers on my wrist, my heart rate went skyrocketing again.

And then the pain started.

I have to admit that I screamed. In spite of the ties, I was twisting and moving around so much that Mark had to get up and hold my arm still.

It seemed to go on and on. I wasn't sure what they were doing and didn't want to look. The two of them didn't talk for a long moment. Doc Brown must have been concentrating very hard on being quick and efficient. The first comment I heard from him was, "Oh, Lord mercy," and then, "Holy cow," from Mark.

I sobbed around the rag in my mouth.

"We found the wires," said Mark. He sounded both dismayed and impressed.

"So which one do I cut?" prompted Doc Brown.

"I'd say sever the capacitor from the Biometric," said Mark, "but it seems to be one unit."

Though he was not actively touching me at the moment, I was still in a great deal of pain and panted shallowly.

"Failing that, cut the leads to the electrodes, but you'd have to get them both at the exact same time to prevent them from discharging and I'm not sure which ones they are—"

I yelled again, muffled into the rag, as there was a sharp jerk on something inside my flesh.

"Right there!"

I'm going to die, I thought, *I'm going to die.*

Then there was a sharp *clip!* And then a horrible ripping sensation and I screamed gratingly with little self-consciousness, somehow totally losing the rag.

"It's out!" said the Doctor.

"It's okay," said Mark. "We got it."

At these words, someone burst in the door behind me, from the house, unable to restrain themselves anymore. I could not see, but in a moment, Mrs. Jones was behind my head smoothing and stroking my hair. "It's okay," she said. "It's all right."

I squeezed my eyes shut and tilted my head back as her fingers caressed me.

"We got it!" Mark shouted again triumphantly. Doc Brown was not quite done yet, and I flinched as he stitched the wound closed. I moaned and sniffed, and Mrs. Jones wiped my eyes dry with her apron.

"It's over," she said. "You're free."

❖

Chapter Twenty-Nine

Suffer the Little Children

Sunday morning dawned bright and clear.

I rode along to the church, bouncing along in the back of the wagon. I was in high spirits. I did harbor a twinge of anxiety about seeing the villagers, including the ones who disagreed with us, in the same place as before. Would they be able to keep the peace?

My arm was bandaged again and had a waterproof plaster layer slicked over it so that it would not be infected by the river. It ached only a little, so long as I didn't touch it.

I'd dealt with a little stretch of time before where the Biometric was out of commission, but this was different. To start with, I couldn't make voice calls. I couldn't access computers—if there had been any around. I had no money. I'd lost access to my Profile and my messages. By the Settlement's standards, I wasn't even a person. Or at least, I was totally severed from the person who had been me.

And I'd never felt better.

As a matter of fact, despite the awful revelations about me to the town, I'd gotten more sympathy in the last week than I'd had most of my life. I supposed that said more about the Settlement than it did about me.

Though I caught the expected looks from the villagers of Hock and Hanfell, it was hard for me to determine their attitude. It was mixed, perhaps. I kept my head down during the service. There may have been some here who had not forgiven me. Did they understand? How was I to earn their trust? I had no way of giving them back what I'd taken.

However, despite the expected tensions, I was pleasantly surprised after service. When I saw Matt Falconer, one of the people who'd been giving me an odd look, I was initially apprehensive. However, he came up to me and warmly shook my hand.

"Ow," I said.

"Sorry!" he pulled away fast. "I just wanted to say congratulations. Not just for your baptism, 'cuz I know that hasn't happened yet, but on…" he tilted his head and nodded like *you know*. "Getting rid of that thing."

"Oh," I said. "Thanks."

"I think that was very brave of you."

I wasn't sure what to say, but his words did make me feel good. Gratitude stirred. "Thank you," I said again, but more warmly this time. I was at least trying to convey sincerity. The prospect of being *admired* under the circumstances was a little shocking. Especially when Matt and his father were going to try to stay and defend their towns. (Die. They were going to die, I thought, and pushed it to the bottom of my mind.)

After the service, a group walked down to the river. We went about a mile downstream of the rapids where I'd washed up prior. The water was wide and calm, if cold. There was a rocky beach of white, rounded pebbles and smooth driftwood.

Less than half the people had stayed, but it was surprising we had as many as we did, given the activities and attitudes of the day. Most of the men who had chosen to fight were elsewhere now, likely continuing to form up and make plans. I'd heard a rumor that Mason had become irritated that Smith was planning to flee with Jones, and was trying to strike a "bargain" with the man to use his forge to turn a number of hoes, rakes, and shovels into weapons, for what Smith decried as a "suicidal" endeavor.

Those who remained sat around on boulders and logs, forming a semicircle. I was not the only one being baptized; there were two children from Hanfell. I did not know them. They went first.

It was a quiet day. The sand squeezed under my toes as I waded into the river to meet the Minister. The current felt icy. The pale sunlight of early October gleamed off the river's ripples. The water itself was dark green. It came up about to my waist when I reached him.

There was a brief exchange of words.

"I baptize you… in the name of the Father… the Son… and the Holy Spirit."

My world went dark. I was forcefully reminded that I'd almost drowned in this river once. Memories of learning to swim with Cam resurfaced. But I didn't have time to panic. The Minister pulled me up and there was light again.

I climbed out of the river soaked through and shivering. There was light applause and I got hugs from everybody I knew and some people I didn't.

"Hey," somebody behind me said. "Where's John?"

John-Michael Jones was sitting on a log, his head came up.

"No, not you. Little John."

***

We'd been looking for little John for nearly two hours. The crowd had thinned even further, but plenty from the village of Hock were still searching with us.

They had spread out up and down the river in both directions. Nobody had seen him after the beginning of the ceremony; he must have slipped off at some point in the middle and nobody had noticed.

At this point, everyone, even Mr. Jones, was starting to get visibly worried. The sun was dropping lower, and we didn't have time for this. The final preparations still had to be made for the evacuation the next day. At this point, every hour could make a difference.

"Somebody needs to go back to the house," said Mrs. Jones. "It's almost dinner time, he might have gone there. He might be at home wondering why we aren't there."

"I'll go," said Gracie, and ran off down the road.

The rest of us kept searching the woods. A chill wind blew. My clothes and hair weren't drying properly, and I was freezing. I shivered some more. "Can I go back too?" I asked. "Just to change clothes."

"Yes," said Mrs. Jones. "There are enough of us here, I think. You keep an eye out for him up there."

I walked up the embankment and out of the thicket, with my arms wrapped tightly around myself. But I kept my eyes roaming constantly for the eight-year-old. "John!" I called, and heard the voices of others much louder and more distant echo back the name.

It was just as I was getting to the road that I heard an ear-shattering scream.

I abandoned my mission instantly and started running in the direction of the voice.

I kept following the noise until I reached the riverbank. It had only been seconds, but it seemed like an eternity. Mrs. Jones and now several others gathered at the top of a steep crag overlooking the river. Down below were rocks and rapids, and a smaller swirling muddy pool.

Mr. Jones was standing knee deep in this pool, coming up out of the river. I couldn't see his face, as his head was down. His wet hair straggled down over his eyes. In his arms was a small, limp body.

Chapter Thirty
The Taste of Death

What can I say about the hours after that?

There were attempts at reviving John, but it was too late. They carried him back to the house, but it was still too late. Doc Brown confirmed it.

We were all in shock. Mrs. Jones, who I had only known as stalwart, continued screaming and weeping for a very long time.

The family was now together in the kitchen. The Minister was there, as well, perhaps trying to console them, but I wasn't sure. I had even seen Mr. Jones, the patriarch, weeping over his son, and it shook me to the core.

I couldn't be there. I retreated into the bedroom and sat myself back in the furthest corner. There I hugged my knees to my chest and cried. It usually took me longer than this to process my emotions, but the moods of the others were having an effect on me. I knew whatever I felt, I hadn't actually expressed it yet.

I guess I was in shock too. It seemed impossible to believe. I'd never heard of something like this happening in the Settlement.

Surely this was someone's fault, but whose? Who should have been there? He ran off, but could you really blame the child for his own death?

What could have prevented this?

Being in the Settlement would have prevented this. *It would never have happened in the Settlement.*

It wouldn't even have been possible. People knew where children were at all times. They were always indoors. There weren't hazards like this. Accidents didn't happen. Children didn't *die.*

Children weren't supposed to die.

It was as if he had been smiling and laughing only a moment ago.

My own words came back at me sardonically. Time to "riot." But against whom? God? Gaia? The river? There was no one to fault.

I waited, unsure what I was waiting for. Then I waited some more. I was hunched right next to the window; and when I looked up under the curtain, I could see the gray light of evening fade into darkness through the slats.

Some time later, I heard soft, quick footsteps. They stopped abruptly, and I looked up. Eva was standing there, having run in, not expecting to see me. She didn't usually come in this room, but was here now, holding a candle on a plate.

She slowly put the candle on the table and then sat down on her parents' bed. She looked at me, and then looked away.

"I didn't know you were here," she said.

Since she had acknowledged me, I might as well ask. "Where's your mom and dad?"

"They're still sitting at the table. I don't think they're coming in here."

"Mark?"

"Went outside. Don't know where. Sam went to the shed."

My mind's eye briefly conjured a vision of Mark going off and getting lost and drowning somewhere too. *No*, that was ridiculous, he was sixteen and nearly as capable as an adult.

"They put Rachel and Mary and Jeremy to bed. Grace is in MY bedroom." She then dug herself under the covers in her parents' bed, and the last I saw of her was a large lump.

Against my will, I started to doze off sitting up. When my head slipped, though, I jolted awake. It was like my heart, which had been standing still, had started again, and thoughts returned to my mind.

It seemed as though the whole world had ground to a halt. In the dark of night, it was easy to believe that the Earth had stopped spinning. Had it stopped for the Joneses too? They had been planning to flee tomorrow morning, with only one day to spare. But now they were paralyzed.

What if—and my heart skipped a beat—what if the taste of death had persuaded them to surrender to the Settlement?

Eva had gone quiet. All was exceedingly still. My ears rang with the silence.

I would have missed it if I had been sleeping. In fact, I would have missed what happened next if there had been any noise whatsoever in the house, or indeed if I had not been sitting up with my ear so near to the shutter. There was no glass in it, and the sound of moving air came steadily through the trees. Then another faint sound.

That was not my imagination; it was the sound of a bell. A distant, far-off clanging bell, carried to us on the wind. The church bell.

I stood up, my knees stiff. Eva stirred.

"Eva," I whispered. "Why is the church bell ringing?"

"What?" she moaned.

"The church bell. What does it mean?"

Eva sat up and rubbed her eyes. She peered out from under the blanket like a hood. "They don't ring the bell in the middle of the night unless something is on fire."

On fire.

DYNTEC was here. For me. And they were early.

I leapt for the door. The Jones family had lost one today, but they could still lose the rest. I couldn't let that happen.

I found myself there in the hallway first, and tugged on the cabinet there. It was locked—damn!

I had on only a knee-length white nightgown with a ruffled edge, but I threw on the dressing-gown on the hook near the bedroom door.

The parents were still sitting at the kitchen table, opposite each other. A burning candle stood between them. Their eyes were closed, but they were not sleeping. They were in perfect silence. I prepared to break it.

DYNTEC is coming. Get in the wagons. Leave now. Run.

But before I could get the words out of my mouth, the front door burst open with a crash. It was Mark.

Both of them opened their eyes with a start, taking in both myself and their son, who was panting, breathless, leaning on the doorframe. His eyes were wide.

"They're here," he blurted out.

Neither of them moved at first, seemingly stunned.

"I—" I started but didn't finish. Mark spoke first.

"They rolled out of the woods and took the road between Hock and Hanfell. Some twenty vehicles and at least a hundred men. Matt and I were keeping watch. We counted them. They set fire to the church. They're splitting north and south to take the towns at the same time."

He didn't wait for his parents to react, but reached the gun cabinet in two steps and kicked the door off in two blows.

Mr. Jones stood up, but only a fraction of a second ahead of his wife. Her face, streaked with tears, had twisted into insensible rage.

"You called them!" she accused me.

I took a step back. "No!"

"You called them to take the rest of my children! You want to put them in the Settlement!"

"No! I didn't! I wouldn't..." I shook my head vehemently, horrified.

"You want to put them in there because my baby is *dead!*" she screamed.

She advanced only one step on me before Mr. Jones got in her way and wrapped his arms around her.

"My baby is dead..." she said it again but broke down sobbing into his shoulder, no longer looking at me.

"It's not her fault," he said, stroking her hair. "She couldn't contact them even if she wanted to. The tracker is gone. We got rid of it."

Her muffled sobs continued, and her hands flailed a little bit. "No… sorry… I'm sorry…"

"We're still not going there. We're never going there."

"Okay."

"We have to run."

"Okay."

With only a passing glance at me, Mark seized a rifle from the closet and dashed off into the night. Seeing this, I did not hesitate to do the same. I grabbed one of the shotguns, scooped up a few shells and packed them in. Then I put on Mrs. Jones slippers, which sat by the door.

"Alex, where are you going?" asked John-Michael Jones. "You're the one who told me… Alex!"

I didn't answer. I just ran. The door slammed behind me, and I sprinted away down the hill, at least as far as I could before the path ended and I had to slow down to avoid stumbling on the long grass. I knew he wouldn't have liked the answer.

I had something the ragtag militia didn't. I was a Settlement citizen. I *knew* these people. I was going to stop them, and if I couldn't stop them, I was at least going to slow them down.

Chapter Thirty-One

Fire and Fury

It was dark, darker than any night in the Settlement would have been. Stars illuminated the sky above me in a stunning display, like a touchscreen with a web of infinite points.

I couldn't see the black vehicles with their headlights off. But I could hear them.

I was twelve minutes past the last house in Hock when the first one passed me with a dull roar. The driver didn't see me. I was off the road, staying up on the ridge on the long grass, looking down on them.

I began to hear the rest of the vehicles up ahead. They were stalled in a group by the church, idling.

Then I saw something else. An orange glow.

I started running.

There were three buildings in the church area; there was the church itself, with its tall white steeple and cross; there was a stable with a sloping roof and a single wall, for horses to be hitched during service; and there was a shed on the south side of the church, used for storage.

I stood on the same side of the road as both the church and the shed. Down there the hill flattened out and the church stood more or less at a level with the road.

It was burning.

It was burning like a torch, like a dry twig, like kindling going up in flames, consumed in a flash as bright as daylight. I knew the pews, the books, cloth, and drapery were burning inside. The fire burst from the windows, licked up the steeple, and turned the building into a black silhouette against its own flames.

I could see the cavalry in its light. There were ten or fifteen vehicles down there, though I couldn't be sure. Most of them were larger than the ATV had been.

When a smaller ATV drove around from behind the stable, I felt suddenly as though the entire landscape had been laid bare. The trees surrounding us, which had seemed like an impenetrable cover for the Kingdom, were now a hiding place for DYNTEC troops. We could be surrounded for all I knew.

The fire of the burning church turned from orange to red and the scene receded a bit into shadow.

If the Joneses knew what was good for them, they were already starting to flee, but what route of escape would be safe? They would be followed, surely.

What was the Kingdom compared to the Settlement?

I bit back my panic.

Before him all the nations are as nothing.

I loaded a shell into the chamber of my shotgun and started down to the road.

"Who's there?" a loud voice shouted, and the lead vehicle's headlights flashed on, flooding the road in painful white light.

I knew that voice. It could only belong to Cam.

He had stepped out of the jeep, and appeared as a black silhouette in the road. I pointed the gun at him, squinting into the lights. "Cam! It's me, Alex!"

"Alex!" His voice was a mixture of surprise and the weakness of relief. "I thought they killed you!" He started walking toward me quickly.

"I have a gun, Cam. You'd better stop."

He stopped, and he showed me his hands, but he kept them at waist level. "Alex, come on. Put the gun down. I'm not going to hurt you. What happened? Your life signs stopped!"

"They took out my Biometric," I said. "Now put your hands up, please."

"This is pointless," Cam warned me. "All my men have their sights on you right now."

"They won't shoot," I said. "You wouldn't let them."

"You won't either," he pointed out, unable to hide his smile. I could barely see him through the light and shadow, but I could hear it on his voice. "Come on. Don't be difficult, Alex, let's get you out of here." He took another step toward me, and I raised the shotgun a little further.

"I have a better idea," I said. I tried to keep my voice steady, to sound dangerous, threatening. "How about *you*, show me *your* Biometric, talk to all your men, the ones in Hanfell too—yes I know about them. Tell them to get back in those cars, turn around, and go right back where they came from."

"It's not that simple," said Cam, and he lowered his voice a notch. "I can't just go back to the Settlement empty-handed. I am here to take prisoners, and that's what I'm going to do. I may be in charge of these men, Alex, but I'm not in charge of the Settlement. You should have learned by now that what we want means nothing. Stop trying to fight. You can't win, only die." I could hear it in his voice now, the despair underneath his layers of humor and irony, behind his laughter over meaningless small rebellions.

"Just do it," I said. "Now." But my hands were shaking.

"Or else what?"

"Or else I shoot you, Cam, it's not that complicated." I gave him a pained smile back.

He struggled, seemingly at a loss for what to do—but only for a moment. "They've brainwashed you," he said loudly, decisively. "This isn't you. This isn't the Alex I know." He started walking toward me, quickly. "Come on. We're going home."

He reached, side-on, for my gun.

"No!" I yelped, barely coherent. I swung it around and shoved him back with the butt end, then before he could recover, I punched him in the face.

Cam stumbled and lost his balance. He sprawled in the dirt but rolled and bounced back to his feet without a pause. He lunged for me again and this time got two hands on the rifle. We struggled over it very briefly. He was stronger. I let go and we went staggering apart from each other. He threw the weapon spinning away into the dust.

I reached into the deep pocket of Mr. Jones' dressing-gown and pulled a knife. It was only a pocketknife, but I flipped it open and brandished it threateningly. "I'm not coming with you."

He made another move, ducking, trying to get under my arm to grab it and put me in a lock. I sidestepped him, but it was a near miss. He rolled past me, and I flipped the knife into my fist, turning to face him. I took a stance with my fist drawn back behind me, in a position to throw a deadly punch. He hesitated this time, sizing me up for an advantage. We circled around each other.

Finally, he sighed and drew his own pistol. "It's over, Alex."

At that moment there was a gunshot. A loud *crack* split the night, above the low rumble of the idling jeeps. But it hadn't come from Cam's gun.

As a matter of fact, the shot had hit the side of the stable somewhere behind Cam. In the spotlight of the jeep, I could see the bullet hole in the wood.

"STAND DOWN!" Cam yelled, looking around at his own men, all hidden in the shadows, behind the wheels or peering around the corners of the vehicles, just beyond the light. "I told you—"

But my eyes were going somewhere else. They traveled up, opposite the bullet mark in the stable, to the roof of the shed across the road. Mark was up there, lying on his stomach with his long-barreled rifle, lining up a second shot.

Without thinking, I threw myself at Cam.

Then my world exploded.

***

"Alex? Alex!"

The next thing I remember was his face, close to mine, looking down at me in frantic desperation. He grabbed me by the shoulders and shook me; I was limp as a rag doll. He stopped, and then I was being moved.

I was still deep enough in shock that I could hardly tell where the pain was coming from. I could barely breathe. There was something wrong; I was straining to breathe, like a heavy weight was on my chest. The world blurred around me.

Now I really was being held down; someone's hands pushed something against my chest. A cloth, or bandage maybe. My sleeves slipped down over my shoulders and away over my hands. I might not have been fully clothed.

"Stay with me, Alex! Stay with me. Alex! Alex, breathe! You have to live." The voice went dull around the edges and trailed off into the distance.

***

The next fit of consciousness I had, I found myself lying on something hard. The feeling had developed into something truly spectacular. My chest was filled with liquid fire. I immediately tried to draw a sharp breath and ended up choking and coughing on blood.

It was still night, and cold. Small but glaring white lights roved this way and that, casting moving shadows. I was in the back of a flat-bed truck.

Cam was crouching next to me, holding his hands under my head as we went over sharp bumps and ruts.

My perception of what was happening sharpened into focus. He was returning to the Settlement, but he was taking me with him. Horror dawned inside me. I couldn't go there.

"No…" I struggled, and coughed again. "Have to go back…" That was the best I could do.

"We are going back," he said. "Back to the Settlement, where you can get proper medical care." His face was set determinedly. He looked me in the eye briefly, then his eyes flinched away, and his throat moved as he swallowed.

We went over another bump.

❖

Chapter Thirty-Two

The Plea

I lay there, half drowsing, for an unknown period of time. It could have been hours, days… surely not minutes?

The first real landmark of my return to the world was when I realized I was in a hospital bed.

Back in the Settlement.

But the panic I should have rightfully felt was not forthcoming. I was under the influence of some sort of drug. I breathed slowly through an oxygen mask pushing air into my face.

My chest hurt more as the imperceptible minutes ticked by. The pain was very large and spread-out; it could have been consuming and all-encompassing if I wasn't floating so far away from it. The drug was pushing me down on the brink of consciousness and keeping me from thinking too much. My general inability to move tempted me to struggle, but I made the quick and deliberate choice to accept it. That was the only way of surviving in the Settlement; by accepting whatever happened to you. Struggling only ever made things worse.

A nurse in a white cap and a white face mask appeared over me. He checked on all of the needles taped into my arm and adjusted some bags hanging next to me, and soon I felt more awake.

I could guess where I was. This was not, strictly speaking, a hospital. They would have taken me to the medical center for DYNTEC operatives. The Settlement invests a great deal of resources and training into its DYNTEC operatives, so they are generally considered valuable assets. Accordingly, their medical center is capable of treating serious injuries that would be considered unsalvageable in the general population.

The Administrators had obviously made a deliberate choice to keep me alive. I checked my wrist quickly, and noted that I was still Biometric-free. That was a choice too.

But now I wasn't sure what to expect. I could only wait.

Eventually a man I did not recognize came in to the white, bare-walled room. He didn't look like a doctor. He was carrying a briefcase. I watched as he pulled up a chair and took a seat next to me.

My bed was inclined very slightly at the head. I would rather sit up while he was in the room, but just tensing caused me pain. I was still breathing through the oxygen mask, and a long hose ran down to a canister under the bed. I moved my eyes, but I hadn't tried my voice yet.

"Hello, Alex," he said, trying to start in a friendly tone, it seemed. "My name is Tony. I'm your appointed legal advocate."

I simply stared at him, wondering what this could mean.

"You've been here about a day," he said. "Good to see you awake. They think you should be able to talk now. That's good because it seems you're in a bit of trouble at the moment."

I remained silent in as deliberate a way as possible. Just because I might be *able* to talk didn't mean I wanted to talk to *him*.

"Besides the obvious, I mean." He tried to deflect with an awkward laugh. "It's okay," he said. "You can be honest with me. Have you ever heard of attorney's privilege? It means that the Administrators aren't allowed to listen to me, or to you when you're talking to me. They can't hear anything you say right now. It's okay."

I opened my mouth. My throat was dry, and my voice was hoarse. It felt a little awkward to try and talk through the oxygen mask. "What happened?" I asked.

"I…" he cocked his head, and paused for an abnormally long time, with a funny look on his face. Finally he said, "You… were shot?"

I almost laughed, but I could easily anticipate the pain this would bring, so stifled it and went for brevity. "No. After."

"Cam Branson brought you back here."

I knew that. I knew that; I vaguely remembered it along with that night ride. The memory hung over me like a shadow. It hurt now, but the pain was only an echo of what it was then. And a threat, too. *Do you remember that?* My body seemed to say. *I could do that again.*

I had thought I was going to die. I'd *intended* to die. Even if it was for only a moment. I'd begged him not to take me back here, but the man wanted me to live, and who could fault him for that? Yet I felt a jarring wrongness at surviving this, as though I had secretly actually died and my soul had been stuffed awkwardly back into my corpse.

Cam was in every sense the sole reason I was here.

"Can I speak with him?" I asked.

"I'm afraid that's not possible right now," said Tony the lawyer. "You've only got me. Now listen. You're accused of some pretty serious stuff." He leaned up on the edge of the seat, hands clasped. "The Administrators think you've betrayed the Settlement. You have no formal violations on record, but they want to push to mark you as a Detractor anyways. They suspect you of being involved in a plot with the Kingdom of Heaven cult to overthrow the Settlement."

Of course there were charges. They weren't idiots. The charge itself was bogus, but they could at least tell that I was no longer acting in their interests. Even assuming Cam hadn't reported on me himself, his men would have.

"It's okay," said Tony. He must have seen the look of chagrin on my face, though it had little to do with hearing the charges. "I'm really very good with the Administrators. I've got them eating out of the palm of my hand. Let me tell you what I've got here." He opened up his briefcase on his lap and pulled out a laptop, which he set up.

"I've negotiated a plea deal for you, one that allows you to get a new Biometric with all fresh accounts on everything. You lose your job at DYNTEC, but that can't be helped. You can go back to whatever job you had before. All you have to do is sign, declaring your loyalty to the Settlement and so forth."

It was a little hard to get my mind around all that in my current state. I can't deny that I was searching in my mind for a way out of the situation, and I guess I hoped that maybe it wouldn't be as bad as it sounded.

"Read it," I managed, my breath fogging the plastic.

Truly, at some level, I almost didn't *want* to know what it said. I wanted to sign and not ask. It would be easier. Might let me live with myself.

But probably not.

There was nothing in the Settlement that I desired. Well, very little. Now that I was here, I could sense the petty concerns of my old world hovering around me like flies. I hated them. The idea of going back to the food labs had never appealed, but now it was the prospect of living in that gray apartment, going to work, and coming home every day for the rest of my life that was too much to bear. It was so alien now; my ambitions from before were dead. I'd dared to build up a new set of hopes and dreams, and they had just been ripped away from me. I had been outside the Settlement. I had seen the trees. It would be impossible to live this way.

"You want me to read it to you?" he shifted in his chair. "All right, then. Yes, I was going to do that anyway. Wouldn't want to make you move around too much. Let's see." He coughed and hunched over the screen.

"I, Alexandra Ortiz, do solemnly swear to be a loyal Settlement citizen from this point forward. I will have no affiliations to outside organizations or entities or any entity besides the Settlement and DYNTEC, its operating arm. I hereby do deny and disavow any involvement in any such organizations including but not limited to: governments, states, cults, tribes, clans, collectives, companies, corporations, businesses, churches, religions, gods, families, or movements. Furthermore, specifically, I regret my former actions in support of the cult outside the walls of the Settlement, which were undertaken without Settlement authorization, and beg the pardon of the Administrators for my actions, which I took under duress after being psychologically manipulated by the cultists. I repudiate all beliefs and ideas of the cult designated by the Settlement as 'Detractive' and agree never to speak of them. I swear never to perform any Detractive action again as long as I shall live, and I acknowledge that any such action would lead to my immediate termination."

He looked up. "And then, under that, it says to sign here."

My heart writhed inside of me, and I squirmed a little bit on the bed.

A stylus. He was holding up the screen. He was trying to push a stylus into my fingers. I wouldn't hold it. It hit the floor loudly and rolled away.

Now? He wanted this now?

"It's the only way, Alex. It's really your only good option. Trust me on this. It's a pretty good deal, all things considered."

"I can't," I squeaked, my voice muffled inside the oxygen mask.

"I'm sorry? I can't hear you."

"I…" I felt winded.

He reached over and pulled the oxygen mask down to my chin. "There you go; start over." Though he had a softened, sympathetic affect, he was ignoring my obvious distress. I was confounded. I was going to feel guilty for not giving him what he wanted, which didn't even make sense. Surely he thought he was doing me a favor. Except this was anything but.

"Alexandra?"

I bit my lips and shook my head. Tears leaked from my eyes.

"What are you saying? Are you going to sign this, or not?"

The forwardness enabled me, and I took the plunge. "I'm not."

"I was afraid you'd say that." The lawyer closed his laptop with a clap, then put it back inside the briefcase and stood up. Something about him had changed in a heartbeat, like a cold wind blowing clouds over the sun.

"There's nothing else I can do for you, then," he said, and turned toward the door.

I watched him go, feeling as though I'd passed some sort of test.

But he wasn't quite done yet. Halfway to the door, he paused. "Although… if it would make a difference, I do feel that you should know. There was a drone strike on the cultists yesterday. Both towns. There were no survivors."

I couldn't take this. Not in my current state. Or maybe in any state. Everything inside of me shattered in an instant. The shock must have showed on my face. I was totally frozen for a moment, for several moments, scarcely able to think or breathe.

But I swept up the shards of my will to live and tried to paste them hastily back together because he was wrong. He had to be.

"No," I said, barely audible through dry lips. I turned my face away from him, toward the wall. "I can't believe that. Surely… some of them must have escaped…"

The next moment he was a bit closer, interested, as though friendly again. "Do *you* think there's any way they might have escaped?"

Surely, yes, some of them might have gotten out in time—they would have run—

Then I realized what he was doing.

Damn. I've already said too much.

I fell silent at once.

"Shame. I told them I didn't think you'd talk to me." He shook his head.

I jerked my head back around, beginning to realize I'd been betrayed, but not sure to what extent. "You're not a lawyer, are you?" I said.

"No."

"I'm not going to get one, am I?"

His lips were flat. "No."

"So they heard all of that."

"Yes."

"The plea. Why?"

"Gauge your willingness to cooperate. Obtain a handy-dandy confession. Which they will get, by the way." He stopped in the metal-framed doorway, smiling nastily. "The next person you talk to isn't going to be nearly as nice as I am."

❈

Chapter Thirty-Three

Sunk Cost

I waited two entire days for this threat to manifest. I would have to come off the oxygen before I could be moved to a prison cell. I wasn't looking forward to it. Especially since I would be losing the morphine. I watched the nurse untape the needles from my arm.

Eventually they did come for me. Who "they" were and what they looked like didn't matter, as they were people I had never seen before and would never see again. It was my first time standing up since being shot, and I tried to take it slow, but they pulled me along. It hurt a lot, and the drug hadn't even worn out of my system yet. I was given some shorts and a white T-shirt instead of the hospital scrubs, but no socks or shoes until we got down to the main doors.

Even such a short walk seemed so far. I was exhausted. I sat down on a bench in the lobby and took as long as I could to put the socks and shoes on. My escorts seemed unsympathetic.

I got up, and we left not through the main doors, but through a bare sublevel, disconnected from the main system and for DYNTEC use only. This one took us to the prisons.

The Settlement's entire prison complex is underground; there is not even one floor above ground level. The West Central DYNTEC headquarters are directly on top of it. Because of this, the only parts of the place I knew were what I passed through.

We walked down a long, empty cellblock. I couldn't take it all in one go, but had to pause, doubled over by the wall, panting. They'd only let me stop for a few seconds before I had to keep moving.

Prisons in the Settlement technically exist, but the system for dealing with Detractors and violations is handled these days mostly with civil penalties, or simply termination for true crimes or incurable cases. Prison sentences are rarely issued, as they are a drain on the Settlement's resources. The fact that I was going here was just another proof that the Settlement clearly believed they'd get something from me valuable enough to offset the cost of keeping me alive.

I felt a sinking feeling in my gut; wishing I could have had one more glance at the sky or even real sunlight. Instead I felt like I was descending into a bottomless pit from which I would never emerge.

At the end of the block, we went down a flight of stairs, where I was dumped unceremoniously into a concrete cell with bars. The staircase was off to the right, and from my place inside I couldn't even see to the top of it. Then I was left unbearably alone.

I wanted to cry, but the tears weren't starting, because I was too exhausted. I sat down, then laid down on the hard bench and waited for the drug to wear out of my system. I tried to savor my last moments of comfort before its effects wore off, but it was too late, they were already too uncomfortable and anxious. So I opted to think instead while I still could.

If they were dead—no, I couldn't allow myself to consider that. Then it would be back to wishing I'd died on the truck bed. They'd had a plan to escape. I simply had to believe it had worked. Somehow. Despite the invasion by Cam's army. I knew some vehicles had taken me back to the Settlement, but I remembered his words about "having no choice" and all that. Nothing about my getting shot necessitated him calling a full retreat. If that village wasn't leveled by now…

I shook my head. No. Couldn't consider it. It was better, my current circumstances considered, to think about their escape plans as little as possible.

I had no resentment whatsoever against Mark for shooting me. He'd only been trying to defend me. And his family and village. I hoped he wasn't dead. I hoped he didn't think *I* was dead. I hope he wasn't letting it eat at him, wherever he was.

I told myself I didn't regret taking a bullet for Cam. I wanted it to be true. What was Cam doing now? Did he realize what he'd done to me? What he'd done to the Kingdom? Did he even care? Why hadn't he come to see me? It had been two whole days.

I tried to pray—for myself, but also for Cam. For the Kingdomers too, presuming they were alive.

I had very little practice composing prayers of my own, so at first I tried to copy the words I'd heard in the Kingdom, but it didn't seem natural. I whispered the words under my breath because just thinking them didn't feel tangible enough, and I'd be tempted to suppose that now that I was back in the Settlement, God wasn't real anymore. I had to say something out loud. But not loud enough to be overheard.

"Please God help me," I whispered.

My attempt at prayer was interrupted by Jesse's appearance.

"Ah," I sat up abruptly, flinching. "Jesse!" I actually felt relieved to see him. Someone I recognized.

He gave me a weary and—oddly—apprehensive look, then settled back to lean across the opposing wall. He hooked his thumbs in his pockets and raised a fuzzy eyebrow.

"I want to speak to Cam," I told him. I could reach one of the bars, from my position on the bench, and grasped it eagerly. "Where is Cam? If *you* can make it down, surely—"

"While you were on mission," said Jesse slowly, "Cam got 'imself a promotion. He's a Level 3 now. Soon's you got back, he was reassigned. He's prohibited from working on your case or seeing you."

Of course. Too dangerous to let us speak; I was the one corrupted by the cult. Cam was still a good and loyal Settlement officer. But he clearly had a weakness for me. Their logic was impeccable; it was actually lucky that Cam wasn't in more trouble than this. Not that I would know about it if he was.

Still, it was more than disappointing. My anger flared out of frustration. Surely we *both* wanted to see each other, but the Administrators were keeping us apart.

"Then you tell me at least," I said. "Is it true? Is everyone in Hock and Hanfell really dead?"

He flinched a little, then an odd look passed over his face, but he said guiltily, "Guess so."

What did that mean? Could it be true, or could he be lying to me also?

"If Cam's not allowed to come," I said, "why'd they let you?"

"I'm not as sentimental as he is." Jesse seemed to settle in a little; he reached into his pocket and pulled out an imitation cigarette. The Settlement had attempted a total prohibition on those things once, but it had been unsuccessful, with poor results, and the i-cigs were soon legal again. Not even the Administrators could curb *all* vice.

"They think I c'n do what needs to be done. Though…" he spoke slowly, twirling the cig. "Admins said I'm not allowed to make you bleed. Too risky. I'm not allowed do anything that would risk openin' the hole in your lung either. Ya might die. You're lucky, kid. You still got time to tell 'em what they wanna know."

I just sat silent on the bench, slumping against the concrete wall, not daring to ask what *that* was. All I remembered was the horrible plea deal I'd refused to sign. Wait, there *had* been a question after that—but my memory of the first day back was already a little fuzzy.

"Hot damn," mused Jesse, shaking his head. "Why'd they send me in here? They should have known I'm too dangerous to sic on ya. I'm not one of those careful, deliberate types. Not really my style. I just rough people up."

I was surprised to hear him say this, as this was far more than Jesse tended to talk about himself. He took a puff on the cig.

"You know, I think you might be the only one of *us*,"—he gestured in a circle, referring to more than himself and I— "who's actually a good person. That's why you're in there. And I'm out here. Tends to happen that way in this godforsaken world. I tried to prepare ya. Tried to toughen you up. Didn't work, evidently. The only way to protect yourself against pain is to stop feeling anything. To stop caring. You couldn't do that. And now you're going to break."

It was neither a boast nor a reproach. It was merely a statement of fact.

"So," he said, "where is the cultists' rendezvous point? You told them we were coming. Where were they gonna flee to?"

There it was.

"You told me they were dead!" My heart beat faster. "Why would you ask me that if they were dead? That means at least some of them survived! Doesn't it? Doesn't it!" I pressed myself against the bars.

"Just answer the question," he said, but the intended force wasn't behind it. He just sounded tired.

"I don't know," I said. "If they had one, they never talked about it."

"Don't be stupid."

"I'm not being stupid."

"Alex…" He eyed me.

"I really don't know. You know me. I'm not that adventurous. I didn't explore around that territory. It wasn't even part of the assignment," I stammered.

"Cut the crap."

I forced myself to quit running at the mouth.

"You're really not going to make this easy on me, are you?"

I sat as though frozen; didn't dare move or say anything.

"All right, I'll cut you a deal. I'll bet that chest wound has gotta be rough. Meds for information. Hm?" He pulled out a little bottle and waved it at me.

I tore my eyes away. I was sure that would sound more appealing eventually, but right now it was too soon. Less than one *day*. If I went for it now, I'd just be ashamed.

"I'll… get by," I said, laying down on the bench.

"All right then. See you again tomorrow. I gotta warn you though. The next person you meet… might not be as nice as me."

Chapter Thirty-Four
Why Did You Do It?

"Wake up."

I jolted awake in the cell, scraping my elbows on the wall as I sat up on the narrow bench. I'd been sleeping for a few hours, probably. It was only my second day down here. I knew my wound was continuing to heal, but it sure didn't feel like it.

Things had, as expected, gotten worse since they'd taken the drugs from me. The exhaustion and general muted soreness had transformed into a sharp pinching sensation deep down in my lung. I struggled to breathe without coughing. There was likely still a bit of fluid in there. The feeling was constant and unabating, and I couldn't quite get comfortable.

Fortunately, last night it had become enough like background noise, albeit the background noise of sleeping at a subway station. I thought my chest hurt even in my dreams.

Now I was faced with one of my escorts from before: a tall, black-haired man.

"You're wanted in the Medical Center."

"For a treatment?" I felt slightly relieved, they were at least going to give me *some* medical attention to make sure I didn't *die*. "It is for a treatment, right?" I wavered as he unlocked the door without answering. "If it is for a treatment," I babbled, "any kind of hint about what it's going to be…"

"Shut up." He kicked me in the leg, and I flinched.

I did not feel like walking and thought perhaps I would have been nauseated even if it weren't for the horrible thoughts filling my mind.

Best case scenario, it was a legitimate treatment. He didn't say it *wasn't* a legitimate treatment.

But the closer we got to the Medical Center, the more uneasy I felt. He wasn't letting me rest enough, and I lagged and got slower and slower.

It was the way the man wouldn't look at me. The way they didn't talk to us at the front desk, even to check me in (I'd been checked out last time). The way we took a service hallway instead of the normal route.

They might be putting my Biometric back, I thought momentarily.

No, that wasn't right. They would view that as a gift. And they didn't *need* it in order to kill me when I was under their power like this.

By the time we got close to the hospital room I'd been in before, the man had to get a second worker to join him to "help" me along. I didn't have the strength to actively resist them, but I did allow myself to be more or less dead weight.

Once in the room, they dumped me and I practically fell onto the hospital bed.

"Fluids," said a nurse, and something jabbed my arm. I laid still. That was a real treatment. Not torture.

"We shouldn't be here when he gets here," said one of the men to the other, though my eyes were shut, and I didn't pay attention to who was talking due to all of the background noise.

"Right. Too dangerous." That was the only response, and when I opened my eyes again, they were gone. I curled up tightly. I wasn't restrained in any fashion, but I wouldn't get far in this state.

A figure appeared in the metal-framed doorway.

It was Cam.

"Cam!" I burst out, struggling to lean up onto one elbow.

He ran to my bed. In a moment he dropped down low enough to see me up close, grasping the polished silver guard rail on the bed with both hands.

I meant to say something like, "What happened?" or "What are you doing here?" But what came out instead was, "Are you all right?"

He laughed a little too loud, in a way that sounded like if he didn't laugh, he might cry. "Hey! That's my line." His blonde hair had lost any semblance of order, it spiked up at odd angles like cut straw. There were dark circles under his eyes. After those words, he seemed a bit at a loss.

"I'm all right," he answered finally, with some reluctance. "Thanks to you. I honestly don't know what to say."

"Thank you is all right." I gave a weak smile of amusement and lifted my fingers to the rail where his hands were.

He shook his head. "'Thank you' is what you say when somebody passes the salt."

I started to laugh, but my lungs couldn't handle it, and the stab of pain left me struggling to breathe.

Stop being funny, I almost started to say, but at the troubled look on his face, I realized he had been quite serious.

"Can't believe it took me this long to arrange—" he started.

"Don't worry about it," I said.

"All right, but Alex, you've got to tell me what's happened to you in all this time. I've been losing my mind. It wasn't easy to bribe you out of *prison.*"

"Can they hear us?"

"They shouldn't. That was part of the deal."

Despite everything, I found that I actually believed him. "I'm fine," I said. "They haven't hurt me or anything. So far."

"You look like you're in pain."

I was. It was hard to muster the will to speak words when each and every single one of them hurt so much. But this was *Cam.* I had to try. "Well, they took away the drugs," I said. "Wouldn't want me to become a junkie, you know."

He looked mortified. "That... that wasn't supposed to happen." Now he was apologizing. "I had to bring you back. You would have died. I thought you'd be *safe* here."

"Cam," I pleaded, "please tell me what happened to the towns."

"I ordered a retreat. I... I don't think they're too happy with me upstairs right now." He spoke in a low voice and stared away, down toward my feet. "They're questioning my judgment. They think I'm emotionally compromised. Not just for retreating, but for going in hot in the first place. We weren't ready, and I pushed it anyway just to rescue one operative. Before I could order a retreat," he said, "fighting broke out in Hanfell. They got a couple of our guys. We don't know if we got anyone. They captured one of our jeeps."

"*What.*"

"Next day, while you were asleep, I was relieved of my command of the unit. They went back to the site in greater force. But everybody was gone."

"They're alive!" a smile crept over my lips. That was enough. I felt as though a great weight had been removed from me. God was protecting them; I was sure of it.

"As far as anybody will tell me, we're still occupying the area to look for clues about where they went. Nobody from this concrete wasteland can track for shit. Also there was hard rain, so that didn't help."

"So… no drone strike?" I asked, hopeful.

"Not yet. They will have to eventually, though. Don't want to let the cultists return to their base of operations."

I gave a small nod. "Right."

"Now your turn. Why were you in prison? That wasn't supposed to happen."

"They put me down there after I wouldn't sign their little thingy."

"You can't be telling me you refused the plea deal." His eyes widened in shock.

"I did."

"No! Alex, no!" He jumped up in alarm. "You don't know what I had to do to get that for you. Dammit, Alex!" He shook his head. "I don't want you to be killed for being a Detractor."

I didn't know what to say to him.

He sat down hard in the chair next to the bed. It was a limp, deflated sort of gesture, and the chair moved back a few inches. There he remained in silence a minute.

Finally he turned toward me again with a deeply intent expression, his eyebrows drawn. He leaned in to inspect my face, taking hold of the bed rail again. "Why?"

It was too broad to answer. "What do you mean?" I rasped.

He hesitated, then his voice wavered. "Why'd you do it, Alex? I don't understand."

"Because," I said. "I *love* you."

He flinched away as though the metal had electrified him. He took two steps back and shook his head fervently, seeming to devolve into some sort of panic. "Love? No, Alex, no. No! I can't... What? What do you mean? Romantically?"

"I don't know," I whispered. I felt my face go ice cold and then red-hot, and I kind of wanted to laugh or cry or die. The truth is that I was attracted to him. But that wasn't the main type of love I was thinking of.

"You can't— you can't just say that! What am I supposed to do?" His demeanor was angry, loud. He sounded furious, but I knew the only person he was battling into submission was himself. "I don't understand. A minute before you were threatening to *kill* me, the next you're throwing your life away."

I chewed my lips.

He paced over to the far wall so he didn't have to look me in the eye, and he leaned on it with both hands. "I don't see any reason why you should even *like* me after everything I've done to you. And other people. You know about that." He started to choke a little. "Your friends. You love them too, don't you? That's why you were trying to fight me."

He looked back over his shoulder at me, and I gave a tiny nod.

His voice was quite strained now. "Alex, it doesn't make sense. How can anybody love anybody else when they can make us hurt each other?"

Like this, I said, but only with my eyes. He seemed to take in the message.

He paced back again, wall to wall, furiously, hands on his head. He was arguing with me, though I hadn't said a word. "All right, but you don't understand. It's not my choice. None of this is my choice. I haven't had a choice in anything since I was a teenager, and I didn't know I was selling my soul." He did lower his volume significantly now, perhaps out of sheer reflex. I strained to make out his words. "I can't get out of the service. If I disobey any of their orders, they'll *kill* me."

I looked at him again meaningfully, as I was, lying in the hospital bed. His eyes traveled over the needles in my arms, and my limp body, covered with a thin T-shirt. The bandages were almost visible. I could hear the sound of these protests falling flat.

"Damn. Shit. Damn!" He kept on swearing more harshly, and finally slammed his fist into the wall with a resounding thump.

After that he seemed to become more self-aware, went to the door, and looked up and down the hall.

Then he came back to me, slowly.

"I was right," he said quietly, leaning over, and he stroked my cheek very hesitantly, so delicately that I thought I really would stop breathing. "You're not the Alex I know. You're *more*. A lot more. What *happened* to you?"

"I—" I started, then was sent into a coughing fit. It hurt spectacularly, and I fought to get it under control. "I'm one of them now," I managed. "The Children of God."

He frowned, but mostly in confusion. "I know you're on their side. The point… the point is… look, you joined DYNTEC, but compared to me you're still so innocent. I might have said a minute ago that I didn't have a choice, but there were plenty of things I did have a choice about. I didn't have to look for promotions, but I did. I've killed and hurt people in the name of the

Settlement, and I wasn't always forced to do it. I'm the Kingdom's enemy, and if you're one of them now then I'm your enemy too. But… you took a bullet for me. Who *does* that?"

The question hung in the air for a moment.

"Jesus does that," I said.

He took a shaky breath. "The cultists' God? He doesn't want me."

"Yes, he does," I said.

"The cultists wouldn't want me if they knew what I did to Paul Tiller. He was the first person to tell me what you're saying right now. And I killed him."

"Cam," I said. "He wanted me, and he'll take you too. That's what he does." The effort of all the talking, culminating in this long sentence, just about winded me. I panted shallowly.

Something strange moved in his eyes as he looked down at me. "You're asking me to adopt their God?"

"Not just theirs. Mine too. He will adopt you." I was filled with an extremely strong hopeful emotion, and tried to reach up to him again.

Cam's eyes filled with tears, but he didn't want to let me see, so he turned his back. He stayed like that for an unusually long time. Finally he wiped his face with his sleeves, turned back around, and said, in a very subdued tone, "I used to work down there sometimes.

I know what's going to happen." By Gaia, he actually looked a bit pale. "I'd rather it didn't."

"Me too," I said.

"I'm sorry. My time's up. Listen." He had a sharpening look in his eye. "I'll see you again. I promise."

And that was the last I saw of him for some time.

Chapter Thirty-Five

Cruel Mercies

The next person who came down to my cell was not Jesse, but Administrator Jamison.

Jamison's hands floated awkwardly; not touching anything from the railings on the stairs to the bars of my cell. He looked around and up and down as though he'd never come to the prison before. "Good morning?" he started. "Or rather, afternoon."

I stared up from the farthest corner of the floor in which I was now settled but made no comment.

He assessed me, squinting, and noticed the reddish line across my wrist. "What happened to your Biometric?"

"They cut it out," I murmured.

"How horrible," he said, with genuine apathy. "Are you ready to begin co-operating with the investigation?"

I looked away from him.

I had already come so far, or it felt like it anyway. I wasn't going to waste the last several days, that I'd spent almost paralyzed, trying not to move or think. Or to give into emotion and sob, though it had happened once or twice. I would be feeling better soon.

"If you do change your mind, simply call for me. I have your drugs on the ready." It was so bald-faced, and yet so bland. Civilized. Disgustingly polite.

What we called "polite society," I felt, was actually a thin skin stretched over the rotting corpse of what used to be a moral framework. Once there had been goodness and kindness and respect for other human beings beneath that façade. Now there was only a writhing mass of maggots and filth.

On the eighth day after I'd been shot, he came in to find me standing and walking slowly around the room of my own volition.

He looked at the capped bottle in his hand. "I was going to offer you this," he said drily, "but it seems you are showing signs of improvement." By comparison with his usual plastic demeanor, it seemed that he was slightly irritated. I allowed myself to feel smug.

His next words were less encouraging. "That's good," he said. "Administrator Dana Morris-Fletcher wants to meet with you."

***

The top of the Central Tower was as before except in one way. Whereas previously, the vinyl curtains had begun stretched over the windows and later retracted, today I entered to a flood of gray light and was promptly greeted by the closing of these curtains.

I watched with a last bit of desperate longing. I had thought I'd never see the trees again, but here—just for a moment—there was a last glance; a reminder that somewhere out there the sun was still shining (though if I'd had to guess, I would have said it was overcast today).

My escorts, the men from corrections, passed back through the door before it closed, and Jamison left my side. There were plenty of people in the lounge today. So many that I thought perhaps *all* the Administrators must be here, even all thirty of them; but they were occupied as usual with their own affairs and scarcely looked at me.

And now as the curtains finished their slow roll, it really was the end. There was a finality about it, like being sealed into a tomb. The trees were gone; the room was lit only by the LEDs on the paneling.

Someone rose from a chair at the far end of the room, a gray silhouette at first against the vinyl, but I recognized her. It was the statuesque, angular form of

Dana Morris-Fletcher. Her shoes clicked across the tile.

"Alex," she said, and feigned friendliness a moment, which I despised more than open hatred. "Why don't you come and sit with me?"

I tried to keep the fear out of my eyes. As the Administrators had clearly run out of patience in their passive efforts to control me, I hoped at least they had decided to make it quick.

We walked over near the window, though it was covered. I kept looking at it.

"Would you like me to open the shade?" she asked.

I gave her a hard look. Unfortunately, her look was always harder, so I felt like a sullen child.

"I'll bet you would," she said. She made no move to do so. "Sit down." Administrator Dana gestured to the plush chair. "Let me show you something."

There was a small table between us. She tapped it twice with a finger, and a screen winked on between us.

A moving image appeared. It was a video of Cam and me, in the Medical Center, taken from a hidden camera somewhere in the ceiling. My blood ran cold.

But he said they weren't watching—

No, I refused to doubt him. It was the bribe. One of his bribes must have fallen through.

At any rate, we were found out, for whatever that was worth.

"You can't be telling me you refused the plea deal," said the tiny Cam on the screen. To witness his distress again from a different angle was almost more painful.

"I did." My obnoxious voice came from the pathetic lump lying on the bed.

"No! Alex, no!" The little Cam stomped back and forth. "You don't know what I had to do to get that for you. Dammit, Alex! I don't want you to be killed for being a Detractor."

"Yes, Alex," said Dana, smiling like a shark. "He did ask for that plea for you. Did you know he actually got down on his knees and begged? Surely you at least care about him, perhaps more than your cultists, since you threw away your chance at life with *them* for *him*." She hesitated only a moment, not long enough for me to interrupt. "You traitor."

And for a moment, I wasn't even sure what she meant I was a traitor to, and the words stabbed through my heart.

I think she could see that she had reached me on some level. There was loathing in her eyes.

"Yes," she said, "you are a traitor, Alex. Despite our explicit instruction and training, you embraced the cult. You were supposed to help eliminate them and the threat they pose. You signed on for that very mission.

And now you are refusing to either complete your mission or reject their ideas. You, who were born and raised by the Settlement. You, who were given everything you have by the Settlement: your food, your water, your money, your home, your Biometric, the air that you breathe, your very *life*…

"You have betrayed us for a foreign power. Through pure reactionary emotion, you sympathized to the bigoted, inbred idiots who propagate their lies in the wilderness. Lies that could undo the very seams of our civilized society. You let yourself be drawn in and now refuse to even acknowledge, let alone apologize."

I had been staring at the tile, but I peeled my gaze off the floor. It felt like lifting a boulder. It was wrong to be ashamed now. She wanted me to feel that way. I'd always held myself back my entire life. Lack of confidence, self-censorship, and uncertainty was how I'd stayed out of trouble. But it was no form of humility to feel shame for a righteous act. Why rebuke in yourself what you would never rebuke in another?

"Of course not," I said.

"A shame."

She looked behind her and snapped her fingers at a woman in a gray suit. That woman moved off to get her a drink from the coffee bar.

I pursed my lips.

"And now this thing with Cam."

I felt a resurgence of panic. I gave her the only line I could think of. "This isn't about him."

"Ah, but it is."

"I thought this was about me and God," I fumbled.

Dana plucked the coffee cup from the hand of the waiting attendant. "I don't care about your god," she said. "But I am not so dense that I can't see how your affair with Cam is a representation of your defiance." She put the cup down on the tabletop and continued to stir it with a small stick.

I pulled a wry face at her characterization of our relationship as an *affair.*

"I might have been deceived into thinking that you'd saved his life out of pure loyalty to him as a Settlement officer… if I didn't have the testimony of his men. And that video, of course." She tapped the fingers of one hand on the table. "You're compromised."

I dug my fingertips into my knees. "What are you going to do?" I whispered.

"Normally our philosophy would require euthanizing you in a situation like this." She took a thoughtful sip of the coffee.

"But I'm willing to give you two options. In the first option, you get to live. Allow me to explain."

She set down the cup and lightly brushed her palms off. "Quiet disappearances don't attract much attention.

That is by design. But when a high-ranking or well-known member of DYNTEC defects, well… sometimes you have to make an example."

I knew she was talking about him.

"He's a Level Three!" I protested. "He's valuable to you! You wouldn't—"

"That's why I've decided to let you live," said Dana. "As an example to him and to others in DYNTEC. He's always been compliant, but when you're involved, he's emotional. That's dangerous. But he's done nothing Detractive. He just needs to be kept in line. So do you. He vouched for you; he claims the brainwashing is not permanent, that he can undo it and keep you in line. Make you a good citizen again. He swore it up and down. So we made a concession. In the eyes of the law, you're considered mentally disabled. He's technically your legal guardian already." Her eyes were smug, half-lidded. "Don't disappoint him."

He was? Now? But she said this was "option one". I could already guess what I might have to do to merit option one.

"We'll get you a new Biometric," she added, "as soon as possible."

My hand moved to my wrist involuntarily.

"You'll need it to go back to work. After all, even drooling idiots must earn their keep. I heard there's an opening at one of your old jobs."

"Educator?" I asked with a glimmer of hope that there might still be something worth doing even in this place.

She smiled coldly. "Not a chance. You're going back to the food labs."

I remembered the back-breaking work of the food labs. "That's hardly better than prison. Not much of a bribe, if that's what you were thinking. I'm not… signing your document… so I can live with Cam but go back to the food labs."

She seemed so amused by this, I thought that if she were the kind of person who could have laughed, she would have. "We can get by without the document. If a high-ranking DYNTEC operative failed to keep their mentally ill dependent in line… well, who knows what might happen to that person. They might get demoted. Or… worse."

So, I thought. This is how they manipulate me—through him. And him through me.

"So that's your first option," she said. "If you cooperate by telling us what we want to know."

"You mean what happened to the Kingdom?"

She nodded.

"So now you admit they are alive." I leaned forward.

"It was worth a try." She shrugged. "Your other option is, well... less pretty. I suppose you might survive."

While I processed that very bitter pill, she added, "Even if you did, there's more than one way to be mentally disabled."

I must have looked confused, because she followed up.

"Legal disability is a very diverse thing, you know. Some people are quite functional. Others... less. Do you want to make this easy on Cam? Or hard? It would certainly be very poetic if we were to grant his request in such a way that he'll look at you every day for the rest of his life and wish that we hadn't." She stirred the drink with a stick. "Imagine being reduced to something so pitiable and helpless you're barely even human. He'll have to feed you through a straw."

I focused exclusively on her lips, trying to comprehend how it was that a human being, ostensibly with a soul, was forming and speaking the words that I was hearing.

"He won't take that," I said, faintly, stupidly. "You'll regret this."

"I don't think I will," she said. "He's a broken man, Alex. He'll do anything we ask. You think those words he said to you mean anything? I spoke with him yesterday. He's already given up. He belongs to us.

Whatever you think you were going to try and convince him of, it hasn't worked."

"I don't believe you," I said. "I don't believe anything you say."

"Then believe him," she said, and tapped the table-screen again. Another video appeared. In this one there was only Dana and Cam.

"You know how this works, Cam," she was saying. "Are you a DYNTEC man, or are you not?"

"Yes," he said. He sat across from her, hands folded in front of him sullenly, eyes looking askance at the corner while she dressed him down.

"You know the necessities. You know the rules. You know what's at stake here. Yes?"

"Yes," said Cam.

"Now don't act soft. I know who you are. You are a torturer. Nothing about that has changed. You were as committed and ruthless as anybody we had. Why should it be different just because it is somebody you know?"

His voice was cold as ice. "It shouldn't."

"True indeed. And where can I expect to see you tomorrow?"

"Reporting to the East Central District, as ordered."

"Excellent."

The video shut down.

I rubbed my lips with my hand.

Administrator Dana followed my gaze to the window. Her mouth twitched slightly. "Don't think you're going back out there. You might as well just forget it exists."

I forced my eyes up to her stony eyes. "You never were going to let us leave," I said, "were you."

"Never," said Dana.

She knew exactly what I was referring to. That distant promise of Gaia's restoration. The ornamental gates. "It was the plan," she admitted. "Once. A long time ago. But it hasn't been for centuries. Humanity will never change. That's why we wall off areas of the Settlement and create incentives to shrink our own numbers."

"Why?" I asked. "What is your end goal?"

She hesitated. "That is not for a traitor to know."

But I was determined. I had her talking. I had little to lose, and wanted to stall my sentence. Beyond that, I truly did want to know the reason for it all. "Why not?" I tried again.

"It was decided by our predecessors, and we carry it out."

"But what is *it?*"

"It is a difficult burden to bear. The public would not accept it."

"You can tell me," I said. "You have me in your hand, and you know it. What am I going to do? Make a post on the Profile?"

She considered me for a moment with a side-eye before evidently deciding that I was right. She lowered her voice, so that the other Administrators, even if sitting nearby, would not listen in. "This Settlement will continue to shrink. In one hundred years from now, we will be one third our current size. In a thousand years from now, there will be less than fifty thousand people living on Earth."

"And then?"

"Eventually humanity must face extinction."

I had to protest the absurdity. "Surely at that point your lie that Gaia is overpopulated would be too difficult to maintain. You couldn't even sustain the Settlement's infrastructure on such low numbers."

"Nevertheless, humanity must end." But it was Dana who broke eye contact now. She would not look at me while saying this, but at the other Administrators, who were sitting or milling around.

"And you tell us it's for survival. The greater good."

"It is for the greater good," she said. "We Administrators hold to a strict philosophy that pleasure and suffering must be weighed against each other in every decision. It is always better to minimize suffering and maximize pleasure."

"You've got a funny way of showing it," I said.

"We must think long term rather than short term. Collectively, rather than individually. Just as the prevention of birth prevents net suffering, some evils are necessary to prevent damage to the Settlement and to Gaia."

Dana continued. "How cruel it is that we are the one creature Gaia has evolved which is capable of reflecting on its own suffering! It is immoral to reproduce, because increasing the number of humans born only increases the amount of suffering in this world."

"And the amount of joy," I said. "And the amount of love."

"For Earth's sake!" Her eyes flashed. It was a rare moment of genuine emotion, and the emotion was anger that was no less intense for the control she held over it. "Look around you, Alex! The immense scope of human suffering surely outweighs any pleasure that we might experience."

"Try looking outside the Settlement," I said recklessly.

"And defile the only goodness that exists by corrupting it with our own misery?"

I plunged on. "I've seen suffering and tragedy out there," I said, "and I still find it preferable to the best you have to offer me in here."

Her face whitened; she spoke through her teeth. "You think you've seen suffering? I'll make you think you're in the cultists' hell." She pushed herself up by the armrest. "I'll make sure to get enough pleasure out of it to compensate in Gaia's logbooks."

�֍

Chapter Thirty-Six

Zeno's Paradox

I hadn't dignified Dana's options with a response, but it was implicit what I'd chosen.

I couldn't stop thinking about her assessment of Cam.

He's a Settlement man.

He wanted me to live, that was clear enough. Yet in the same breath he'd begged for a chance to prove me loyal to the Settlement. But I wasn't. Did he care anyway? Even if he did, he had a point. If he defied the Settlement, they'd kill him for sure.

He would have no choice but to wait and see if I lived or died.

From the cell, the Level Ones took me to interrogation. I was in the clear now, supposedly; my wound healed enough. My lungs could take it. That was their opinion. I didn't think they were right, but no one asked me.

I had drowned before.

Several times, actually.

The first time didn't really count; I'd swallowed water while Cam was "teaching me to swim." It had been scary anyway. The second time, I'd been knocked unconscious in the river and didn't really remember it. The third time was this morning. The fourth time also this morning. The fifth time also this morning. The funny thing about drowning is that you never really get used to it.

It was shaping up to be a long day.

I fell to my knees, coughing up water. Water dripped from my wet hair, painting small black dots on the concrete. So I would die the same way as the boy John. It seemed appropriate.

The Level Ones were quite rough, and very loud.

They didn't know me, but they hated me fiercely. No, it was not me, but the idea of me that they hated, and it was surreal to know that only a few weeks ago, I too had hated the idea of me, and had given violations to Detractors to prove it. So now when I thought about these Level Ones, I felt sad. I was occupying the role of a criminal in their world.

This wasn't like the fear of barbarity at the hand of some mysterious cult. This was the homeland, the Settlement. An impersonal, yet intimately familiar machine. In a sense, I was occupying the role of a criminal in my own world as well.

One of the men knocked me back into the wall.

"Where are they?" he snarled.

I just slid down.

I'd already told them that I didn't know, just like I had told Jesse. But they hadn't listened, so I didn't bother anymore. There was nothing to communicate.

The world seemed to spin. I closed my eyes and tried to conserve energy.

I had never successfully defied anyone before. Not Jesse, when he tried to teach me. Not the teachers at school. I hadn't even been able to handle the food labs; they wore me down until I gave up.

I didn't feel defiant. I didn't think I had it in me to act that way. I was small, meek, foldable.

It was hard, then, to believe that I hadn't folded yet.

Jesse had been right; I was going to break soon. Probably in five minutes. Not this second— it helped that they scarcely gave me long enough intervals to cough up water and get my voice back—but I couldn't take this much longer.

It was five minutes away. No more than five minutes. *Just five minutes,* I said to myself, like a sleeper reluctant to wake.

It had been five minutes all day.

Sometimes I astonished even myself.

In school, I had learned about Zeno's Paradox. Zeno's Paradox is a philosophical theory based on the idea of infinite divisibility. It states that nothing should ever be able to get anywhere, because it would have to traverse an infinite number of points in order to get there. Ultimately, the Settlement said, on a fundamental level, the universe just doesn't make sense. But that wasn't why I thought of it now. Like the arrow in Zeno's paradox, there was a point that I continually approached, closer and ever closer, yet seemed unable to actually reach.

Some amount of time passed, the duration of which would be meaningless to describe.

A hard adrenaline crash left me lying on the floor as though floating. My whole body felt numb and limp and warm, my mind fuzzy and unwilling to feel emotions any longer. People moved around me, but I didn't care.

Everything we ever learned in school or from our parents was geared toward survival in the environment of the Settlement, toward surviving the whims of the Administrators. Though it was called "collective" and "cooperative" and idealistic, it was actually personal survival that we learned, at the expense of all else and all others.

The Administrators believed that to ensure a comfortable life for oneself was the highest moral good.

How could they ever understand the Kingdom, then? The Kingdomers could never come to the Settlement if it meant giving up their faith.

To accept a life full of suffering and danger for the sake of an *idea,* a *message* that would not guarantee happiness until the next life must have looked like lunacy to the Administrators. They didn't believe in another life. Only the ever-present now.

(The ever-present now was looking like kind of shit from my vantage point.)

These were the enemies of God, and I had not betrayed them, because I didn't belong to them anymore.

He was in spite of all the suffering in the world.

He was the reason why the Settlement held no meaning, the reason their entire empire was a hoax, the truth exposing their duplicity. He was the light outside the walls of darkness, the open air and freedom, the warmth of human affection.

I felt better, not afraid, like my anxiety had been purged and flushed out, like even if I died I would be fine.

As it turned out, the doctor had been quite wrong about my lungs being in the clear for such rough treatment. That was how I ended up in the medical center, dozing off not from any comfort or ease, but out of pure exhaustion.

Chapter Thirty-Seven

The Sublevels

I woke with a jolt as hands shook me awake. It was dark in the room, but strips of moonlight came in between the blinds. I struggled, pulled away and yelled out in fear and pain from the movement. A hand clapped over my mouth, muffling my scream. Then I saw Cam's face and did my best to go slack. He slowly removed his hand.

"*Cam.*"

"Sorry! Sorry. Quiet!" he whispered. "Get up. Put some real clothes on." I was wearing a loose T-shirt and pajama shorts. He shoved at me what could have been a pair of jeans out of my own home and a blue DYNTEC jacket.

"What are you doing here?" I tried to keep my voice down, but he hushed me anyway.

"You're coming with me. Right now. We have to go."

"I can't believe it. It *is* you." I could scarcely contain myself, but rushing him with a big hug like I wanted to would have been disastrous.

"Couldn't wait a minute longer. I waited too long." He grimaced. "I should have gotten you out last night, but I couldn't."

I sat up slowly and got to my feet carefully on the tile. He took down a backpack and threw a wad of socks at me too, and tossed over some tennis shoes. I didn't bother with modesty but slipped the clothes on over what I was already wearing.

"Where are we going?" I whispered.

"I can't tell you here. Just hurry."

He waited for me to finish putting the shoes on, and then took off out the door. He looked back to make sure I was following him as he ran down the hallway.

I panted, jogging slowly after him as best I could while breathing shallowly. With Cam present, I felt quite distracted from any pain—it almost didn't seem to matter. Still, one wrong move and I felt that I would tear something. I trotted doggedly on down the hallways. Some of them were dimmed for night hours, some (and these made me more nervous) were still lit as if it were daytime.

A door at the end of the hall, merely a partition between wings, slipped automatically open in front of Cam, and then shut behind him. I shuffled to keep up, and the darkness of the room seemed to press behind me. I thought I heard footsteps somewhere in the wing, and looked over my shoulder, breaking momentarily into a run. I caught up with him but my chest ached again and I slowed.

"Come on," he said. "We're almost to the elevator."

He took me by the arm and pulled me along, looking both ways nervously.

I stumbled a few hundred more feet along with him and then slumped to my knees inside of the brightly-lit elevator. He hit the buttons forcefully, then turned to me, letting his backpack slide off his shoulders.

Kneeling, he asked, "You all right?"

I nodded. "I'll be fine in a minute."

"Good. We have a long way to go." I could tell he was trying to maintain his usual coolness, but a brief look of anxiety passed over his face before he squeezed my shoulder and stood up.

The elevator dinged for the sublevels. The doors opened, and I forced myself to get out.

The sublevel was partially dimmed for the night, and the glass skylights were lattices over black voids. The shops on either side of the row were shuttered. Two people walked up a flight of stairs far away, but didn't turn around to look at us. Apart from them, the shopping strip was empty.

"Where are we going?" I asked.

"Not yet," said Cam, signaling that this was still a bad place to talk.

In the center of the plaza was a signpost with several arrows. We were now under the 1st Central district. One of the arrows pointed back to the Central Tower, one south to 3rd Central in the direction of the tenement building in which I was housed, one pointing away toward the departure bays for the city subway.

We didn't follow any of them, but proceeded toward the 3rd North district. This place was oddly liminal at night, though I knew we weren't alone in any meaningful sense, as the cameras could still see us. Eventually, the strip forked, and the corridor narrowed. There were no skylights here, as the ceiling was lower. There were still shops, though. Light came from thin tracks in the ceiling. We passed a generic clothing chain, and even a candy store.

Those were the highlights. As we kept going, the sights downgraded to snack stores (still open despite the late hour), public bathrooms, and dubious art installations consisting of amorphous bronze sculpture or framed panels of solid color. We passed only a few people on their way to or from night shifts.

Cam hung a hard left at a service hallway. It was narrow and even dimmer than the main court. We leaned against the walls next to an open closet with a bucket and mop.

"Now we disappear," he said.

"What about your Biometric?" I asked. "They can still track you."

In response, Cam held out his hand. He was wearing black fingerless gloves and clutching something in a sweaty fist. He slowly uncurled his fingers to reveal an object. I didn't know at what point he'd taken it out of the backpack. It was a small, thin steel ring, about four inches in diameter, with what looked like a bead on it. This ring was bisected with a hinge and a clasp.

Cam studied it for a moment, with some implacable emotion brewing. It was the look of someone who was about to drink poison. I knew immediately that whatever that thing was, it was going to hurt him.

"Cam?" I said. "What is that?"

Seeming to break through some sort of trance, he carefully pressed a tiny button on the bead, and a miniscule green light appeared. With a flicking motion he slapped the bracelet around his wrist, where it latched shut.

His lips twisted into a rueful yet sardonic smile. "Signal jammer."

"Wait... what?"

"It emits a frequency that jams the signal to my Biometric. I'm cut off from the network. They won't be able to track us from here."

"Oh," I said, my eyes widening. "That's super convenient. Wish I'd had one of those, might have made things easier."

"No, you don't," said Cam. "I wish I had what you had. But there's nobody to perform extremely delicate emergency surgery on me, so it is what it is."

"Why?" I asked, unable to comprehend why he would wish for surgery when there was an easier way. "What is it going to do to you?"

He hesitated, then shook his head and muttered, "nothing."

"But—"

He gave me a chilling look. He was uncharacteristically tight-lipped after that, at least for a few minutes.

At the end of the service hallway was an old, grungy-looking doorway with a manual twist knob. On the other side it was even darker. There was a set of concrete stairs with metal railings leading down to a wide, echoing hall.

This appeared to be some kind of abandoned access shaft or disused subway tunnel. It was very dark at the bottom, and quiet. I could see only light from Cam's flashlight reflecting off a slick of water on the floor and hear far-away dripping. Our shoes slapped across the shallow puddles.

"Come on, Cam," I said shortly, breaking the silence. "You can't lie to me. I know that thing is hurting you or something. Are you sure about this?"

He was silent for such a long moment that I could hear his breathing. He stopped walking long enough for me to catch up to him. He pointed the flashlight at the floor. We were coming up on the old subway's boarding area; there were tile stairs ahead of us and a weak moonlight coming down from broken skylights where the place opened up somewhere beyond. There was a faraway look on his face.

"The signal jammer isn't what's going to do it," he said. "It's the Biometric."

I just waited.

"Once your Biometric is out of network for twelve hours, it automatically kills you."

I made a strangled noise. "But… what? That's impossible. Cam, there's no way. That can't be true." I found myself talking faster. "What if there was a system outage? What if somebody just wandered off and got stuck in a hole without service?"

"Be honest," said Cam, pointing the flashlight back ahead of him and continuing to walk. "Has there ever been a system outage lasting longer than one hour in your entire lifetime?"

"I—" I couldn't say that there had been.

"They don't need to plan for that. And you can't just wander off grid without trying. Even if you're so well hidden that your GPS tracker doesn't work, the main system puts out a search and rescue alert for anyone who drops out for more than four hours."

"So you're telling me that in four hours, the Administrators will be notified that you're gone?"

"If they haven't pieced it together by that time."

After ascending the wide stairs, we came into a large abandoned court. There was glass and plaster on the tile, and two of the panes overhead were broken. From up above, a breath of fresh, but chill air came down. We were still under the 2nd North District of the Settlement; I could see orange lights up there. There was green scum in the puddles on the floor, but it appeared almost black.

Cam seemed to know where to go, out of the five available directions.

"What are we doing, then?" I asked. "You obviously have to get rid of the jammer before the twelve hours are up, and if you want to avoid getting caught, you have to be back on the system and somewhere plausibly normal within the next four hours. And with a damn good alibi, unless you're planning to put me back in that room."

"Three and a half," said Cam. "Also, no. We need to be as far away from here as possible by then."

There was another loud drip from ceiling to floor, and a faint gurgling noise like a drain.

"But Cam!" I protested. "It's going to be hard for you to pacify them if you wait so long that they discover you've gone missing. They'll know you disappeared at the same time as me. You have to go back! Just tell me how to get out, and I'll make the rest of the trip on my own. I appreciate everything you've done for me, but I won't have you dying on my account."

He turned the flashlight directly into my face. "Alex," he said softly, "that's not going to happen. There's more at stake here than just you." He closed his eyes and rubbed the bridge of his nose, lowering the light a little. "I can't take it off because they will definitely have a termination order on me by the end of the next twelve hours."

I froze and just stared at him in shock.

"No."

"Yes. Alex, I'm sorry."

"No no no." I pressed up to him and started trying to pull the bracelet off his wrist. It was too small to go over his hand, and he didn't even have to resist. When I found the latch, he raised his arm over his head and I was left jumping up for it like a baby reaching for candy.

"No!" I pleaded. "It's not too late! You can still undo this and go back there and put me back where I'm supposed to be. Cam, why?" I growled as tears started from my eyes. "Why do you think I took a bullet for you? It's because you're not prepared to die! But I am."

He put his arm down and took a step back. "Just hear me out."

I hugged myself tightly and frowned.

"Keep walking," he said, "And I'll tell you everything."

We walked, taking a dark, wet path that sloped downward.

"Where do I start?" he mused to himself, swinging the flashlight almost randomly around the walls of the train tunnel.

"At the beginning?" I suggested.

Chapter Thirty-Eight
The Life and Times of Paul Tiller

I introduced myself to Paul Tiller by kicking him in the head.

They had brought the man in earlier that same day. From the jeep, he had been taken down from the garage to the sublevels, and then they threw him into the holding cells. That is to say, they put him near the front of the Central prison complex for easy access. You were there yourself, Alex; on your way in you must have passed the place where he was held.

I found out that there were people living outside the Settlement only an hour before meeting him.

We had a short briefing prior to being assigned to the interrogation team. That's a common way for Level One grunts to be assigned, especially when they haven't got any specialization. We were to find out everything he knew. And that meant *everything*, in this case, because there were so many unknowns. At that point we didn't even know his name.

He looked exactly like what I imagined someone from outside the Settlement might look. He was sweaty and dirty, wearing some kind of jacket—I was told it was fur and leather—with worn-out brown leggings. The only difference is that he wasn't very tall, and I might have thought that anyone clinging to such a primeval mode of existence (I supposed he probably lived in a cave) would be old and stooped over, but he wasn't. He was young, maybe twenty-two. He had pink cheeks and dark, curly hair. He looked pale, but anyone probably would have in his situation.

He had big, brown eyes, like a sad puppy.

After I finished beating the crap out of him, we set him down at a table. I said something like, "What's your name? Where do you come from?"

"My name's Paul Tiller," he said, and he rubbed his neck, and looked me in the eye. He was glancing me over, carefully observing whether I was about to get up and beat him again (I wasn't; softening him up was just standard protocol), but he wasn't even trembling, so I was forced to reevaluate him. I thought, *maybe he's not as pathetic as he looks*. Maybe he's had a hard life, not 'on the streets' per se, but the cultist-land equivalent. He'll be a tough nut to crack.

Then he said, "What's yours?" and I'll be damned if he didn't actually crack a smile.

I waffled on my assessment. I would have said that he didn't know what kind of time he was in for if I hadn't just pounded him into a wall.

"I'm Cam," I said, and I hit 'record' – not on my own Biometric, but on the table screen, which he seemed to find fascinating. He kept tilting his head to read his own words, and feeling the surface, watching the way that little bubbles of light appeared under his fingertips when the screen squished.

The next words he said to me were, "Have you heard about Jesus Christ?"

I said, "No."

He said, "I'd like to tell you about him, and about how you can be saved."

I didn't know what *that* meant.

Yet.

"Well," I said, "I want you to tell me everything you know, so you might as well get started."

It was all a bit confusing to me. My actual memories of this time are fairly blurry. Me and the boys traded off taking his lengthy statements. Eventually, as we learned more about his religion, I thought I had built up more of a context for these and other similar types of comments that he made. Mythology stuff, a god who became a man and was two, maybe three people—did they have three gods?

I wrote "three gods?" in my notes, and he saw that and immediately started correcting me, so I stopped trying to take notes, and just glazed over and let the a/v do the work. Understanding his religion wasn't my problem.

"I'm not doing a very good job, am I?" he said, and seemed a bit distressed.

"No, you're not," I said. "Let's talk about the villages."

I showed him the satellite photos of his village. Were these the only villages? Were there any other villages? How many people lived there? Who were they, what were their names and ages and so forth? He was pretty mum about that.

We had strict orders at that point to make sure he stayed alive, lucid, relatively healthy, and so forth. The Administrators wanted to speak to him, and they hadn't had the chance to do so yet.

It was all right. It wasn't that he wasn't willing to talk. He talked for hours. Just not about anything we wanted to hear.

It was all a bunch of garbage, of course. Just, like, pages and pages of totally useless intelligence about ancient cities and creation myths and things like that. The others would interrupt him when they thought he was wasting their time.

Not me. Why bother? I was getting paid by the hour.

The problem is that I actually kind of liked him.

You could tell he had a life outside the Settlement. He didn't say a lot about it, obviously, but sometimes he seemed like he was pining for it; that's why he was sad.

Finally his date came up for the meeting with the Administrators. One day I came in, but he wasn't in his cell. They had taken him up to the Central tower. We waited. It wasn't very long.

When they brought him back, everything was different. I could sense from the boys' attitude that something had changed. The mood was darker.

I tried to find out what had happened up there, but I couldn't get anything but rumors. The Administrators were livid. I never thought he'd deliberately tried to piss us off, so I wondered what he could have done.

That's when our orders changed.

He couldn't just ramble anymore, the Administrators said. We would get specifics by any means necessary. And after that— well, DYNTEC knew the drill. If he couldn't be induced to become ill of natural causes, it was going to be a suicide.

I tried not to feel upset about it. After all, you're not supposed to feel pity for a Detractor, and he was worse than a Detractor; he was a cultist. I had to make myself believe it; after all, it wasn't my decision. But even though I didn't feel as justified as I had with other prisoners, I still followed through on my orders."

Cam was silent for a long time.

"We beat him every day after that. It started taking a toll on his health, like it was supposed to. I would see him every third or fourth day. He was half drowned a dozen times, shot up with drugs, sleep deprived, and they sorta stopped feeding him."

Cam was glazed over, as though recounting something that had happened to someone else.

I asked him things like, what do *your* people know about *us*? And there were questions like what kind of arms do they have? What defenses? What level of technology?

He told us most of what we wanted to know, eventually. But it took a pitifully long time.

We didn't have to actually go through with the suicide, because he succumbed to a brain bleed eventually. I don't even know who actually struck the fatal blow. I'm sure I contributed.

If you want to know how I sleep at night, the answer is that I didn't. Not for a long time. I got the promotion to Level Two a week after he died, and I took it just to transfer out of there. Not long after that, I stopped talking to those guys.

The upper offices felt totally different. I tried to put all of that behind me and just forget about it. I liked going to the gym, going to the bar with my new kind-of friends, feeling like a normal person. And that was how it was for about three years.

Until you came along.

I left you out there, dropped you off, and then I suddenly felt as though I'd made a terrible mistake. I dunno. I was afraid I'd killed you. But there was nothing I could do about it.

After we met up on the ridge, about a mile away from the cult, I drove back to the Settlement alone. When I came back inside, Jesse surprised me with the news that I was getting a promotion. The next day we had the promotion ceremony, and I was made into a Level Three.

It wasn't a *real* surprise; I had been angling for it for some time. The work I was doing with you on the cult project was above my pay grade all along, as you might have guessed. I'd intended to get myself placed on this project because it was more novel and important than other garden variety law-enforcement; and then after that, my goal was to become indispensable to the project, so that when Jesse retired, I could replace him.

I was being ambitious, and it worked. They figured the work I was doing was too important for a Level Two, so they could either get rid of me, or make me a Level Three. So I got the promotion.

That's kind of how you got dragged into all this in the first place. When I first transferred to the project, I suggested your name. The only real reason was—was—well, I thought you were cute, and wanted to keep working with you. That's it. I made up some bullshit about how you showed extraordinary promise and so forth, and so—I should be apologizing to you, probably, for all the trouble I've gotten you into. But anyway.

I'd wanted you to be able to be there for the ceremony, but obviously that wasn't possible since you were with the cult.

After you left, I kept a close eye on your vital signs with the Biometric, as you might have guessed. I started off looking at them every day on the computers. I kept thinking about what the cult would do to you if they found out you were a spy. I kept checking, more and more, every hour, twice an hour. When I found myself wanting to stay later at work just so I could watch your biofeed, I... well, I couldn't bear to go home and wait all night just to find out in the morning if you were still alive. So I synced your feed to my Biometric, and it was easy to check on you anywhere that I went.

I was listening, all day, all the time, those first two weeks. It made me feel better, to know any time I could just attune my Biometric and... hear your pulse as a steady electronic beep. Sometimes it was slower, sometimes faster. When it was fast, I worried a lot. When it was slow, I found it sort of calming. Maybe it was kind of weird, but... we're spies. Listening is what we do, isn't it?

Jesse was at the ceremony, but he doesn't have the ability to promote people to his own level. That's why they had to have an Administrator present. Dana met us on a floor just below their sky lounge. I was sworn in as a Level Three in a room with windows looking out over the green. You were out there somewhere. My heart wasn't in the oaths. We all say pledges all the time, even in school as a kid. It never meant anything to me then, when I was too young to understand the words about loyalty and all that. Why should a pledge mean anything to me now? It's just... mouthing words to pass a checkpoint. The only reason I even thought about it was because for some reason this time I disliked it.

I was thinking about the words you said on the ridge, about how the cultists were minding their own business and not hurting anybody. I was swearing to oppose the enemies of the Settlement while thinking about how I didn't really care, personally, if the cultists went on doing their thing, and maybe the best outcome would be if they were somehow absorbed back into the forest, and we never saw them again.

Dana told me, 'Congratulations,' and shook my hand. I tuned my Biometric to your pulse, and I felt like you were right there.

After I became a Level 3, I got a lot busier. I tend to appreciate that sort of thing, though, because it keeps my mind off... things. At first it seemed like it was all filework. Level 3s have access to audio-visual logs, like the kind made on the security cameras around the city and even most of the ones in the DYNTEC buildings. As the new head of the cult project, I was specifically given access to the files surrounding the cult, and I was expected to be up to date on all of them. That included the a/v logs from the incident with the captured cultist three years back.

Now, I don't think the Administrators actually realized that I was the only person still working on the cult project that had been around back when they brought in Paul Tiller.

That made me the only person currently working on the project who had actually met him in person.

And I remembered. Boy, did I remember. Not all of it, of course; there was some of it that I'd pushed down to the point of almost forgetting. But it came back to me as I was reading the logs.

Of course, most of them, even the ones we got out of him under torture, were lifestyle details and the kinds of things that were in the lecture Jamison gave you. Stuff he told us about "working the land", as he called it, raising and eating animals, stuff that was ultimately of little tactical interest.

Then of course there were the religious sections. I reviewed the transcripts. It was surreal to come back to it after such a long time.

I didn't want to watch any of the videos. I felt it would pull me back too much, make me feel things I didn't want to feel. There was one video that tempted me, though, that kept pulling on me like a gravitational force.

There *was* footage of his meeting with the Administrators.

Of course logically it had to exist somewhere, but I was still surprised, as I'd half expected it to be destroyed. None of us who ever worked with him had watched it. I sensed it was something the Administrators wanted to keep deeply hidden and buried. Probably because it made them look bad.

I had told you that I didn't know what he said to the Administrators that got him killed. I do now.

When I clicked, it was like walking into a trap, but your words about the cultists only being simple farmers made me want to go in and find something to prove you wrong. Rereading the logs, I was only finding information that proved you right. I thought maybe this video, the one so inflammatory they killed him for it, would provide the answers I was looking for.

But I also knew that I was on dangerous ground, because this was my last bit of evidence, and if this video didn't provide that answer, then you'd be right. And I had to believe there was something in it that justified Paul Tiller's death. I didn't want to risk finding out that I was wrong. But I watched the video.

It's a wide angle, a little distorted.

He gets taken into the room. They let him out of the elevator into the sky lounge. There are two of our guys holding him, but I don't know which ones, because they're wearing motorcycle helmets. Dana gestures to let go of him, and they just stand there.

The Administrators are all standing around, just staring at him. All the heads turn. Next to them in their fancy suits he looks like some kind of wild man from the desert, except small and short and sad. He stands up straight, with those huge eyes that I forgot about on purpose.

"Who are you?" Dana asks.

"I'm Paul Tiller," he says.

She definitely already knew that from our reports. But the Administrators had to get a look at the circus sideshow with their own eyes. They'd given him over to us first hoping to avoid pushback when they finally summoned him in person.

"Where do you come from?" she asks.

"The Kingdom of Heaven."

"And this Kingdom, who rules it?"

"His name is Jesus Christ," says Tiller.

"Who is that? How many are there in this kingdom and how far does it extend?"

He is a little daunted by the two questions at once. "Why—the world. The entire world. Jesus is the son of the living God, and his rule extends over all creation."

"I see," she says, and she starts to walk around him, "I see—an expansionist cult, are you? And I suppose you hope to claim the Settlement for this kingdom?"

"I do hope so, God willing it were possible, ma'am."

"Well!" She looks back on the rest of the Administrators. "Well, you heard him. Details, then! What is your cult planning? How do you propose to do this?"

"By speaking the truth," he says.

"And that is?"

He must have looked to them like he was staring off into space. But he wasn't. It was like he was looking directly at me.

"That Christ, the God who made the world and everything in it, died for our sins. That He became flesh, and dwelt among us, in the likeness of sinful man. That it was necessary for him to be punished by God, beaten, and mocked, and crucified, so that we might be considered righteous.

That he was buried, and that he was raised to life on the third day according to the scriptures.

That no one is righteous, but all have sinned and stand in need of this sacrifice for their forgiveness.

That Christ, who gives everyone life and breath, who made all the nations from one man, is the Lord of heaven and earth. And He commands everyone everywhere to repent, for one day there will be a judgment; that He will return to judge the evil in the world, cast down the wicked and the proud, and lift up the humble and the righteous.

That you personally must repent for your actions as an enemy of God and accept the man Jesus Christ as your Lord and King, for He will save anyone who calls on his name. Only then can you too be saved."

Chapter Thirty-Nine

The Last Straw

That was when you died.

It was the same day, the same hour.

I felt you die. I felt your heart speed up, faster—faster— hard and quick turned to shallow fluttering, not like exercise. Not a quick startle, either. It went on for longer than that. That was when I knew they were hurting you. It seemed like forever. I was losing my mind, Alex. Just sitting there, tense but drained, feeling as though I could hear you screaming in pain, and I couldn't save you. I couldn't do anything.

And then it stopped. Suddenly it stopped.

You were dead.

And it was my fault, inasmuch as I was responsible for bringing you onto the project, putting you out there.

I thought I'd prepared you enough for the cruelty of life, I thought I'd prepared myself for losing you the same way I lost everybody else. But it turns out that you can't desensitize yourself like that. It just doesn't work.

But at least, suddenly, I didn't need the video anymore to prove that the cultists were evil. Any doubt I ever had about them being evil seemed to evaporate out of my mind for the moment. This was proof enough. They killed you, and I was going to kill them. That was how I felt about it.

But it takes time and work to set up a raid.

When Jesse found out that I was planning an attack, he took me aside and said, "Hey now, slow down, y'know she may still be alive."

I didn't buy it. "How?" I asked. "Her biofeed stopped."

So he showed me the signal jammer. Supposing they had you stuck in a stone hole, like a well, or they were generating some kind of interference, like Jesse could do from this little bracelet. Then maybe you had another twelve hours to live.

It was little comfort to me, only anxiety as I waited for your biofeed to come back on, and it didn't.

I would have started out immediately to save you, but I couldn't get the requisitions through that fast. On the paperwork, it said "rescue mission." I'm not sure "revenge quest" would have gotten approved. At any rate, after 12 hours, even Jesse had to admit you were probably dead.

We started out on Sunday evening, and got there Monday AM, as you know.

I thought more likely than not I'd find your body, then burn the place. If you were alive, I'd take prisoners. The Administrators would forgive me for anything that happened as long as I didn't actually lose to the cultists. After all, I could just say they were too heavily armed to take alive. But there was little danger of that; we had superior firepower and I wasn't worried about it.

But obviously, when I got there, you *were* alive.

You know what happened after that.

I prayed to your God on your behalf for you to live—I thought He might even listen to me as long as it had something to do with you—but by the time we got back to the Settlement, I was thanking Him that you were unconscious.

I tried to follow you to the hospital, but the nurse stopped me at the desk.

"You can't go in there," she said.

"Why not?" I demanded. "I'll have you know my clearance is Level Three."

I wanted to be the first one there when you woke up. You were compromised, but I thought I could mitigate the situation by talking to you before anyone else found out about it.

"Overruled," she said. "I've been specifically ordered not to let you in."

"By whose orders?"

"Dana Morris-Fletcher's."

So I had to sit it out.

On the second day, you were still unconscious. I put in a written request to Dana Morris-Fletcher to see you on the grounds that you were under my command.

She wrote back, saying, "Alexandra Ortiz is no longer in your unit. This is because an urgent matter has come up in the East Central District, and they are in need of a Level Three. As of today, you've been reassigned to East Central. Please report there tomorrow morning."

Well, I knew that was a load of garbage. I was inconvenient and she was getting me out of the way. That was most likely because she was investigating the incident. She needed to know what went wrong. And most importantly, she was investigating *you,* and she'd be questioning my men, and as soon as one of them spilled what *actually* went down out there, she'd know you were compromised.

And then you'd be as good as dead.

Well, I'd already been through that once. Helpless while you were dying. I wasn't about to hang out in the East Central district waiting for you to be condemned to death.

I arranged a personal meeting with Dana myself.

Went up to her office. Not one of the lounges this time, it was a private meeting. She'd allowed it for some reason. I think she knew I was about to spill.

When I got there, I found out I was right. One of my men had already talked about our little altercation—you defending the cultists and all that. So I went ahead with my sales pitch.

"She said you begged for my life."

"Begged? Well, that's one way of putting—"

"She said you got down on your knees."

"She told you that?"

"Yes."

"Well… anyway.

The point is that I was able to convince her, or so I thought, that none of this was your fault, but really mine for picking a weak-willed person to begin with. You were brainwashed by the cult, but you could go back to being a model citizen. And I said that I would be able to undo the programming and—stop laughing! Of course I was lying my ass off, but I still thought the plea deal would be a good option. No, I didn't write it. I thought it was the only way to keep you alive, and I hated myself for suggesting it.

I even suggested that she didn't have to keep you on Settlement resources—I would take you on myself if that was a problem. She was reluctant but seemed to eventually agree.

She still wouldn't let me go back to my old command, and I still wasn't allowed in to see you. So... I had to take care of that myself.

It was horrendously difficult, that's why it took me so long. With my access to the a/v, it was easy enough to verify that Dana had held up her end of the bargain and that you were still alive, but by the time I had found some nurses corruptible enough to let me go visit you, you were already in jail.

Luckily, I have friends in the jail. I was able to bribe one of the doctors to prescribe a false medical exam, then I took care of the video cameras... well, all the ones I knew about.

And everything seemed to go according to plan.

But when I visited you, you forced me to think about... Tiller, and the videos, and... well, that's when a lot of things changed for me.

Finding out that you did *not* sign the plea deal was a... setback. Not—not that I blame you for that *now*, of course. I knew that if you hadn't signed the plea deal, and you were still alive, that could only mean one thing. She wanted you for information.

And yet, somehow, when you refused to sign it, I felt *relieved*. Not at first, obviously. But later when I had time to think it over.

At least somebody had integrity, I thought, although it wasn't me. It couldn't be me. At least, I didn't think so yet. But I knew now which side I was on. If Paul Tiller was wrong, then I didn't want to be right.

I realized I had to get you out. But because you were going to be interrogated, I had to keep it a secret from you until the last possible moment. That's why I didn't send any word.

Instead I made preparations, acquiring the signal jammer and so forth.

I was still in loose contact with Jesse, you see, and eventually he told me he had heard you were healing from your injury. I knew that meant you were running out of time. But I didn't know how I could get you out of the prison again—another false medical exam wouldn't work a second time.

I just needed time to think of something and I thought I might be able to buy more time by asking for another audience with Dana. It was risking a lot, but I was desperate.

I decided to see her again.

"I'm told she's healing well," I said. "Why didn't you turn her over to me as promised?"

"Well you see, Cam," said Dana, "she didn't sign the plea deal." She sounded quite pleased about this, actually. I wondered why until I realized she never really expected you to, it was just there to placate me and estimate you. It made her look fair.

"That doesn't necessarily mean you won't get to be with her," said Dana. "Just not right away."

"When?" I asked.

"You can have her if she survives."

I couldn't hide my anger from her by this time. She must have seen it in my eyes. She went ahead and broke the news.

"Ca-am. We know you went to visit her in the hospital."

That was when I found out that I'd been betrayed by one of the nurses and we'd been watched. I knew it was my life on the line and I tried not to react, but she did her best to goad me. You know how she is.

Cam paused speaking.

I realized this had to be the source of the video.

"All I could think about was that you were about to be tortured for information that you didn't even know," said Cam. "And she made a great point of telling me that I was too late to prevent it. And I was. I was under her thumb. All day yesterday, I was busy on a pretext, with Jamison watching me personally. I tried to do paperwork but couldn't concentrate. Couldn't think; could barely write.

"When Jesse told me you were back in the hospital, I knew it was the only chance I was going to get. I'd been betrayed by the staff last time, so this time I had to get in secretly during night hours, without actually telling anyone, which is harder than it sounds.

"So here I am," he said. "I don't know if the cultists would ever forgive me, or if there is any place for me to go in this world outside the Settlement. But if *you* can forgive me, then it is possible that your God might, since you obviously got something from him."

I nodded rapidly, but stood stock-still, almost petrified.

"I guess I've just learned that... God is real and... what else is real? I don't know. It's been a pretty tough pill to swallow. First off, that the Settlement isn't God and that maybe somebody's judgment matters more than theirs. And they might even be defeated, eventually. And then after that, I realized that I can't go on working for DYNTEC anymore."

I lowered my eyes.

"Come on. You know it's true. You made that decision for yourself already when you chose to get that thing out of your body. You know that choice could have killed you."

It could have. But I'd chosen it anyway; it had been an important moment for me. He was right; he was facing the same choice.

"So," he said, "for the first time in my life I found some hope, and then realized at the same time that it's going to kill me." He gave an ironic laugh. It died in the echoes of the court.

This time when I ran to him, I hugged him as tightly as I could manage and still breathe. He hugged me back. I sobbed into his chest. There was no one down here to overhear, so I didn't care about crying loudly. After a minute Cam let go of me, but I kept clinging on. He relented and put his arm back around me and let me keep crying into his shirt.

Eventually I remembered that we needed to keep walking.

"We have to go now," he said, as I wiped my eyes with my sleeves. "It can't wait." He had a more definite tone, like he was trying to sound brave. "Now, don't tell me to go back. I can either honor your wishes by staying alive or I can honor your wishes by converting. But I can't do both. Tomorrow, unless we do something about it, they're going to find those people and kill them."

❉

Chapter Forty
Flying Machines, Revisited

So soon.

I felt sick to my stomach. "How are we going to stop them from doing *that?*"

"There *will* be a drone strike on the towns," said Cam. "There's nothing we can do about that. They would also like to strike the cultist's current location… if they knew where it was."

Of course.

"Normally the satellite imagery would help. After all, it's not easy to hide that many tracks for miles and miles, wherever they have gone. They got lucky that the hard rain obscured their initial flight. But the Administrators could have found them quickly… if it weren't for this week's persistent cloud cover. And you know how it's gone for us in the past trying to fly over with the surveillance drones. They say Dana was just about pitching a fit not getting the information that she wanted."

"You don't have to remind me," I said. I scratched my arms, trying not to relive any of that. It was hard to imagine one of the Administrators projecting anything other than smooth or cool confidence that they would always come out on top; Administrator Dana had definitely veered into "schadenfreude" and "disdain", but in front of me, she had never seemed to doubt that she would win.

"But the cloud cover is expected to clear out tomorrow. The cul— er, Kingdomers need time and space to keep moving, and if we can't get natural cloud cover," he said, taking the stairs determinedly two at a time, "then we will have to make some."

"Make some…"

"We're going to start a fire."

"What?" My mind blanked.

"A big one."

"Bigger than the one at the church?"

Cam flinched. "Yes, it will have to cover a wide area."

I was astonished. My own devotion to Gaia had once been sincere; Cam apparently had either never possessed such qualms, or had dropped them seamlessly without looking back. This was undoubtedly the most destructive application of fire I'd ever imagined.

And yet. Was this a necessary evil of the kind the Settlement often spoke of? Or was it more like the Joneses' woodstove? Or the bear? A sacrifice of Gaia to preserve human life?

Either way, as much as it pained me, I knew he was right. We had to do what we could to blind the sat-cams.

"Are you sure this is going to work?" I asked.

"I don't have any better ideas," he said. "You could pray for a miracle," he added, in a completely sincere tone.

"Oh," I said.

***

We came to a flight of stairs. They were a spiraling metal contraption that seemed to float dangerously toward a spot of light, detached from anything solid. They groaned under my weight.

When we emerged, it was from a circular manhole. The cover was already removed. I could smell by the air that we were outside the Settlement. The ground was covered with a green moss, and a cloudbreak sent moonlight spilling down on the world. We were in one of the abandoned sectors, outside the Wall.

There was not much to see, not at first. We were jammed between the Wall and a derelict building with a curved roof.

Part of this building's roof was missing, either collapsed or blown away. We walked around the corner to the doors. They were giant gates, at least twenty feet tall, made of corrugated steel. One of them was open by a couple of feet. We slipped through the gap.

The interior of the building was completely open. Moonbeams fell down through the missing panels in the ceiling.

Some strange objects sat on the expansive floor. Hulking monsters, it seemed. Huge, rusted machines. They had propellers, and… wings.

Flying machines.

Were these… drones? No, I didn't think so. I saw a seat for a human driver in one of them. A manned flying machine, how strange. It simply wasn't done in the Settlement, probably due to the prohibition on seeing over the Wall.

"Planes," said Cam. "I used to come out here all the time when I was a teenager." He ran his hand across the wing of one of the planes. There was moss and lichen crusted along the metal surfaces, and other dripping wet scum.

"My parents were killed for being Detractors," said Cam. He said it, then he paused to reflect. "I... I don't think I've ever put it in those words before."

"I'm sorry," I said. That was something that hadn't happened to me, and I felt awkward, unsure how to sympathize.

"I lost my chance for a normal life a long time ago. DYNTEC took everything from me. And in exchange I got, what? Power? Money? Being hated by everyone for the perception that I'm better off than they are?" he scoffed.

"This is where they found me," he said. "I was fifteen. They told me I'd come too far. I'd discovered things that ordinary people weren't allowed to know about. They gave me two options. I could join DYNTEC and learn more; become a cool agent, and stop the bad guys. Or I could go to prison until I turned eighteen. That way I wouldn't be able to tell anybody what I'd seen before I got old enough to be ruled a Detractor for it."

I teared up again. He was dry-eyed, though. He'd gotten plenty worked up over me, but as for his own fate, he was stoic.

He seemed totally lost in his memory for a moment. It was easy to imagine him as a fifteen-year-old. He still acted like one sometimes. In my mind's eye I saw him playing around and climbing into the cockpits of the planes. I saw DYNTEC agents walking into the front door on a search-and-rescue mission, with a group of armed men and bright lights. That image was a little *too* vivid, perhaps. I looked back over my shoulder at the door.

"None of these are operational," said Cam. "We have to keep moving."

"They have working ones…?"

"Yep. There's still a few of them. I've never technically flown one, but I was really good at the simulator."

"Oh boy," I said.

Then I remembered he was also on a ticking clock. "What if something happens to you while we're in the air?" I asked.

"Not…" he grimaced. "That's not for a while." He tried to be reassuring. "I have the signal jammer, remember."

I had a hard time trusting any innovation to stave off the will of the Settlement, but I held my tongue.

There was a smaller door on the far end of this building that led out into an alley. We followed the alley to an abandoned, dark street more reminiscent of the ruined streets outside the Settlement than the layered reality I was familiar with. Old streetlamps that didn't shine bent over us.

There was a compact building with a modern-looking front somewhere down the way. I didn't see anyone surrounding it, and all the windows were blacked, but it was totally intact. We went behind this building. The back was made of brick, giving the lie to its modern façade. It was actually of a slightly more dated construction. Cam pointed up to where a fire escape clung to the side of the building.

"We have to get up there?" I balked.

He clambered onto the closed lid of a dumpster, then jumped up to grab the bars. He was climbing over the metal railing before I knew it, then leaned over and extended a hand. "Come on. I'll pull you up."

Getting onto the dumpster was hard enough; it was slippery. I was sure I was loud enough to alert anyone nearby, but Cam seemed unmoved. He reached down and I reached up. I gritted my teeth, and he pulled.

I grasped the iron and managed to throw a leg over the fence. Ah. That felt wrong, something was wrong. I hoped I hadn't ripped my stitches. No time to worry about that, however. We kept going.

"Almost there," said Cam, seeing my tired face.

It was still early morning; the sky in the east was just beginning to gray. The stars were visible here, but sparely; still mostly muted by the orange lights from the city next to us. I could not see the horizon. Old sections of Wall here still obscured it, along with vacated buildings.

We came out onto a wide, flat rooftop. It was not quite tall enough to see back over the Wall, of course, but close.

On this roof there was a helicopter. It was bigger than I'd imagined it. The machine had a large rotor atop of it, more than forty feet across, I estimated. The body looked like some sort of large insect; a comparison I could make only because I'd spent time outside the Settlement. There were two additional spinners on the tail, and underneath it had three wheels that looked strangely puny compared to its size.

Cam came up beside me.

"It probably hasn't been used in years," he said. "They mostly use drones nowadays. We still have—" he checked his Biometric. "two hours until daylight. It's six A.M. now. I need to hurry and try to fuel this thing."

He started to walk quickly around the machine, but came back to me in a hurry.

"Oh, blast it. It's what I was afraid of: no fuel. There is a fueling tank up here behind that wall"—he pointed at a short retaining wall—"but it's all turned off and disconnected. I need your help."

"With what?" I asked.

"You'll have to go inside and turn on the pipeline. There's a valve inside, to the left of the elevator, on the ground floor. You can't miss it, it's red. It's a big wheel, just turn it."

"I…" I started, a little confused.

"Here's the thing," he said. "Neither of us have functioning Biometrics anymore. That means that the only way to leave the building once you're in will be through the fire exit. When you do that, the alarms will sound. I need enough time to fuel the chopper, so you have to go in there, turn on the fuel line, wait for me to finish fueling, and *then* come out through the fire doors and get back to the roof."

"But if we don't have Biometrics," I said, "how do I get in? And how do I know how long to wait?"

"Easy," he said. "About thirty minutes. And I can get you in… if we hurry…"

There was a raised level on the roof with a white painted, scratched door set in it. He rattled it, but it was locked.

"Blast," said Cam again. He hesitated just a moment. "What time is it?" he asked himself, checking his Biometric. The device's internal clock still functioned, despite being offline.

"Oh no," I said, reading his mind.

"I figured the place might be locked. My Level Three clearance might get us into this place if it hasn't been revoked yet."

"Don't even think about it," I said, putting my hand on his wrist. "You can't go back on network."

"We've still got five minutes," he said. "I can do this."

I gripped his wrist harder.

"Come on," he said. "We can't have come all this way for nothing. I'll turn the jammer off and right back on. They shouldn't even notice my position immediately. The activity will be logged, so they'll figure out what we're doing sooner than they might've otherwise, but on the plus side, my timer gets reset and I gain four hours, so that's a plus."

"If you don't die *immediately*," I said. "It's been almost four hours. How do you know they haven't already noticed you're gone? You could have a termination order on you *now*."

"Alex, we don't have enough time to argue about this." He jerked his arm away. "That's a risk I'm just going to have to take."

He placed his hand close to the door, and pressed the button on his bracelet.

I held my breath and bit my tongue.

There was a *click*.

The door swung open.

"Hurry," I urged, but Cam was already re-activating the bracelet.

I stepped inside. There was an elevator in there, which had also been activated. Cam reached around and hit a starred button for the ground floor. I was just about to ask him another question when the elevator doors slid shut, leaving him on the other side, and I began to descend.

The doors slid open on something like a warehouse, filled wall to wall with tall metal shelving. There were forklifts on the floor and a few other automated vehicles that were deactivated, not moving. The items on the shelves were crated and labeled with numbers, not anything that I could read. There were also rolling ladders here and there along the shelves. It was clear enough to me that though this place was seldom visited, it was not truly abandoned.

I paced side to side a few moments, but found the red valve without too much difficulty. It was a large wheel, and the metal was cold under my touch. It was tightly jammed and squealed loudly as I turned it. I prayed there was no one else in the building.

Once it was all the way open, I looked around, but no one seemed to be coming.

Now I had to find somewhere to wait for 30 minutes. I felt open and exposed, standing in the middle of the floor, next to an elevator that I could not use to return to the roof. I needed to at least locate the fire door.

I turned down one of the aisles, running my hand along the boxes.

As I did, I heard voices.

There *was* someone in here. My heart sped up.

The voices echoed around the warehouse—there were at least two people. "…and they say she disappeared a few hours ago."

"Good Gaia. If they don't get her back soon, we'll never hear the end of it."

"And the worst part is, she doesn't even have a Biometric, so they can't track her. She could be anywhere by now."

As they rounded the corner onto my position, I lay flattened on the third shelf, between two boxes, looking down through the iron lattice. The ladder rolled away from me, slightly, almost imperceptibly, and I hoped they didn't notice its movement.

I could see them down there, walking around on the floor, where I had been standing a moment ago.

They were two men in white coats. One of them made a gesture toward the elevator.

What?! Were they going to the roof? They'd discover Cam! I was barely able to keep still, but the other man said, "No, not that elevator. We're going down."

They walked away, on to the next aisle, where I could no longer see them, but still hear them.

"Grief, what's taking it so long?"

"It isn't like the others, it's a manual," said the second man. "Give it a minute."

There was suddenly a loud noise, so that I startled, but I could see nothing. It was the most awful clanking and rumbling and grinding I'd ever heard, and it seemed to be coming closer and closer. Finally, just as it was right upon us it stopped and there was a steamy hiss.

"So…" said the first man nervously. "Sublevel 35, then?"

My ears perked up. They were talking about it as though it was real.

"Goodness, no. 33. Nobody actually goes down *there*."

Then there was another clang and the voices of the two fell muffled. The noise roared up again and then vanished into the distance the way it had come.

I got back onto the ladder, and climbed all the way to the top this time. This turned out to be one of my better ideas. I was able to make out a fire exit sign, glowing faintly red on the adjacent wall.

I slipped down onto the ladder and made my way to the floor.

I turned round the corner, cautiously, looking where the men had gone.

There was a door at the end of the aisle.

And unless I was very much mistaken, it was another elevator. Unlike the one I'd come down in, it wasn't the Settlement standard steel and black glass. It was a more gold-bronze color, edged blue with corrosion. I pressed the button, almost just to see what would happen.

There was that racket again, the rattling of gears and clanging, growing louder and louder, but this time I knew what it was.

Then, anticlimactically, there was a tiny "ding" and the door slid open.

I stepped cautiously inside and looked at the panel. Instead of going up to the roof like the other elevator, this one had buttons for a series of sublevels. This elevator only went down.

I retreated again. Interesting, but it was too risky to hide on another sublevel. Who knew what I might find? But as I started walking away, I heard another voice echo through the warehouse, and saw a hint of a white coat in the distance behind the shelving.

Oh no—more people.

And this time I didn't have a convenient ladder to climb out of the way. They were going to see me.

I stepped back into the elevator and pressed the button to close the door.

Not a moment too soon, as the voices drew closer. They were coming here, of course—*idiot*, I told myself. They were going to get inside *with* me.

Panicking, with only seconds before they reached the door, I did the only thing I could think of.

I slammed the bottom button.

The floor lurched.

Then I looked at what I'd pressed, and was filled with immediate regret.

Sublevel 35.

By the time I got to be an adult, I'd eventually learned by experience that the lowest sublevel, the mythical sublevel of the child's bogeyman, either didn't exist, or wasn't accessible from the shopping corridor. There simply weren't thirty-five sublevels. That was too deep even for the Settlement to bother digging. It was only a story made up by adults to frighten children. Except that it wasn't.

With a terrifying *clang,* the elevator began to descend.

Chapter Forty-One

Shrine of Glass

I'd never had an elevator ride this rough before.

It was terribly slow; the machine lurched and ground and jolted as though it hadn't been used in many, many years. Terror gripped me every time I could feel it catch. I was sure it was going to drop me, and in a moment I'd be *splat!* on the bottom of the shaft. It had never occurred to me for a moment that DYNTEC would leave any of their machinery in less than working order. Even worse was the fact that I would eventually need this thing to take me back *up.*

The numbers changed one by one, until the box, with me in it, eventually ground to a halt on Sublevel 35. The doors opened.

If only I could go back up, right now, this minute. But they were waiting at the top. There was only one floor I knew for certain they weren't going to: this one. They said nobody ever came here. That would make it as good a place as any to wait. I stepped from the elevator, and a pair of soft outer doors closed in front of it.

I could barely hear the machine now—its noise was muffled by thick concrete walls. But I knew it was leaving, called back up to the surface.

I found myself in a large open space.

The walls, floor, and ceiling were made of rough gray concrete. This room was almost totally empty. However, it did not have the sense of being abandoned; there was an intentionality to its emptiness.

In the center of the room was a censer. A bronze bowl stood on top of a pole and burned with a tall, flickering flame. I approached until I could feel the heat, and stared at it for a moment. It was a puddle of burning oil.

This in and of itself was odd; I had never before seen fire in the Settlement. It seemed to contradict the Administrators' values, and yet here it was, outside the Wall, though perhaps not beyond the reach of the air filtration system. It was hard to say. However, upon inspection, I could not see any fuel inputs to the censer.

I shrank back, my insides tightening with fear. This place had to be maintained. Regularly. Someone came down here to keep this flame burning.

But why?

There was another door, if it could be called that, at the back of the room. It was merely a rectangular opening in the wall.

Curiosity drew me through, but as soon as I had stepped through, the hairs rose on the back of my neck. A sense I'd been repressing before registered more strongly the further I continued into this place. There was a deep silence: the silence of underground chambers. I moved without daring to break it.

Through this door was a second antechamber, this one with another strange sight. This one had hundreds of strings hanging from the ceiling, each with a piece of paper tied onto the end.

I reached up and touched one of them. It fluttered slightly. There was no breeze down here. I had the sense of being inside a tomb.

There were words on the papers in many different strains of handwriting. A cramped scrawl on some, large block letters for others.

For Gaia, conquer

Another said, END OUR PAIN

I didn't know what to make of this, and let go of the scrap, stumbling back into the quivering sea of prayers and petitions. To what? To whom? By whom? I should go back. I should turn around now. How long had I waited here? Too long.

But there was another doorway.

In the third room, there was a person.

I pulled back quickly, and pressed myself around the corner, heart racing. Their back had been to me, they hadn't seen me. I knew who that was, too. I'd know her anywhere, with her stone-gray hair in its smooth, plain updo.

Dana Morris-Fletcher.

In my panic-induced haste, I risked another glance around the corner. She was kneeling on the stone floor, in silent contemplation of what appeared to be some kind of sculpture. There was no one else in the room.

There was nowhere for me to hide. She could come out of there at any moment, and then she would see me. Even if I went back now, she could turn around at any—

And she was. I could hear a rustle and soft scrape of cloth on stone in this silent place. There was an echoing footstep.

I didn't know what to do. I held my breath and pressed myself flat against the wall, praying that she wouldn't see me.

Administrator Dana didn't turn around. She walked up the room, right past me, through a nearly invisible pathway in the midst of the dangling strings. They bowed out around her with the movement of air. She continued on, to the room with the flame. I couldn't see her anymore.

I stayed there, waiting, barely breathing, until I heard the soft close of the elevator's outer doors. I didn't hear the machine start up, but that was because of the muffling effect, which was the same reason she hadn't noticed me coming down.

Now that she was gone, I peered again into the room she'd been sitting in.

It was flat and empty like the others; but in the center of it was a large, jet-black sphere. It was recessed slightly into the floor, and not able to roll.

This was the only room so far with an object large enough to hide behind. What if she, or someone else, came back? I had to get to that elevator, but what if it was occupied? I wasn't sure how soon I could get out of here and was terrified of being trapped. Eventually I'd have to try.

And what about Cam? I had no way of warning him that there was an Administrator in the building. What if he came down to look for me? What if they found him?

There was a slight mark on the ground where Dana had stopped to kneel and contemplate. I looked at it, but it wasn't dirt or anything she had left behind, just a slight discoloration in the stone as though too many people had sat there for too long.

I walked around, examining the sphere from all sides. Yes, it was large enough to hide me – about twelve feet high and the same in diameter all round.

But as I circled behind it, I noticed a hole cut into the back. Small, but large enough for a person to enter. To my surprise, the space inside was dimly illuminated.

On the pure instinct to seek a hiding place, I first looked, then squeezed myself into the sphere.

It was not as small in there as I had assumed; the surface of the sculpture was a thin, hard shell of black metal. But I felt cramped, swallowed, digested. I sensed that I was standing somewhere no one had stood for years, perhaps centuries. A place where no human was ever meant to be. I didn't even know where I was yet, but it felt wrong. It was as though I'd crawled into the palpitating ventricle of the Settlement itself; some vast, malicious entity whose skin I'd crawled over my whole life without knowing.

The interior of this sculpture was concave mirrored steel. But this was more than a sculpture. It was some kind of machine.

There were a few wires, a box—maybe containing computerized parts, I thought, but it had no screen— and there were things wired up all around me, spaced out on the inside of the sphere. I began to realize they were likely some sort of explosive charges.

Was this a bomb? Perhaps it was mobile, despite being unusually large. But who would make a bomb of such an unwieldy size? Why?

There was also a skinny plinth in the middle of the dome, which crowded me, and I had to bend and crouch around it. On this stand was a small metal sphere, about six inches in diameter, in what I thought could be the exact middle of the dome. The color of the sphere was golden-bronze.

I waited here for moment after moment. I had to get out. I had to go back to Cam. I'd have to risk the elevator eventually.

It occurred to me, belatedly, that this center orb was likely the main explosive charge. The others around the ring were aimed to point at it. Likely if they fired, they would set it off, creating an explosion of more devastating effect.

If this was some kind of weapon, I couldn't let them keep it.

I reached out and picked up the bronze ball. It was much heavier than I'd imagined. Then I peered out the little doorway. There was no one around that I could see, even when I looked all the way down the three chambers.

I steeled my nerves and walked back toward the elevator. Since I didn't have a backpack, or a pocket, I shifted my trophy back and forth hand to hand as I walked.

I had to wait a long time for the elevator to return to me, but eventually it lurched into place. There was no one inside. I pressed the top button.

Despite my apprehensions, it did, in fact, go up.

But not for long enough.

At about Sublevel 15 those numbers changing on the board started to slow; at Sublevel 8, I watched with terror as they came to a stop with a ding.

Someone had called for the elevator.

I didn't even know what was *on* sublevel 8. Not out here. Not in this building. I shrank back.

The door slid open on a white hallway.

Dana Morris-Fletcher stared blankly into my face.

Chapter Forty-Two

Two Women in a Hallway

I stared back for a second, only for a moment as we both tried to process what we were seeing. Luckily for me, the element of surprise was on my side, as she had more to process than I did. She was still trying to get past the confusion of seeing me here, outside the Settlement, in the flesh, when I dodged around her and started running down the hallway.

"Stop!" she called, weakly, and then again, more forcefully. "STOP!"

I didn't stop.

She turned to come after me. I looked ahead briefly, in the direction I was running. There was a pair of automatic glass doors at the end of the hallway. I couldn't keep my eyes off her as I ran. It slowed me, but in my mind she was more than human, like some sort of creature with unknowable powers, that followed without having to walk.

The side of my head collided with something hard. I found myself lying on the floor, groaning. My chest swelled instantly with such a huge ache that I could barely breathe.

I had run into the automatic door.

But of course; it was Biometric activated.

I started to push myself up onto my hands, but she had caught up and was already standing over me.

The sphere, the bomb component, was rolling away. I looked around for it and located it about two feet to the left and rolling lazily—slowed by its own weight.

I reached for it, but just as I took my hand off the floor, Dana's sharp shoe-point kicked my supporting arm, and I fell back down.

"How did you get here?" she asked, somewhere far above me. Her voice was like a sliding steel knife.

I ignored her and made a faster grab for the metal ball. This time I actually got my fingers around it and pulled it close to me. Dana seemed to notice the object for the first time.

"What have you got there?" She sounded a bit interested, but not as interested as she should have been.

I pushed myself up to my knees, holding the sphere in one hand, and then went to stand.

Dana again kicked my leg out from under me, shoe on bone, and it hurt, too. I grunted softly, and stumbled to the floor again, but didn't let go of the ball, keeping it clutched tightly to my stomach.

"No, you stop trying to get up. Why won't you tell me what that is?"

But at the same moment, she seemed to be having a realization. She could barely make it to the end of her sentence; her face changed. Her eyes widened, and her lips shrank to a small pale point.

At the same time, I was having a different realization. I was half-laying on the floor, on one elbow, with my feet towards her feet.

Why won't she let me stand up? I thought bitterly. *It's not like I could do anything to her. It's like it always is: there's security; there's somebody standing just around the corner just waiting to help—*

I stopped.

What if there *wasn't?*

We were outside the Settlement now. Nobody lived here. Not in the abandoned district outside the Wall. Dana could have confidently made this pilgrimage completely alone, with the expectation of total safety.

For once, just once in my life, there were no cameras, no surveillance, no listeners, no Biometrics, and even if somebody had been observing, they were many floors away and couldn't make things any worse for me. Indeed, there was no use sitting around waiting for them to come. I had no social credits, and no charged-up capacitor inside my body. There was nothing holding me back anymore.

It was just me. And her.

Just two women in a hallway.

"Give me that," Dana demanded. Ruffled as she was, her tone still anticipated my compliance.

I looked her in the eye, finding I was no longer afraid to do so.

"No."

She didn't have long to register her surprise before I kicked her legs out from under her. She hadn't picked good shoes today. She fell hard, with a smack on the tile, ill-prepared for the attack, and now she was with me, on the floor.

For only a couple seconds we didn't touch each other, preoccupied as we were with scrambling to our feet, sizing each other up, almost unsure what was going to happen, like two teenage girls who've slapped each other in the classroom while the teacher is out and are trying to decide whether they have enough time for a full catfight.

But I had one advantage on her: I'd actually been given a little training in hand-to-hand.

I took a wide stance and grabbed for her forearm.

Despite that I was weak, wounded, exhausted, and had recently been physically tortured at her command, Dana's first move was to try and run away. She pulled away from me as I caught hold of her wrist. She grabbed with the other hand to loosen my grip, but it was too late. I pulled her off balance and kneed her in the stomach.

She stumbled backward, then went down, bringing me with her. She clawed at me, trying to reach my face with her fingernails. I held her back with the arm that was holding the orb. She went for the metal object, and I was forced to drop it; it went spinning away from both of us. I struggled to get control of her hands as she kept trying to claw me in the face, rolling this way, then that.

Now that she was forced to fight me, I could see why she didn't want to. Somehow, I'd thought she'd be stronger than this; strong enough to win easily, but maybe it was only an impression that had formed in my mind based on her status and power.

Dana screeched in frustration and tried to kick me off, I positioned myself with a knee on her chest and my arm across her throat.

"Give it back," she rasped madly.

I leaned a little harder, and she sputtered.

"That's it," I said. "That's your final solution down there. Isn't it?"

Dana made an almost growling noise, struggling. Finally, she gasped with a high, feminine sound and went slack, as though defeated. I let up a little bit to let her speak.

"I'm not going to set it off," she wheezed. "It wouldn't be me. Not in your lifetime—" I could see the sweat coming through her foundation. It was like she was begging me to agree with her.

My eyes narrowed. "I don't care. You're never getting it back."

She struggled again suddenly, but it was only a test, I hadn't released her a bit. I pressed back down on her neck. "Now listen. You're going to do what I tell you. You get on your Biometric, call up whoever's in charge of that drone strike, and tell them to call it off."

She still managed to look at me with disdain as she spoke through her teeth. "You know I can't do that."

"I think you can."

"What are you, stupid? It won't work. It was a decision of all of us in council. I don't have the authority to call it off by myself."

My heart dropped a few inches. I leaned down harder. "I'd like to see you try it anyway."

Dana coughed and choked. "Uyghhg. All right! All right. Let me.. let…"

I nodded, and sat up, continuing to sit with my knees on her stomach.

She took a few seconds just to breathe.

"Well?" I said after I'd judged it had been long enough.

She slowly brought her wrist up toward her face. I grabbed her forearm and kept it tightly in my grip to make sure she wasn't going to try anything.

"I need my other hand to activate it."

"No, you don't," I said. "Use voice."

"Biometric activate," said Dana.

The tiny blue pinprick lit up.

"Call Central Tower Command."

There was a moment's pause.

"I don't hear a ring," I said.

"I can't loop you in," she said. "You don't have a Biometric."

"Use this," I said. I could see a small tablet in her pocket, and I pulled it out and showed it to her.

"Volume to Dana's tablet," she said, and the voice that picked up came through the tinny speakers.

"Central Tower Command Center. How can we be of service, Administrator?"

I glared at her.

"Request... request cancellation of the planned strike," said Dana, her eyes on me.

"Confirm? The strike on coordinates 38492734 by -23849370 at O-seven-fifty?"

"Confirm," said Dana. "This is my recommendation."

"Administrator, please allow the Administrators to confer on your recommendation. Are there any additional comments you'd like to add?"

"I'm not taking questions at this time," Dana snapped.

"Confirm," he said, and his voice sounded a little funny. There was a beep before we were put on hold.

I waited. The silence stretched out painfully. I wondered how long it was going to be, and shifted a little. Dana chewed her pale lips. Minutes? Hours? What time was it now? Had they just ignored us? The hold tone kept playing.

The operator at Command Center came back. "Administrator?"

I nodded at her.

"Still here," said Dana.

"Your request has been confirmed. The council has voted. You will be understood as compromised and temporarily relieved of duty."

No.

I shook Dana by the collar so hard her head smacked against the floor, and then I froze promptly, a bit horrified at the noise. She groaned a little and began to struggle again. She evidently wasn't hurt too bad, as she pulled her head up and pried at my hands.

My anger returned. "*You used a code*," I said. "Some sort of code. Didn't you?"

But she'd had long enough to get her wind back, and my hands were off her throat. She threw her weight sideways, rolling us both over, but I kept us moving, and came out on top again. This time I remembered to keep both hands on her throat.

I could only see red.

Her hair had come undone, spread out on the floor. She looked totally blank, eyes wide, almost girlish. She let go of me and went totally limp. "You're going to kill me now, aren't you."

I hesitated.

"You might as well get it over with."

There was some bitterness in her voice.

Did I really want to kill her? Would that even be the right thing to do? Surely it would be; she'd caused so much pain and suffering to others, and ordered so many deaths. But… Cam had done horrible things too. And I'd refused to let *him* die. Would killing Dana Morris Fletcher stop or even weaken the system that had done so much evil? Did I want to be her executioner?

I remembered her own words to me. Dana seemed to hate life itself. I wondered what kind of despair could make a person not only feel that way but embrace it as a philosophy.

There was only one way out of this for me; I could not give her what she wanted.

"No, Ms. Fletcher," I said. "I've decided to let you live."

I let go and jumped back quickly, but ultimately it was unnecessary because she did not get up. As I backed down the hall, Dana continued lying on the floor, staring at the ceiling.

I slowed, unsure. Had I killed her, even accidentally? Surely not. I took the bomb component from the corner it had reached and made for the elevator.

Finally she started moving, one arm flopping across her body. I pressed the button for the elevator. I didn't wish to be trapped here with her, after all. She pushed herself to sit up against the wall. She looked at me, with only a glare, as if to say, "what are you waiting for?"

I didn't know. The elevator doors opened.

Then, a ring tone from that tablet.

I tensed, waiting.

She tapped a finger to her wrist, eyes still on me. A voice spoke out loud.

"Hello, Dana. I'm sorry to have to be the one to tell you this." By the flatness of his voice, I couldn't tell whether he was sorry at all. He could have been brokenhearted or gleeful, but the operator maintained absolute professionalism. "The Administrators have decided that in your current position you are a liability.

For the greater good of the Settlement, you have been terminated."

"I—" she sat up straighter a second. Fear flashed in her eyes, and it was the fear of a person who suddenly realizes at the last possible moment that they don't want to die. "Wait. It's not like that. You have to retake the vote. Let me talk to Jamison. I need to talk to Jamison."

"I'm sorry, Dana," said the operator. "The vote was unanimous." There was a soft click.

I backed into the open elevator doors.

The betrayal registered in her eyes for only a moment before she gasped and clutched her chest.

The doors slid shut.

Chapter Forty-Three

Drone Strike

I was still oddly numb as the elevator opened on the warehouse floor. I couldn't bring myself to speak or shout yet, but I knew I had to find him. I was trying to put the next steps in order in my mind, but couldn't quite get past what I'd just witnessed. My knees were shaking; I had to stop and collect myself, leaning against a wall.

Cam must be back on the roof, waiting for me.

Dana was dead. Dana Morris-Fletcher, the most powerful Administrator in the Settlement, was dead. Because of me.

I killed her, I thought, only semi-rationally.

I climbed one of the ladders again, this time going all the way to the top of the shelving, and surveyed the room. Fortunately, this time there were no visitors. I slipped around the shelves and made my way over quietly to the fire exit.

When I pushed the door open, the building alarm began to sound.

It didn't matter at this point. They were on to us already.

It was still early in the day. We had passed several hours in the tunnels, and then there had been the thirty-minute fueling period—perhaps I was even late. But the sun was only now just dawning over the horizon. It could be seven A.M., possibly.

I pulled myself doggedly up the stairs, my footsteps echoing on the metal slats. I leaned heavily on the handrail. This was an exhausting day and it had barely even begun.

At the top Cam spotted me instantly and called to me. "Finally!" He said. "What happened? I thought I had lost you."

"I…" I started. "It's a long story," I said.

"Well… we're all fueled up and ready to go."

Cam flipped through his checklist, turning knobs and switches until the blades on the helicopter began to turn. They went slowly at first, but faster and faster until I could barely see them.

I came up to the door where he sat and held out the metal sphere. "Take this," I said.

"What is it?"

I gave it to him. He wasn't prepared as it fell into his hands. He caught it low with a barely concealed "oof".

"What *is* this?"

"Never mind," I said. "Let's just go. They know we're here."

"All right then," said Cam. "Hop in."

He directed me to the other door, the one I'd assumed was the pilot's side. It was not, however. I climbed into the cockpit and sat on the left; Cam sat on the right. There wasn't much to be heard in here except for the chopping sound of the blades and the whine of the engines. He pointed to an odd gangly device hanging overhead. He had one like it and put it over his ears. I copied him; and the noise was dampened a bit. I could hear him again.

"There you go," he said. "Intercom's working. Then he hesitated while flicking some switches. "Shall we have the radio on, or off?" He laughed drily.

"Wouldn't they hear us?" I asked.

"No, it's push-to-talk. We might get some intel until they figure out we're listening."

"They have," I said. "No more stunts from you, Cam. They know where we are. I met Administrator Dana in the building."

"What? Well then—" the chopper was beating harder. "How did you get away?"

"She died."

He did manage to sneak a startled glance at me.

"The Administrators killed her."

"I…" his voice crunched over the intercom. "Was going to say… don't distract me. I haven't actually done this before. But uh. Wow."

"Sorry," I said. I felt around and tried to figure out how to belt myself in.

The machine lurched.

"Whoa," said Cam, and I could see his lips moving before hearing the sound through the intercom.

Cam gripped the controls carefully, steadying us. We had liftoff.

We rose up from the building, until I could see through the plexiglass windshield out over the wall of the Settlement. Cam was already taking us away and forward, but I sat up a little taller to get a look as the buildings dropped away.

The Settlement was small in some ways but vast in others. The continuous metro stretched for twenty miles in both directions, eating up the skyline behind us. Even from the air, we could not see the whole city at once. I could make out the shapes of the districts though, laid out like a grid of thirty-six squares, and in the center, the Central Tower, the one from which I'd originally looked out on the world. Even that shrank and fell below us. We were higher than I'd imagined it was possible to be.

Ahead was the green.

I struggled to match the terrain to what I had seen on the map. There were some fields, a river. I thought I could vaguely match these objects to the pictures in my mind.

Now that I was used to seeing green, the Settlement looked like a blight. Even the difference between the city and the consumed ruins on its borders was stark. They had been overtaken with green, but the Settlement looked dead and lifeless.

The mountains were far in the distance. We were moving at such a speed that I felt something I had never felt before—the mountains were real, and if we continued at this rate, we might eventually reach them. It was a stunning idea.

In spite of everything, I saw a smile struggling to break through on Cam's face. He split into a grin as we rose higher into the air. He twisted the throttle, dipping the nose of the craft, and we began to accelerate. He glanced back over his shoulder, then ahead, and hollered over the noise. "WOO HOO!"

I found myself tearing up again, and wiped my eyes on my sleeves.

"So… how are we going to start the fire?"

"Well," he said. "I was thinking we'd have to do it before we find the Kingdomers. In order to cover our six. But look around. The sun's up. I'm thinking the Settlement is going to do our job for us."

"What do you mean?" I started saying. Then I saw it.

There was a small, sleek object like a black arrowhead, sweeping low over the land. Its elevation was below us. Cam looked.

"It's the dr—"

But before I could finish, a burst of fire ballooned out over the trees.

Then the puff collapsed, and there was nothing but the buildings, burning, burning, all of them on fire. And then a second billow of flames up the road, which I knew was Hanfell.

I knew that no one was there, but I felt something fall inside of me. It was gone. All of it was gone. Forever.

And fire raged up from the ground. It licked over the cornfields, the grass, and towards the dry trees.

"All right," said Cam steadily. "Not our problem."

I couldn't stop looking. Smoke kept rising from the land.

They weren't there, I told myself. *Nobody was there.* It was hard to believe.

"New problem. We have to find everyone and relocate them to a safe place."

"A safe place?" I repeated. "What safe place is there?"

The next thing he said shocked me.

"They don't have sat-cams everywhere."

"What?" I almost started from my seat. "And you tell me this *now*?"

"When else?"

"Maybe back there in the sublevels."

"Slipped my mind, sorry. It's only been a few hours."

"That's all right," I said, remembering that he only had a few hours left to live.

"What time is it?" I asked.

Cam checked his Biometric. "Almost eight A.M."

By my reckoning, then, he had only until about six P.M. this evening, though I didn't say it.

"I don't understand," I said. "Don't the satellites, like, orbit or something? And can't they just send up a new one or move the ones they have?"

"It's not really like that," said Cam. "The sats they have right now have been up there for hundreds of years. They were built to last, but nothing lasts forever. They don't have any fuel left in them to reposition them, and the Settlement no longer has the infrastructure to build or launch more of them. It's not like they forgot how, but doing something as energy-inefficient as a launch is against their ethos, so I doubt it will happen soon. Sure, there used to be tons of sats all over the place, but as they started to take attrition due to age, the functional ones were repositioned in a stationary orbit over the Settlement and the surrounding areas.

That means most of the earth is actually dark to us now."

I sat back, a sense of amazement washing over me. This was a surprise almost on the same level as learning the world outside the Settlement wasn't a barren wasteland. There were parts of the world that the Settlement not only couldn't dominate but couldn't even *see?*

Cam finished his thought. "So, there are vast regions over the continent without any kind of available imaging."

"And that's where you want to take them?" I asked.

"Right. The only problem is that I don't actually know where the cult—um, the Kingdom folks are. They were able to evacuate before the Settlement troops moved in. And now obviously there's no one there. But other than that, all we have to go on is the lay of the land and the Settlement can see that too—"

"They're by the river," I said, "In that space between the two foothills." I pointed a ways off to the right.

The roar of the chopper was loud in the face of Cam's stunned silence. He actually twisted around in his seat, taking his eyes off the horizon, to look at me. "You're kidding," he said.

"No," I said.

He was forced to get his attention back to the sky, as we had started to drift. He swung the chopper around to the right in a wide turn.

"Alex."

I blinked.

"Alex."

I wasn't sure what to say.

"You *knew*?!"

I gave him a tiny wry smile.

"Oh Gai— um." It seemed he didn't really know what to curse by anymore.

�֍

Chapter Forty-Four

It's Just Me

"There," I said, pointing.

I had known for some time. After the dinner when I agreed to have the Biometric removed, Mr. Jones had told me of their rendezvous point with the other families who were fleeing. It wasn't hard to remember: at the place where the river met the foothills, there were caves in the mountain. They couldn't stay there, of course. It was still too close to the Settlement. But it would provide a temporary hiding place and shelter.

We found a spot clear for a landing there beside the river, and we began to descend.

The dark fir trees came up closer and closer, until they were on both sides of us, and we were still going down, a little too fast, I thought—I braced; the floor slanted under my feet.

"WE'RE CROOKED!" I screamed.

We came in roughly, one wheel hitting before the other. My shoulders jammed upward against the seat belt and my chin hit my chest. The rotor blades slowed with a deeper and deeper chopping sound.

I rubbed my neck, feeling an odd crick in it and a possible headache starting to develop. Cam seemed all right, though he was twisting the bracelet on his wrist.

I looked up. Through the glass windshield, the first thing I saw was the jeep.

And they were there too. Several of the men were in the jeep. More than a dozen other men were cautiously advancing on us from the trees with guns raised.

I released myself from the belt and jumped to the door. I heaved it open and jumped out without waiting to ask permission from Cam.

"Wait!" I shouted, as loud as I could. "Wait, don't shoot! It's me!"

Several heads turned; several eyes lit up in recognition. John-Michael Jones lowered his weapon, then Mark, and then Matt Falconer. Then the others, though not all at once, but a few at a time. The last barrels only went down, in confusion, when they looked around and saw what everyone else was doing.

"We escaped," I said as the noise from the helicopter died off. "Don't be afraid. We're here to help."

Cam chose this moment to open his door and step out. Before his feet even reached the ground, every gun in the clearing was drawn again.

"No!" I yelled, and nobody fired on him, but the tension remained. Cam put one hand in the air—the one he wasn't using to hang on to the side of the helicopter.

He spoke for himself. "Hey, listen," he started. "I know I haven't exactly earned your trust. But I swear to— to *God* I'm trying to save your lives here."

"He's telling the truth," I said.

They stopped pointing the guns at him, but their expressions still held doubt and suspicion. Mark knew, however. I could see that on his face. Cam jumped down from the helicopter.

"We have to get you all far away from here," said Cam. "Further than you can go on foot. They're sending drones. They've already destroyed your villages."

As he spoke, I looked beyond the men, and saw more people beginning to emerge from the trees. First there were the women, who had evidently been pushed into hiding, then lastly the children, who had been placed even further behind. Among the women, I noticed Ruth Tiller, one of the few who was not running to their husband.

There was hushed talking I couldn't hear, and then one of the children burst loudly into tears. "Our house! Mom!"

Looking even further around the clearing, I noticed the wagons, and the vast variety of *stuff* that had somehow been hauled to this location.

(Yet, it was not enough. So much had been destroyed.)

"You have to go now," said Cam, bluntly, looking directly at the elder Jones. "Otherwise, they will find you and do the same thing at this location."

"But where?" It was the man called Mason. Though he had opposed Mr. Jones at the council, he now seemed less combative. He and his men had fought a battle and won a jeep, and it must have looked like he had a point right up until a few minutes ago. But at the loss of the villages, everything he'd argued to preserve was gone. He had a subdued countenance, looking quite shaken.

"Over the mountains," said Cam.

I could see on Mr. Jones face that he'd already had a sense this was the answer.

"I'll take some people there, in the helicopter," said Cam. "I can if we start now."

"Who?" asked Falconer. He was right there next to Mason. "We can't all go at once. How long will it take?"

"Women and children go to safety first," said Mr. Jones.

"No," said Mason. "What if it's not safe where he's going? We barely know that we can trust him. What if he's taking them back to the Settlement?"

I sighed my deepest sigh.

"We should send one man with him and then back," said Mason, "Just to make sure—"

"We don't have time for that!" snapped Cam. "Volunteers. I'll take volunteers. We can probably get twenty people on board. Hell, this is an emergency, we can probably fit more. Who's coming?"

"I am," said Mark, stepping forward.

"Great," said Cam, not recognizing the boy who had shot me. If he had, I wondered if there would have been any hard feelings.

"How long will it take?" asked Falconer. "Can you make more than one trip?"

Cam's eyes lowered. "Fair point, I suppose. We can't take all of you this way. I don't have enough…" he hesitated, "…fuel. Some of you will have to go over land, using the jeep."

"What about the wagons?" asked one of the women.

"The jeep is strong enough to pull at least a few of them over the pass."

"There's a pass?"

"Yes—the lowest point in the mountains. There used to be roads there, too."

With that revelation, some of the men immediately set about at fixing the wagons to the jeep, end-to-end.

"I'll go," said Mason.

"All right then," said Cam. "We have enough capacity to lift eighteen more people, but maybe more if they're kids. I'm going to start the engine again."

"I'll go," said Ruth.

Mrs. Jones raised her hand. I looked at her in surprise.

"Samuel, Grace, and Eva will go."

They were her three oldest children, after Mark, who had volunteered himself.

"Are you sure?" I asked, scarcely believing she would now trust us this much.

"Anyone who stays is in danger," she said.

That did set off a new wave of volunteers, or rather nominees, mostly between the ages of nine and sixteen.

Jones and Mason exchanged a look.

"For those of us who stay," said Jones, "We have to hide."

Cam stopped, sitting in the pilot's seat. The blades were starting to turn again at a low speed. "Yes, stay hidden. This place is not good enough, though. It's too exposed."

"There's a cave in the mountains," said Jones. "I know where it is. It will keep us hidden for a while—a few days perhaps, though we may use up our supplies."

"Good enough," said Cam. He handed down a map, which Jones studied with some interest. "Mark where it is. I'll come back and meet you near that location."

Villagers started climbing up into the chopper. I helped them up from the ground.

Mrs. Jones lifted Eva up into my arms.

I hesitated.

Her eyes met mine.

"Yes," she said. "I know you are taking them to a safe place."

"I don't believe there is a place outside the Settlement that is perfectly safe," I said, in complete honesty.

"No," she said. "Perhaps not. Eva."

She reached up and took the hand of her daughter, who was standing on the deck of the helicopter. "Listen to me. Do you know why I am sending you out there?"

Eva chewed her lips, with tears starting from her eyes.

"Because," she said, "you *are* the future. Not just because you have physical life. You have something even more important. You have spiritual life. Now go." She let go of Eva's hand.

"You too, Alex," said Çam.

"Me?" I asked. The world seemed to snap back into focus.

"Yes, I want you to know the way."

I was surprised, but jumped on board.

The engines roared up, and the sound of it frightened many of the children, but I held their hands until they quieted down. We rose into the air.

As we came up over the trees, I saw the twin columns of smoke from the villages rising into the air, higher, and bigger, and thicker than before. They darkened the sky with a hazy gray.

Chapter Forty-Five

The Eleventh Hour

The mountains passed under us. Bold, majestic, unspeakably massive. They were closer than they had appeared. We had flown for only about two hours in total, but at a speed I couldn't quite comprehend.

Half the children were excited at the idea of flight, the other half seemed terrified. Mark was taking it well. He pointed out the window, talking to Eva. "Hey, bet you didn't think we'd ever be in an actual flying machine. Cool, huh?"

The adults were trying to be brave but were mostly silent. They had relaxed a bit once they could tell we were definitely not heading toward the Settlement.

But when the green mountains dropped away behind us, we saw something I'd never imagined I would see in my life. It was something I had almost as much trouble visually comprehending as I had the first time I had seen the green outside the Settlement.

There was a great flat. All the way out to the horizon, there was a shining, sparkling darkness. It shimmered blue and yellow and white and black, and as we got closer, I could see that it pulsed in tiny movements. It was as big as the whole world.

"Is that the Ocean?" I asked Cam over the headset.

"That's it," he said, and he sounded as subdued as me. He had never seen it before either.

We landed on the white beach, and even before the helicopter blades had stopped spinning, I could hear its noise.

There was a deep, pulsating roar that blanketed my senses, an undercurrent of everything, but somehow also a silence, and when the helicopter quieted, I could make out a soft slapping and washing of the waves on the beach.

It was mid-afternoon.

We disembarked. Cam was rather in a hurry to get everyone off the aircraft, and I understood why. Mason didn't, but he immediately took charge of the refugees. He helped the children down off the helicopter and began shepherding them toward a group of scraggly trees up the beach.

"When will you be back?" he asked Cam.

Cam looked rather stricken, he started shaking his head. I knew instinctively that we did not have time for a second trip.

"We don't have… fuel," he said.

"But you will come back by land?"

I spoke up for him quickly to head things off. "The rest of the group will come in the wagons," I said, "with the jeep. How long do you think that will take, Cam?"

"A few days at least," he said. "Maybe a week. I don't know exactly; I haven't made a trip like that."

Mason looked like he still had more questions, but Cam dodged and got back into the pilot's seat.

I found Ruth's eye among the adults standing on the beach. "I'll be back," I said.

She leaned in for a hug. As she did, she whispered something in my ear. "He isn't going to," she said. "Is he?"

"No," I said.

"I can tell," she said. "He doesn't want to say. But it's eating him."

"I *will* be back," I said.

***

It was just Cam and me on the way back over the mountains. He continually glanced at the map to locate the spot where Jones had marked.

"Almost there, I think," he said, and looked down again.

The whole sky was now full of a faint haze, even out over the Settlement. I could still make out the Wall, though, and some of the buildings. As my eyes hovered in that direction, I saw something that sent a jolt through my heart as though from the Biometric.

"Cam!" I said. "Look!" I pointed out to the horizon.

There was something coming toward us.

Cam took only a second, but he saw it too.

"Shit," he said, through his teeth.

He quickly twisted the throttle, and we started to bank left, away from the landing spot.

"What's going on?" I ventured anxiously. I looked back. We were definitely being pursued.

"They've sent another chopper after us," said Cam.

Whoever was monitoring the airspace around the Settlement not only noticed we were gone, but had seen us returning.

"They have more than one?!" It could scarcely be believed that multiples could exist of the man-made wonder which we now inhabited.

"Bit too many surprises for one day, isn't it?" Cam managed a quip, which was impressive, under the circumstances. "They're following us to try and figure out where we're going. We have to draw them off."

"How do we get rid of it?"

"Maybe we can lose them. Outrun them." Dismay swept over his face, but then the relaxation of someone who is totally resigned. "Might take a while though."

"I don't know about that," I said. "Looks like they're gaining on us."

They were.

Cam led them around the south side of the Settlement, as we rounded the corner of the 3rd Southwest District. The further we could make it, the better.

I looked behind us again. Our pursuers were slowing. More than slowing, they were stalling. They dropped away. Cam slowed as well. The Settlement chopper was realizing they had been fooled; they were leaving our tail and heading back to the West side.

"Hold on," said Cam grimly. "I have a plan."

My stomach lurched as we bobbed and pivoted in the air; I placed a hand to my mouth. I really was going to be sick if this continued.

But "this" proved to be nowhere near the end; it was only the beginning of the roller coaster. He put on speed again, demanding the other chopper's attention as we raced toward them head-on.

The Settlement chopper increased altitude in an evasive maneuver; Cam moved up to match them.

"I don't think—" I shouted into the intercom over the noise.

Our chopper and the Settlement chopper came full circle around each other.

"You know I don't think you're supposed to try this sort of thing on your first day—"

Cam laughed so loudly it seemed almost a little bit unhinged.

The Settlement chopper had gotten the superior position; they had positioned themselves over top of us.

"Rats!" He pulled some levers I hadn't seen him touch before, and a scope moved on the dashboard. The other chopper turned, and my stomach flipped as we dropped like a pendulum swinging out of the way.

"They're trying to force us to land!"

There was an explosive noise. We swerved left and right. They were *firing on us.*

I didn't think we were hit. Yet. Cam swerved again to dodge, taking us closer to the mountains.

"I don't think they'll follow us. We'll just—"

We sped towards the mountains as the craft above descended, forcing us lower and lower. At this point even I thought we were far too low. One of the foothills reared up ahead, and Cam dropped even further.

"I have to get lower," he said. "Make them think we're going to land—"

"It's too much!" I yelled. We were almost clipping the treeline, and there suddenly a cliffside popped up in front of us almost by surprise.

Cam pulled sharp to the right.

There was a loud *cracking* noise.

The Settlement chopper whizzed by us overhead. As I followed them with my eye, I could see a bit of a tree falling off down below. We'd hit a tree on the underside, I was sure of it.

And then the Settlement chopper hit the cliffside.

I could tell Cam wanted to look around, but he didn't. We pulled up again.

"They crashed," I said.

"We're damaged," he said. "Should land ASAP."

We puttered back towards the landing site, trailing a line of smoke through the already smoky air.

"And we don't have a lot of fuel left. Need to conserve some."

"What time is it?" I asked him.

He checked his Biometric, and then hesitated. "Five thirty P.M."

I remembered what time this morning he had started his twelve-hour time limit.

"Oh no," I said. "Cam!"

He continued, faster, seeming to ignore the emotion in my voice, as if he had to get through his piece without looking me in the eye. "I don't think we'll be lifting off again, but the amount of fuel it takes to fly this thing will keep that jeep going for a really long time, so you better just use the jeep, and besides, you don't need me to drive that."

"Cam!"

"What? I'm just saying. We know how this ends for me."

"Cam," I said reproachfully.

"It's not like there's anything I can do about it."

He put the helicopter down in front of the mountain. It was a worse landing than before. There was a hard jolt, and a tilt that was wrong and wronger.

We scratched into the sand, grinding at approximately a thirty-degree angle as the blade slowed. Fortunately, the blade did not hit the ground, as that might have flipped the craft.

"It's a wheel," he said. "We lost a wheel."

I could see the cave mouth from here. He'd found the right place. I'd never seen a cave before. The entrance was marked mostly by a dirt ravine, but quickly fell underground into darkness, and I couldn't see anyone. Either they were well-hidden, or they hadn't made it yet. I hoped strongly for the former.

The chopper blades continued beating predictably. Cam took off his headset, and so did I. The moving air over my ears felt strange after the hours wearing the puffy headphones.

We just sat there for a minute.

"That was amazing," I told him. He deserved to hear it. "I can't believe that actually worked, but it was brilliant. You did great."

He looked at me, but it was a bit ruefully. He seemed to be trying to collect himself.

I tried to calm my hands, which were still shaking from the near-death in the air and the near-crash a moment ago.

"I want to go in and meet them, all right?"

I glanced at the cave. Tears welled up in my eyes.

"I want to see them," he said.

After he'd done so much for them, he deserved that much, I thought. I sighed shakily. "All right, Cam, if that's what you want."

He pinched the bridge of his nose. "Please don't…"

I sniffed.

"…make this weird."

I nodded.

"Really. I don't want… to alarm anyone. There are children. We'll just go in for a few minutes and then out."

"Okay," I said, trying to be brave. He was being so brave, I had to keep up with him. "Fine."

We disembarked and walked to the cave entrance.

I peered into the shadows.

A small girl ran out of the cave at full speed, slamming into me and hugging me tightly around the waist.

"Mary!" Hadn't she been on the chopper? No, she hadn't—I'd sensed that one of the children was unaccounted for, but I was thinking of John, perhaps.

Cam jumped like we'd been ambushed, but I saw him relax again. Mrs. Jones followed out of the dusky interior. "Mary… Alex!"

"We're back," I said, awkwardly. "Mrs. Jones, I just wanted to give you a proper introduction. This is Cam. Cam, this is Sarah Jones."

She was holding her one-year-old in her arms, but she managed to shift the baby on her hip and nod. Mr. Jones emerged behind her, looking solemn.

"And John-Michael Jones. This is Cam," I said. "He helped me escape from the Settlement. We can trust him—but I know you know that now."

As my eyes adjusted, I could vaguely see Dr. Brown and the Minister further back in the cave, with some other people.

"I guess you've probably heard a lot about me," Cam started in a husky voice.

"Sir," said Mrs. Jones, "thank you for helping my children."

He lowered his eyes, nodding.

"Quite," said Mr. Jones, and held out a hand to shake. Cam took a moment to figure out what to do with it, but Mr. Jones gave a firm handshake and he seemed to catch on. "We appreciate the risks you've taken on our behalf. Especially in acquiring this… machine."

"It's damaged," said Cam, looking back out the cave. "I'm sorry."

The Joneses both looked rather taken aback.

"You'll have to take the jeep. Alex will help you find the way. Siphon the fuel out of the helicopter to fuel the jeep. It will be several day's trip one way."

"Oh." Mrs. Jones tried not to let her disappointment show, but I could tell this new challenge was an unpleasant surprise. It was better than their plan before Cam showed up, though, so she tried to keep brave about it, and I could tell Mr. Jones was thinking the same thing.

"Ah, well, very well, though if we could get the helicopter going again—if only my son Mark were still here, he would be able to help, I'm sure."

I was skeptical about the realism of this but didn't say anything.

"Alex," Mrs. Jones said anxiously to me, "What was it like over there? How are they doing?"

"They're waiting for you," I said. "It's quite nice, and I'm sure they'll be safe. I saw the ocean," I supplied.

"The ocean?"

"The seaside will be a nice place to live, I'm sure."

She nodded hesitantly.

None of them had seen the ocean any more than I had before today.

"We just have to get there," said Mr. Jones. "As soon as possible."

"I'd like to meet the others," said Cam. "If that's all right." I noticed his glance at his Biometric.

I nodded at him. I went to the cave wall and pulled out the Minister by the arm. "Cam, this is the Minister. He told me all about Christianity."

The Minister was attentive, but a bit confused. He let himself be led up to the light.

Cam shook his hand. "I'd like to apologize for burning your church," he said awkwardly.

The Minister's eyebrows raised a little bit. "Oh." It took him a moment to gather himself. "Well," he said, "The church is not a building. But I appreciate that. We forgive you," he said. "Besides," he added wryly, "I doubt it would be standing now in any case. I was able to save…"

He reached into a bag slung from his shoulder. "Six Bibles. And a couple of hymn-books."

Cam's eyes widened. "Is that really all?"

"And the families will have their own."

"Good…" he was looking down at his wrist again.

I lowered my voice to him. "How long…"

He was looking a bit pale. I took his hand, it was clammy. "Excuse me," he said to the Minister and to the Joneses. "I have to go outside."

Mary tugged at his shirt. "Hey mister! Come look at my chicken! I bet you've never seen a chicken before."

I saw him start to tear up as he gently separated her hands from his shirt. "I'm sorry… what's your name?"

"Mary!"

"Sorry, Mary, can't go look at a chicken. You're very sweet," he said, a little glazed over. "Have to go outside."

"Is everything all right?" said Mrs. Jones, bouncing her baby.

"I just need a bit of air. Feel like going on a walk. You know, all that time flying. Come on, Alex, let's step out."

"I'll come too," said Mr. Jones, and the tone of his voice suggested that he'd sensed something wasn't right.

"No, don't worry about it," said Cam. We were already moving into the sunlight. I hurried to keep up with Cam.

"Where are you going, Alex?" Mrs. Jones started. They were both following, which flustered Cam greatly and me as well as I tried to get the situation under control.

"Nowhere," I said. "Not too far."

He grabbed my hand and pulled me further out into the ravine. He seemed to be trying to take us back to the chopper for some reason. Privacy, I realized.

"How long?" I asked him under my breath.

"Six minutes." His breath caught.

"What are you talking about?" demanded John-Michael Jones.

It was too much for me.

"He's dying!" I shouted.

"Dammit, Alex!" Cam groaned. "I told you not to make this weird." But he was so rushed, there was no ire in it, only fear.

We stumbled down the ravine away from the cave.

"What?!" demanded Mrs. Jones. "Why is he dying?"

I tried, breathlessly, to explain, even as we got farther away, and they chased after us. "He's dying because his Biometric... his hand..." I gestured helplessly.

Then I pulled loose of him.

My eyes had lit up with a kind of frenzied hope, and he could see it, and he was momentarily confused.

"*Cam,*" I said. "I have an idea." I grabbed his right hand below the wrist and held it up between us.

"What? What are you talking about?"

"It's this—this!" I pushed his arm towards his face. I was incoherent, but he seemed to get the idea.

His eyes widened.

"It's better than death!"

"I can't! I'll be… a burden on you… injured… a liability… Alex you can't be serious, you'll have to drag me around like—"

"I don't care!" I yelled. "How much time?"

"Three… three minutes…"

"Three minutes?!"

"Alex, it's too late."

"It is bloody well NOT!" I shouted, loud enough for Jones to hear. "It's the Biometric! It's that thing in your hand! It's going to kill you! Better just to cut it off!"

I could see Jones starting to move down at the bottom of the ravine. He was tapping on Falconer's shoulder, saying something urgently.

"How much time?" He shouted up.

"Now!" I yelled back. "Now, right now!"

Cam just stood there, bewildered and pale.

Finally he shuddered and gave a tiny nod.

Jones and Falconer reached the top of the ridge a few moments later, the latter man dragging a long axe. There was no time to hesitate. The men shouldered me out of the way as they tackled Cam and pulled him off to the side, where there was a fallen log. He fell to his knees.

"You'll thank me later," said Jones.

I pressed my hands over my eyes.

The axe fell.

Chapter Forty-Six

The Seed

Cam lay on the floor of the cave like a sack of beans. He'd fainted almost immediately upon losing a hand; and now I thought he was still in shock.

Doctor Brown thought so too.

It was thirty minutes past his projected time of death.

We didn't have a Biometric to tell us that; instead, there was a small analogue antique clock that Ann Baker used in one of the wagons. It made a ticking noise as little needles moved across a clock face. I couldn't tell time by it, but she could.

We were all struggling to regroup. Doc Brown hadn't gotten up from where he knelt beside Cam's form, and he was taking a pulse yet again.

The man's forearm was gone just below the wrist, enough to take the Biometric with it. It had been cleaner than I expected, but there was blood, a great puddle of blood on the sand outside, and just to keep him from bleeding out was a full-time job. Doc Brown had demanded a fire be lit to provide what he needed to cauterize the wound.

I recognized the generous use of the limited medical supplies. Bandages, cloth of any type, would be in short supply.

Mrs. Jones lit a candle. The light expanded the interior of the cave, showing the ceiling to be higher than I'd thought, and the back to be deeper, with more rooms inside.

The majority of the Kingdom was back there now, all waiting, hidden under the earth and now under the smoke from the drones, the satellites, the eyes, and the fire.

Once the smoke dissipated, there could be problems. But I felt confident they wouldn't find us today.

"He's going to be all right," Mrs. Jones said, putting a hand on my shoulder.

I nodded.

"She's right," said Doc Brown. "He's stable now. I feel confident that he's going to live."

"What next?" I asked, shakily.

"Rest," said Mrs. Jones. "We have a long journey ahead of us."

I continued sitting there. Cam was definitely conscious again, he groaned occasionally, making my heart want to burst, but he didn't speak yet.

It wouldn't be easy for them. It would be dangerous, in fact, very dangerous. Not just for them, I realized. For me, too. But we'd have each other. And we'd be free. I'd be really free for the first time in my life. As a matter of fact, I was. I already was.

And Cam, too.

It was an hour later when he opened his eyes a crack for the first time since losing his hand. I inhaled sharply.

"Well," he said, finding his voice drily. "Looks like I owe you my life a second time."

I laughed, tears falling down my face. "You made it," I said.

He got a distant look. "Is this it? We're... we're never going back, are we?"

"I can't leave forever," I said, and I didn't really know it until that moment. It came to me as I said it. "Not like that. Someday I'll have to go back. I have to help more people escape, at least. I'd like to bring God into that place."

"In there?" he smiled a tiny bit, in amazement. "Yeah, I guess, why not?"

"When do we leave?" I asked Mrs. Jones.

"Tomorrow," she said. "Not all of us. The first group. The second group will move to another cave, farther from this area, and follow when the jeep returns."

"What about me?" I asked. "I don't think he'll be ready to leave." I held on tightly to Cam's left hand. Tomorrow suddenly seemed awfully soon. I didn't want to part with him again so quickly.

She looked thoughtful.

"I was supposed to lead the way," I said.

"I understand," she said. "You'll have to speak to my husband. Perhaps something can be done about it."

"It's like I was afraid of," Cam groaned weakly. "I'm slowing you down."

"No!" I insisted. "Don't start talking like that. You're alive, and that's what counts."

"But you should go. You have to. That's why… you flew with me."

"Are you sure you'll be okay without me?" I asked, and then I winced. How could I trust him to tell me the truth? This man hid the fact that he was dying from me.

I exchanged glances with Mrs. Jones.

"I'm sure the doctor and this lady know what they're doing," he managed.

"We can take care of him," said Mrs. Jones. "And we'll be right behind you. We'll meet up again soon."

***

We had said our goodbyes early, and emerged from the cave, squinting, into the sunlight.

The jeep's engine huffed and rattled as it bounced along on the broken road. I sat next to Smith, who had been the one to originally commandeer the vehicle. He had asked me if I wanted to take the wheel, but I didn't have any experience driving either.

Three wagons were hitched up behind us. Consequently, we were forced to take it slow.

The road was broken by roots and obstructed by light debris, but was otherwise passable. We sometimes had to stop and move tree branches, or roll slowly over long, jagged cracks.

Along the sides were twisted streetlights and faded signposts. Occasionally, there was a collapsed house or a glimpse of a barrier wall underneath mounds of ivy.

"Which way from here?" Smith asked, as we came to yet another faded octagonal sign. I pointed straight ahead. It was a long road, but it was straight nearly the whole way from here.

As we passed on, I fell silent, listening to the peeping voices of the children in the first wagon. Mary's voice was loudest. "What's that?"

"That was somebody's house once," said a voice I recognized as the Minister's.

"Really?"

"Yes."

"What about that one?" said one of the other children.

"That was… I don't know what that was."

He paused.

"A place of business, maybe. The place we're passing through used to be some sort of city."

I looked back at him. All the children were gathered around listening intently, as if waiting for a story.

"Imagine all the people who used to live here. Everything was clean. New. Impressive. Inhabited. They probably thought that the things they built would stay the same forever. But now they're abandoned, and the trees grow over them.

"That is how buildings are destroyed. Every tree starts as a seed, but when it grows, its roots can crack stone. Just give it a couple hundred years, and it will conquer even the proudest palace.

"The kingdom of heaven is like that. The kingdom of heaven is like a mustard seed, which a man took and planted in his field. Though it is the smallest of all seeds, yet when it grows, it is the largest of garden plants, and becomes a tree, so that the birds come and perch in its branches."